# Running Clear

# Running Clear

▼

*Emil Mihelich*

Writers Club Press
San Jose  New York  Lincoln  Shanghai

**Running Clear**

All Rights Reserved © 2002 by Emil Mihelich

No part of this book may be reproduced or transmitted in any form or by any means, graphic, electronic, or mechanical, including photocopying, recording, taping, or by any information storage retrieval system, without the permission in writing from the publisher.

Writers Club Press
an imprint of iUniverse, Inc.

For information address:
iUniverse, Inc.
5220 S. 16th St., Suite 200
Lincoln, NE 68512
www.iuniverse.com

Any resemblance to actual people and events is purely coincidental. This is a work of fiction.

ISBN: 0-595-21641-2

Printed in the United States of America

"The fool doth think he is wise;
The wise man knows himself to be a fool."
William Shakespeare
'As You Like It'
Act V, Scene I

To wise men and women everywhere,
and especially to my wife whose love
always has run clear.

# THE ARRIVAL

# I

No one ever would confuse Lebanon, Oregon, with being a Catholic town, although St Edward's Catholic Church sat on the corner of Main Street and Tangent at the north end of town across from the junior high school that used to be the high school in an earlier era. In fact, no one ever would confuse Lebanon, Oregon with being anything other than another western Oregon lumber town and farming community—typically Protestant—situated in the heart of the fertile Willamette Valley and sandwiched between metropolitan Portland, 80 miles to the north, and socially conscious Eugene, 40 miles to the south. But a man has to begin a teaching career somewhere, and Lebanon was as good a place as any. At least that's how Ron Petrich felt in the winter of 1967 after he finished his BA degree, with an English major supported by history and philosophy minors, at Seattle University, a Roman Catholic Jesuit school that had given Seattle, Washington—and America—the premier basketballer, Elgin Baylor.

Now, Seattle University, almost two years after the conclusion of the Catholic Church's Second Vatican Council and steeped in its tradition of St Augustine and St Thomas Aquinas, gave Lebanon, Oregon, and the Willamette Valley 22-year-old Ron Petrich, who wasn't aware he was being given to anyplace by anything. He was a 22-year-old English teacher who needed a job, and Lebanon had one available at its Union High School. He didn't have much choice in the matter, with his only other options being the Army and its promise of Vietnam or Halfway, Oregon, with its promise of a position as a typing teacher. Ron couldn't type, and he had no idea what Halfway, Oregon, was halfway to. And the Army was to be avoided if at all possible. So, considering the circumstances, Lebanon, Oregon, looked fairly inviting that winter of 1967.

Confident of receiving a 2-S occupational deferment from his draft board, Ron considered himself lucky to have this opportunity in the middle of the school year. He looked forward to beginning his teaching career in Lebanon, not ever concerned about his own Catholic background that had taken him from Tacoma, Washington's St Patrick's Parish School to the Jesuits' Bellarmine Prep High School and finally to Seattle University. He was more than willing to follow the job wherever it may lead and had no idea that in nondescript Lebanon, Oregon, he ultimately would face a conflict of obedience that would force him to choose, like the fictional Huckleberry Finn, "forever betwixt two things."

There was nothing immediately special about Ron Petrich. Physically, at five ten and 160 pounds with brownish blonde hair and blue eyes, he wasn't imposing by any stretch of the imagination. He wore his hair in the traditional cut—without sideburns, off the ears, and tapered in the back along the neck—as reflective of his identity with the established, but now in 1967 the threatened, order of things. If anything distinguished him, it was his nose that appeared to have been chiseled out of granite in keeping with his Eastern European, Slavic heritage and by his honest curiosity more closely related to that of the biblical Eve than to that of the biblical Adam. Accompanying this honest, natural curiosity was his just as natural understanding, imprinted on him as a direct result of his personal, historic past, that an individual should be more inspired by responsibility than attracted by rewards.

He wasn't always without fear, but his fear never was of life itself, which had to include time and death. Before he was ten, he had witnessed the death of his favorite uncle an his father's side and of his grandmother and grandfather on his mother's side. His Uncle Tom died at 40, and his grandmother and grandfather died at 70; but, still, their deaths, regardless of the age disparity, seemed more natural than unnatural. He saw grief and mourning, but he didn't see despair. Instead, he saw a celebration of life, that had to include death, built around the rhythmic cycle of the natural year reflected in his Catholic Church's liturgical year and even in his mother's and father's conducting of their everyday lives. His mother went about her housewife labor more with a sense of satisfaction than resentment, and his father went about his work at Tacoma's Asarco copper smelter in the same manner.

Ron and his older sister never knew wealth as a result of their parents' labor, but they never did without, either. He came to Lebanon from a simple and dignified life built around a home created by a man and a woman who definitely were opposite but at least appeared to be equal. It was a home that seemed to live more in celebration of time rather than in resigned consumption of it, and his mother and father practiced their Catholicism seriously but quietly. They had their religion. They had their movies and later their television. And his father, although not totally exclusively, had baseball. In short, Ron Petrich came to Lebanon, Oregon, from a Tacoma, Washington, life of quiet acceptance and affirmation.

He had no fear of the nature of life itself, but there was a time when he feared that he may not find a place for himself within it. He had worked at "manly" jobs during his high school and college summers, but he never quite felt comfortable in that male fraternity, although he respected it and initially aspired to nothing else. He was a willing worker but thankful he had college to put off, for four years anyway, his entry into the adult work world. He was a boy governed by Love, and college offered a continuation of that adventure inspired by the rock n' roll music of his formative high school years. He never was pious, but he always was religious. With his fear of finding his place temporarily forgotten, he entered Seattle University in the fall of 1962 obedient to the promise of Love celebrated with consummate vitality by Ricky Nelson and 'Hello, Mary Lou.'

Seattle University, as did most—if not all—Catholic universities, offered Ron an extension of his high school, Tacoma's Bellarmine Prep. He was only 35 miles from home but he was at college. And it was Seattle University, if not Seattle itself that no self-respecting Tacoman ever would embrace, that became the center of his life. He was close to Tacoma, but even if he had been separated from his home by thousands of miles, he never really would have left home because the shadow of the Catholic Church stretched far and wide. A product of a Jesuit high school and a Jesuit university, he was solidly educated "in the shadow of religion," as D H Lawrence would say. And that religion was as expansive as the Christian world had to offer as Western civilization entered the final decades of the 20th century.

Ron's youthful fear took second place to the enchanting promise of Love until the spring semester of 1966 when he faced the fact that soon he would have no more college to attend. His adventure had been inspiring, and it had led to his decision to major in English rather than in the more practical math. But that adventure hadn't led to any job prospects nor to the discovery of a suitable marriage partner for whom Love held the same enchanted promise. His immediate future looked bleak from all angles as he began the spring semester of his senior year. But during that semester of anxiety, marked by English major indecision, the possibility of student teaching came to the rescue.

It came to the rescue only because Ron had to try something after the mathematical and business worlds proved to be as uncomfortable for him as did his father's smelter world. He found that he couldn't swim in any of those waters, and with the very real prospect of the draft staring him in the face, he decided to try the waters of education. He was a person of duty who was not necessarily part of any antiwar sentiment in reference to Vietnam, but he decided to pursue student teaching in the fall and then take his chances rather than simply wait for the draft to make his decision for him.

To his delight, he found that he could swim in the waters of education and student teaching. He may have lacked a solid and thorough understanding of literature and writing, but he didn't lack in personality and balanced psychological temperament. He had a sense of humor grounded in his still unconscious acceptance and affirmation of the nature of life just as it is experienced. At the same time he discovered that, for whatever reason, he had a presence in a classroom that even affected his fellow student teachers and high school student role players. He didn't have to understand much to effectively give a 20 minute presentation to his peers, but he couldn't help recognizing he was swimming in comfortable waters when they sat quietly in attention to him and to what he essentially had memorized.

Armed with this initial success and with the confidence it brought, Ron enthusiastically and successfully negotiated the waters of his student teaching experience. Respected by students and experienced teachers alike, he felt ready to join the adult work world he never actually feared and to which he always aspired. It made no matter that Lebanon, Oregon, although only five hours south of Tacoma, would turn out to be a long way from home. Lebanon Union High School had an opening for a senior English teacher beginning with the second semester in the winter of 1967, and Ron Petrich was convinced he was the man for the job. He knew we wasn't an accomplished teacher, but he did know he was inspired and able. He knew he would go as far as his inspiration and ability would take him, and his sense of adventure knew no boundaries. He already had taken a healthy bite out of Eden's apple, but as yet he was unaware of his identity with his biblical and fictional counterparts found in the likes of Adam and Eve and Huckleberry Finn.

# II

Dr George Harrison, the superintendent of Lebanon's Union School District, wasn't particularly interested in any individual to fill the position at his high school. He was more interested in getting a teacher as quickly as possible, and after talking to Ron Petrich on the telephone and after reading the recommendations in his placement file, he felt reasonably assured that Ron, regardless of his effectiveness as an individual teacher, would not be an embarrassment to the district or—even more importantly—to him. Thus he considered Ron's subsequent interview a mere formality and simply one of the motions he had to go through. Dr Harrison had the extensive formal education required of a person in his position, but such education was deceptive. He was an administrator more interested in the security of his own position than we was in the lives of individual teachers and individual students. He was not unlike the paternal head of a family whose children learned at an early age that they were more subject to the will of the father than they were to that of their emerging individual natures.

However, such a thought remained completely foreign to Ron, who was pursuing his social role of teacher more as a result of obedience to his own discovered will than he was out of obedience to any imposed, paternal will. Maybe it would have been different for him had not his father been a smelter worker for whom the position of teacher held considerable respect, but Ron's freedom wasn't curtailed as a result of growing up in the Petrich family. In Dr Harrison he would not find an extension of his own father, although he would find an extension of the Old Testament pulpit Father who sometimes surfaced in the more altar-centered Catholic Church. Ron had a hard time, given his obedient heart, reconciling the pulpit God the Father with his own personal, historic father, which always led him to think seriously about the meaning of God and Christ as the Son of the Father.

It was all fairly confusing, but freely and not coercively obedient to his own emerging will, Ron Petrich still managed to drive into Lebanon, Oregon, on a typically rainy, late January afternoon in preparation for his interviews the following day—with Dr Harrison at 10:00 AM and with Mr Bill Polk, the high school principal, at 2:00 PM. Ron knew nothing of Lebanon, and at the age of 22, only one week removed from the protective confines of Seattle University, he had never even rented a motel room for himself before. But it was all part of the continuing adventure of his life as he drove into Lebanon from the north, past the identifying sign that welcomed him to the comfortable, if not comforting, Willamette Valley lumber and farming community of 7,500 residents.

To the 19th century pioneer the lush fertility of the valley of western Oregon's Willamette River had to offer a vision of paradise not far removed from their biblical image of the lost Garden of Eden. It only proved that human beings will endure incredible hardships if the prize at the end appears worth the effort. And there was no doubt that the Willamette Valley delivered on its promise of greener grass beyond the plains and beyond the Rocky and Cascade Mountain ranges. But that admirable 19th century pioneer spirit was a Protestant spirit as well, and in its wake it left tightly knit and exclusive communities built on a morality of biblical abstinence that only grudgingly tolerated any public deviation from that code. Thus the hard working lumberjack had his tolerated tavern haunted by this Protestant moral code, and the just as hardworking farmer had his Grange Hall supported and upheld by his Protestant church. By the late 20th century and the time of the arrival of Ron Petrich, the Willamette Valley had been deprived of a great deal of its natural inclusiveness.

Ron was neither a lumberjack nor a farmer, but he was an inspired and prospective teacher of both. He knew nothing of the governing mythology of Lebanon, but he knew he had a job to do, should he be selected to fill the vacancy for a senior English teacher at its Union High School. But for now, he was mostly concerned with finding a motel room in a town that was as obscure to him as it would be to any city-bred young man venturing out on his own for the first time. At 22 he was six years older than his immigrant Uncle Steve who, family legend had it, left Bulgaria alone at 16 to find his life amongst the coal mines of America and eastern Montana. Ron was of a different generation, but he was thankful for that immigrant past. It gave him the courage to face his world that, for him, was as formidable as was his uncle's in an earlier era when college was a luxury few could afford.

He drove down Lebanon's narrow Main Street that, although it was not without a certain pedestrian charm, never would be confused with the setting for a Norman Rockwell painting of Americana. He was used to Tacoma (and to some extent Seattle) with its downtown retail center—only recently threatened by the extensive Tacoma Mall still spreading on a once open acreage of scotch broom just beyond the city's 38th Street near its southeastern boundary—and neighborhood shopping areas. Lebanon's downtown, bordering either side of its Main Street, reminded Ron of his own Proctor neighborhood and retail district of Tacoma's residential North End. But Lebanon's downtown seemed more cramped. He drove past hardware stores and clothing stores and smiled at the familiarity of the Kuhn Theater and JC Penney's and the Town Tavern. In the space of a few minutes he was through downtown and driving past real estate agencies and grocery markets and drive-ins and car dealerships on his way south toward the next town of Sweet Home when he discovered the welcomed sight of the Gables Motel on the left-hand side of the road that now led out of Lebanon.

Through the familiar rain he saw the vacancy sign and turned left into the Gables' parking area, as close as he could get to the office. It certainly wasn't Ellis Island, but the Gables Motel still offered a strange room in a strange town. He stopped his 1965 Chevelle Malibu in the parking lot nearest the motel office and for a time sat in silence, wondering what he was doing there in the first place. As long as he was going to teach, why didn't he hold out for a job in the Tacoma School District that offered four high schools of the approximate size of this Lebanon Union High School with its 1,500 students? He couldn't help thinking that maybe he had chosen the wrong path as he sat in the family car, that now was his car, outside the office of the Gables Motel that didn't look the least bit inviting as the rain beat on the light blue Malibu and ran down its windshield, obscuring the red neon office identification and attendant vacancy sign. He thought about returning home, but remembering his heritage, he opened his driver's side door, stepped out into the rain, and sprinted for the office door.

Once inside the office he wiped some of the rain off his forehead with his back-pocket handkerchief and lightly punched the bell that sat on the office counter. A smile crossed his face in recognition of never before having rung such a service bell. In a few seconds a middle-aged woman with neatly combed brown hair and dressed in navy blue slacks emerged through the doorway directly behind the office desk.

"Can I help you?" the woman asked in a pleasant voice as Ron stood in nervous anticipation on the other side of the counter.

"I would like a room for the night if you have one," he answered.

"With one bed just for yourself for one night?" she asked, looking him directly in the eye.

"Yes," he answered, meeting her eyes, "just for myself for one night."

"I think we can accommodate that," she said with a smile. "Just fill out the registration card," she added, sliding him his room key at the same time. "You'll be in room number four."

"Thank you," Ron replied as he turned his attention to the registration card.

"Do you mind if I ask you what brings you to Lebanon?" the woman asked as he completed the card.

"No, I don't mind," Ron answered.

"Well then," the woman responded, smiling again, "what brings you to Lebanon in January?"

"I'm here to interview for a teaching job at the high school," Ron answered politely.

"The English teaching position?"

"Yes."

"If you don't mind my saying so," the woman added, "you don't look much older than a high school senior yourself."

"I don't mind. You're not the first person to make that observation. I'm used to it by now."

"Does it bother you? I mean being a teacher and looking so young."

"Not any more. But I used to think about it a lot when I first decided to try teaching. I thought that maybe I didn't look old enough to create the necessary discipline."

"What changed your mind?"

"My experience as a student teacher."

"What happened?"

"I found out I could do it. I could create discipline and teach."

"How did you do it?"

"I don't know. I didn't do anything special. I just tried to teach as well as I could with as much sincerity as I could, and with just as much understanding and compassion. I didn't seem to have any serious problems."

"And now you're ready for the real thing?" the motel woman asked, still smiling.

"I think so," Ron answered. "At least I want to give it a try."

"In Lebanon?"

"I have to start somewhere and I guess this is as good a place as any."

"Yes, I suppose it is at that. Who are you interviewing with?"

"Dr Harrison at ten o' clock and Mr Polk at two in the afternoon."

"Oh, yes. Dr Harrison is the superintendent and Mr Polk is the principal of the high school. Dr Harrison is an import, but Bill Polk is a native."

"You know both of them?" Ron asked somewhat incredulously.

"Sure," the woman answered. "Lebanon is a small town and the high school is all we have. Dr Harrison is a little distant from it all, but Bill Polk is another story. The high school is his life. It's his school, and he's proud of it and of what it can accomplish. If you can fill the position without embarrassing anyone, you'll be okay with Dr Harrison. But Bill Polk will expect more. He'll look at you more as an individual. He's a good man."

"Well, whatever happens," Ron responded much more relaxed now, "I'm looking forward to the interviews and I'm looking forward to teaching, if they give me the chance."

"I wish you luck," the woman said. "And if you ask me, you have a good chance. By the way, do you like baseball?"

"It's my favorite sport. I learned it from my dad who calls it The One True Sport. I don't know what he'd do without it."

"That sounds promising. Bill Polk is a baseball fan. From what you said about your dad, I'd say that he and Mr Polk have a lot in common."

"Now I'm really looking forward to meeting him tomorrow," Ron said.

"I'm sure you'll conduct yourself admirably," the woman replied. "I have a feeling that you'll be around here for a while if you want to be."

"As I said, I have to start somewhere. And it might as well be in Lebanon, Oregon."

"Might as well," the woman added as she filed Ron's registration card.

"Well, it's been nice talking to you," Ron said as he turned to head for the office door.

"Nice talking to you, Mr Petrich," the woman replied, reading his name correctly, with a short 'e,' from his registration. "That's not a Lebanon name. But maybe we can use some new blood in the old town."

"I hope so. Could you recommend a place to eat tonight?" Ron asked as he opened the office door.

"Bing's Kitchen is the best place in town," the woman answered. "Just head north back toward town and it'll be maybe a half a mile down the road on the left-hand side, You can't miss it. Great Chinese and American food."

"Thanks, I'll try it," Ron said, opening the office door.

"You're welcome and good luck tomorrow," the woman offered.

"Thanks again," Ron answered. "I'll just be honest and see what happens," he added as she leaned on the office counter. He felt confident as he walked through the rain to his waiting Malibu, opened the driver's side door, slipped behind the wheel, started the engine, backed up, and headed for Bing's Kitchen.

He had little trouble finding the restaurant, but he paid little attention to it or to his dinner of breaded veal cutlets. He wasn't a part of Lebanon yet, if ever he was going to be, and breaded veal cutlets under those circumstances were no different here than anywhere else. His mind was preoccupied with his interviews scheduled for tomorrow, and Bing's Kitchen was just another Chinese-American restaurant that happened to be the best restaurant in Lebanon, Oregon, according to the motel woman. He sat quietly and anonymously, eating his breaded veal, and it occurred to him that from what he learned from his conversation with the motel woman, he would lose his anonymity should he be offered, and should he accept, the position of senior English teacher at Mr. Polka's high school. But that eventuality still lie in the future. Immediately, he was concerned with finishing dinner and with finding out just where he had to go tomorrow. He finished his breaded veal and with regard to his concern about tomorrow, he resolved to ask the motel woman in the morning. He left the appropriate ten percent tip on his table and walked toward the cashier's counter. He paid his bill that came to four dollars, including his glass of milk, left Bing's Kitchen, and headed toward his Malibu for the short drive back to the Gables Motel and an evening of television in preparation for the next day's date with destiny.

Thanks to television the evening passed quickly, and after an hour and a half of 'The Virginian' and an hour of 'The Smothers Brothers,' he was ready to try to get some sleep in preparation for his interviews the following day. He brushed his teeth, removed his contact lenses, and found his way into bed only to discover that he couldn't immediately go to sleep. He wasn't worried about the interviews tomorrow, and he wasn't worried about his inspiration and ability with regard to teaching. But he couldn't help worrying about not having much to teach, even though he had a degree that said he had something to teach. He could write and he could read literature, but did he understand either? He felt he understood more about writing, and watching the likes of 'The Virginian' and 'The Smothers Brothers' didn't contribute much to his fledgling understanding of literature. As a prospective teacher of the same, he felt no superiority to television. If anything, he liked it and wished he could sense in TV drama a popular expression of that which he could sense in Shakespearean drama. Knowing that he had to learn how to understand what he sensed so that he would have something to explain and thus to teach, he finally drifted off and slept soundly until the next morning when the logging trucks returned to the Santiam Highway that connected Lebanon with Sweet Home just 30 miles to the south.

Ron never before had awakened to the rumbling of logging trucks, although his hometown of Tacoma, Washington, housed the corporate headquarters of the Weyerhauser Company, the Pacific Northwest's timber giant. He had heard the whistles at the Asarco smelter as a comforting sound of life, but the whirring sound of shifting gears on laboring logging trucks, being entirely foreign in nature, offered him little solace as he opened his eyes to the wet and foggy January morning that would lead him to the first two interviews of his emerging professional life. He looked at his watch, which said seven-thirty, and was startled and surprised to hear his room phone ring.

"Hello," he said, rubbing the sleep out of his eyes and picking up his bathrobe that he always laid on the floor to the left of the bed and on top of the pillow which he never used.

"Mr Petrich?" the woman's voice asked.

"Yes," Ron answered, tying the sash on his brown, terrycloth robe.

"I thought I'd call you just to make sure you were up. I remembered your interviews this morning and I didn't want you to sleep in."

"Not much chance of that," Ron said in answer to the motel woman's voice. "I knew I'd wake up in plenty of time. Besides, those logging trucks make a pretty good alarm clock."

"Maybe you'll have a chance to get used to them."

"Maybe so," Ron said, "but I think I'll always prefer whistles."

"Why whistles?" the motel woman asked.

"Because that's what I grew up with in Tacoma where I'm from. We live close to the Asarco copper smelter where my dad works, and the whistles always blow to signal the end of a shift and the beginning of another. There's a rhythm to the day that the whistles remind you of. I guess I've come to count on those whistles, and the sound of the logging trucks is more grating than comforting."

"Maybe the sound of the logging trucks is as comforting to us as the sound of the whistles is to you," the motel woman offered. "Maybe it's more of what you get used to."

"Maybe," Ron answered. "I guess I'll just have to wait and see how I take to the new sound if I stay in Lebanon."

"Well, stay or not, you'd better start getting ready to greet the morning and Dr Harrison and Bill Polk."

"Thanks for the call. I think you're right. By the way," he added, "how much do I owe you for the room?"

"That's right," the motel woman answered. "We forgot all about that, didn't we? I guess we got too caught up in the high school. Anyway, it's ten dollars."

"Okay. I'll pay you as soon as I get ready. Besides, you have to tell me how to get to the superintendent's office and to the high school, too. I have no idea."

"No problem," the motel woman answered. "As I told you when you checked in, Lebanon's a small town and things are easy to find. I'll direct you to where you have to go."

"Well, thanks again for the wake-up call. I guess I wouldn't have to live near the highway if I were to stay. But wherever I live," Ron continued, "I know I'm ready to teach, even if I don't quite know what to teach."

"To begin with," the motel woman said, "don't be late for the interviews. I'll be here when you're ready."

"Okay. I won't be long. Thanks again."

"You're welcome. Goodbye."

"Goodbye," Ron answered and hung up the phone.

It was almost seven forty-five when he turned on the shower and stepped under the warm water. Ten minutes later he stood in the steamy bathroom, drying himself and thinking of what he was going to be asked later in the morning and early afternoon. He smiled when he realized he didn't know what the questions would be so that he couldn't plan his answers in the first place. But as he dried himself and thought, he did resolve to present himself honestly and to tell the truth. He knew he would be wrong to try to impress Dr Harrison or Mr Polk by telling them what he thought they wanted to hear. He wouldn't deceive because he realized he would have to continually keep up any deception he would create. He finished drying himself, wiped the steam from the bathroom mirror with his towel, and looked at his youthful reflection. He wasn't resigned to being Ron Petrich from Tacoma, Washington. Instead, he was proud of his identity. And that's how he would present himself. He knew he could teach and he was eager to start. With such resolve his butterflies vanished, and he readied his young face for his morning shave.

He shaved deliberately, as was his customary practice, and splashed on his Old Spice aftershave with the same care. He liked his daily shave partly because it was relatively new to him. He was a late bloomer in his teenage years. But he had no fear of time and all that it guarantees and, therefore, performed his morning routine with the proper ceremony more in celebration of time than in resigned consumption of it.

Accordingly, when the time came to get dressed in his interview clothes, the ceremony only continued. Ron learned his sense of ritual from the altar-centered Catholic Church. In his individual life he was the celebrant. He was the priest. In a sense his life was a reenactment of the Sacrifice of the Cross with the sacrifice lying not in death and in how one dies, but rather in life and in how one lives. Thus the sacrificial act associated with Christ wasn't his death by crucifixion or by any other popular means. The sacrificial act, instead, involved how Christ lived with the subsequent sacrificial life resulting in his crucifixion. If Ron Petrich didn't consciously identify with Christ as one of his fictional counterparts, the seeds of such conscious awareness definitely were planted. And watching him put on his dress slacks and coat and tie, as if they were sacred vestments, left no doubt that his conscious recognition of oneness with the sacrificial Christ would occur in time. To Ron the coat and tie were garments of the teacher. They were vestments, and he was fully aware that for him to be worthy of them, he had to live up to the responsibility they represented. Clean shaven and properly vestmented, he was ready to meet Dr George Harrison and Mr Bill Polk.

# III

"Well, you certainly look the part," the motel woman commented as Ron walked through the office doorway.

"Thanks, but I just hope I don't look too nervous. I've never had an interview with so much at stake before."

"There's nothing to worry about. Just be yourself and tell the truth. What more can you ask?"

"Nothing. But I can't help being a little nervous."

"I bet that once you start answering questions, the nervousness will go away. You're confident, aren't you?"

"Yes, I am. I know I can teach and I know I want to teach."

"Well, seeing as how Dr Harrison and Bill Polk need a teacher, and seeing as how it's the middle of the year, and seeing as how you'll come cheap, you'll have a job by this afternoon if your confidence is authentic."

"But I have to go home and get my clothes and then come back here to find a place to live."

"I think they'll allow for that," the motel woman said with a smile. "They don't expect you to start tomorrow."

"I can be ready soon," Ron said, "but not that soon, " he added with relief. "Anyway, where do I go?"

"Dr Harrison's office is in the junior high school, which used to be the high school. You passed it coming into town yesterday. Just head back the way you came and you'll see it off to your left, just past the welcome to Lebanon sign."

"I think I can handle that. Now, what about the high school?"

"Bill Polk's school is on Fifth Street, which is four blocks west of Main Street. It looks like a school, so you can't miss it."

"And what about breakfast?" Ron asked as he reached for his wallet for a ten dollar bill to cover the room charge. "Back to Bing's Kitchen?" he continued as he handed the motel woman the money.

"That's right," she answered, taking the ten dollar bill and giving Ron his receipt. "The best food in town breakfast, lunch, and dinner."

"Well, thanks for everything," Ron said as he took his receipt and headed for the door. "You've been a big help, and you made me feel right at home."

"You're welcome," the motel woman replied. "Stop by this afternoon and let me know how everything went. Okay?"

"Sure," Ron answered. "I'll stop by before I head back home," he added, opening the office door to the morning mist and fog. "One way or the other, I'll stop by."

"I'll be expecting you," the motel woman said as Ron walked through the doorway. "Goodbye and good luck."

"Goodbye and thanks. I'll be back this afternoon," he said as he closed the door behind him and walked in the foggy mist toward his '65 light blue Malibu parked in the space in front of room number four.

His breakfast of sausage and eggs at Bing's Kitchen was no more significant than his last night's dinner of breaded veal cutlets. Lebanon, Oregon, had no special hold on him, and thus its food was simply food. It wasn't like his mother's cooking, for example, that, supported by their family heritage, occupied a special place in his heart. There was magic in her cooking whether it be standard fare, such as sausage and eggs, or Slavic, ethnic fare, such as apple strudel or sarma—a combination of hamburger, sausage, and rice rolled up and wrapped in individual cabbage leaves. There wasn't much difference between his church's altar and his home's dinner table. In either case the preparation and serving of food provided the central act in a potentially affective ritual. But he felt no ritual and no affect power as he ate his sausage and eggs at Bing's

Kitchen. They tasted good because he was hungry, but there was nothing beyond the taste. After he finished breakfast and paid his bill, he found himself with half an hour to kill before his ten o'clock appointment with Dr Harrison.

With some time to spare Ron thought he would be adventurous and explore some of Lebanon and the surrounding country, all the time keeping track of Main Street that ran north and south, splitting the town. He decided to head a little farther south past the Gables Motel where he discovered, off to his left, a road that cut in front of a lumber mill to intersect with the main road leading to Sweet Home and points south. He turned left onto the intersecting road and headed back toward Lebanon, this time along River Road that followed what he came to know as the Santiam River, at least partially known for its annual steelhead run. But for now it was just a river, running through the January fog and mist, that didn't provide any challenge to Ron's native Puget Sound country of western Washington. His identity with Lebanon was anything but immediate.

The Puget Sound country of northwestern Washington had left its mark on him, and no other geographic location was going to easily replace it. Besides, Ron was from Tacoma, which bred in him an equally solid identity, probably due to the fact that Tacoma lived constantly in the shadow of Seattle, hailed as the crowned jewel of Puget Sound and the Northwest. The Sound, named after the 18th century explorer, Peter Puget, cut a majestic path through western Washington from the Straits of Juan de Fuca, near its northernmost boundary, to the state capital of Olympia, more than 100 miles to the south. The Santiam River, running parallel to Lebanon's River Road, seemed tame an insignificant when seen in relation to the waters of the Sound. It seemed especially so when seen in relation to Tacoma's Commencement Bay and the wooded majesty of its Point Defiance Park that thrust itself out into the Sound just to the north of the Tacoma Narrows, guarding the southeastern entry into the Bay.

From his front porch at home in Tacoma's Old Town district on North 28th, just east of McCarver Street that led from Tacoma Avenue to the south to the Old Town dock on the southern shore of Commencement Bay, Ron could see both Point Defiance and the expanse of the Bay that led to its northwest entry at Brown's Point. Commencement Bay seemed to open to an unlimited expanse of land and water beyond the Olympic Mountains to the west. The Olympics and the Cascade Range, lying more than 200 miles to the east and dominated by the snowcapped presence of 14,000 foot Mt Rainier, created a natural, expansive setting that made the wooded wetlands of Lebanon's River Road and the Santiam River seem uninspiring and confining.

To the native of western Oregon perhaps the Santiam River setting proved to be as potentially affective as did that of Puget Sound, the Olympics, and the Cascades for the native of western Washington. But Ron Petrich wasn't native to the country he was tentatively exploring as he drove up River Road toward the north end of Lebanon and ultimately to the office of Dr George Harrison, the superintendent of the Lebanon Union School District. He couldn't help feeling closed in by the confining space of the Santiam River country that cut through the heart of the Willamette Valley. Besides, the Willamette Valley was farm country and, still unbeknownst to Ron, Protestant country. In contrast, Puget Sound—Commencement Bay especially—was industrial country, smelter country and—most significantly—Catholic country. Tacoma's original city of Old Town was settled not by American Protestant immigrants from the nation's heartland, but rather by Old Country, predominantly Catholic, immigrants from the long-established traditions of Eastern Europe. No wonder Ron felt somewhat confined and out of place as he continued his exploratory drive along the banks of the Santiam. The fog and the intermittent mist didn't help as he finally decided he'd better turn left on an intersecting street and find his way back to Main Street and his ten o'clock appointment with Dr Harrison. He needed a teaching job and he had to start someplace.

It was almost nine-fifty when he discovered Main Street once again, but in a town the size of Lebanon having ten minutes to get someplace on time could seem like an eternity. He found himself close to the north end of town, and he turned right on Main Street as he headed for Dr Harrison's office in the old high school building. He saw the building sitting off to the left as he neared the sign that welcomed both natives and travelers to Lebanon. He turned left at the intersection just in front of the welcoming sign, drove past what he would come to know as St Edward's Catholic Church, and, two blocks past the church, turned right into the school. He had five minutes to spare as he got out of the car, locked his door, and headed toward the main entrance of the new junior high school building that housed the administrative offices of the Lebanon Union School District.

The building looked comfortably like a school was supposed to look, being made of red brick and rising at least two stories from the ground level. Ron wasn't much of a fan of the modern educational architecture that favored campus-style schools of one-story, glassed and straight-angled buildings. He preferred the stately dignity of the established architectural design with its inspiring, multistoried brick structures and rounded archways that always seemed to grace the main entrance. The main building at his Tacoma high school, Bellarmine Prep—named after the 17th century saint, Robert Bellarmine— reflected such a design as did the Administration Building at Seattle University. The fact that Lebanon's old high school building reflected that inspiring style as well told Ron that the new high school, Bill Polk's school as the motel woman said, reflected the recent trend toward the campus style that, by itself, didn't appear to command the respect Ron associated with school buildings. He wished this building was still the high school. But it was 1967 after all. He did need a job, and he had to start somewhere. After admiring the architectural grandeur, he pulled open the solid oak entrance door and stepped inside.

At once he was struck by the familiar smell that took him back to his days at Bellarmine. It seemed like yesterday that he left the pungent, musty smell of Bellarmine Prep with its crucifixes, holy water basins, and black-robed Jesuits. Seattle University was Jesuit as well, but its size and secular character helped soften that influence. Thus Ron found his Bellarmine experience to be much more memorable. His high school was more enclosed; and within its walls, supported by the sacramental objects of the Catholic Church, you could see, feel, and smell the presence of majesty. And that constant, majestic presence supported the black-cassocked Jesuit priests and scholastics. For Ron and the rest of his generation, it had been two years since the conclusion of Vatican II. The changes implemented as a result had diluted, to a large extent, he thought, that presence—exposing the less than impressive individuality of many of the men once supported by the black cassock and the religion it represented. Ron liked majesty, quiet majesty, and felt uncomfortable with its dilution, no matter how well intended. As a public school teacher, he knew he would have no black cassock with any affect power to support him, but he was determined to be enough of an individual to compensate for the lack of that institutional support. In fact, he was beginning to learn that no one could count on it in the first place.

He couldn't help wishing he could get his start in a building such as the one in which he was standing. Even without Catholic sacramental objects and black-robed Jesuits, such a building by itself had the power to command—or at least to suggest—respect for education and maybe even to awaken a sense of awe in expectation of its prospects. He had seen progress in Tacoma with the construction of Woodrow Wilson High School in 1958, following the popular, campus-style design. And even though he could understand how anyone could welcome its cleanliness and open-air accessibility, he couldn't help thinking that one would have to sacrifice the warmth and comforting, musty educational smell of his own 1924 vintage Bellarmine Prep to partake of Woodrow Wilson's progressive atmosphere. Ron wasn't consciously aware of it yet, but he was primarily an ancient teacher in a modern era. As such, he was committed to fulfilling the ideal suggested by the architectural grandeur of the educational past.

For now, however, he simply found himself in the market for a teaching job inspired by the fact that, in the face of his fears, he had found something he was suited for. He felt comforted by the familiar smell of Lebanon's old high school building. Alive with the subsequent inspiration, he looked for the sign that would direct him to the superintendent's office and spotted it painted on the wall of the main hallway at the top of a short flight of stairs. He walked up the four stairs and followed the arrow that pointed to the right. As he turned to walk down the hallway, he saw the sign identifying the superintendent's office extending from the archway of the first door on the right, or east, side of the hall. Based on what the woman at the Gables Motel had told him about Dr Harrison, Ron wasn't expecting an individual of black-cassocked majesty. He walked into Dr Harrison's office with one minute to spare for his ten o'clock interview.

"May I help you?" the secretary asked, looking up from her neatly organized desk set comfortably in the center of the large room. Surveying the expanse and initially oblivious to the secretary's greeting, Ron stood and stared out the windows opening to the building's green-grassed lawn that stretched to the sidewalk which ran parallel to western Oregon's Santiam Highway, leading into and through Lebanon to points south.

"My name is Ron Petrich and I have a ten o' clock appointment with Dr Harrison," he finally answered, trying to regain his composure

"Oh, yes," the secretary replied, smiling. "Dr Harrison is expecting you. I'll tell him you're here," she added as she stood up from her desk and walked toward the door to her right at the north end of the room.

She was an attractive woman about 30 years old and Ron watched attentively as she walked across the room to Dr Harrison's office. He had an eye for beauty that Dr Harrison's secretary had awakened, even though he realized she was a bit old for him. She wasn't seductive by any means, but Ron couldn't help noticing her gracefully proportionate figure as she walked to Dr Harrison's office door and back to her desk.

"Dr Harrison will see you now," she told him, smiling in awareness of his acknowledgment of her mature womanhood. "Right in there," she added, pointing in the direction of Dr Harrison's office door.

"Thank you," Ron said, feeling a slight flush in his cheeks. "Do I just walk in?"

"Yes," she answered pleasantly. "He's waiting for you."

"Okay," Ron said as he returned her smile and walked toward the open door at the north end of the room.

He never had seen a superintendent before, but from what he had been thinking and imagining, even he could tell that Dr Harrison, with his aloof presence, looked the part and that his office, framed by its book-lined walls, only reinforced that image. The books at least suggested that Dr Harrison was learned, but Ron remembered the woman at the Gables commenting on his distance from it all.

"You must be Mr Petrich," Dr Harrison said, extending his right hand as he met Ron just inside his door, having moved out from behind his desk.

"I'm sorry, but it's Petrich with a short 'e,'" Ron politely said, shaking Dr Harrison's outstretched hand as firmly as he had been taught.

"Oh, excuse me," Dr Harrison replied, relinquishing his grip on Ron's hand and moving back behind his desk. "We don't get many names like that in Lebanon. What kind of a name is it?"

"It's a Slavic name. Croatian to be exact."

"That's nice," Dr Harrison said, settling in behind his desk in his swivel chair. "I'm from sturdy English stock myself."

"I see," Ron said, somewhat awkwardly still standing in front of Dr Harrison's desk.

"Oh, I'm sorry," Dr. Harrison said, recognizing Ron's awkward plight. "Sit down," he added, pointing to the straight-backed chair sitting in front of his desk and slightly to the left.

His office truly was impressive both in its size and in its wealth of books, the majority of which were of the textbook variety dealing with education and its various rational approaches. The office took up more than half of what used to be two high school classrooms, and it wasn't hard to tell that Dr Harrison was impressed with his nameplate that identified himself and his social position. His windows opened to the same green-grassed lawn that stretched out to meet the Santiam Highway, but, in contrast to the curtainless decor displayed in his secretary's office, Dr Harrison had them neatly draped in a deep maroon color with gold trim that fit the dark wood paneling of the walls. The outside light shined through open venetian blinds and was absorbed by a plush, dark brown—almost chocolate—pile carpet that covered the office floor wall to wall. His textbook library seemed appropriate for a room of ostentatious elegance that never could be confused with stately dignity, and Dr Harrison himself represented the exact opposite from what Ron aspired to as a result of his obedience to the heritage of his personal, historic past. While Ron, even unbeknownst to him, was more inspired by responsibility than attracted by rewards, Dr Harrison obviously, and certainly more consciously, was a man firmly attached to the rewards of his social role with little or no regard for the responsibility involved. As Ron's motel woman had commented, he was distant from it all.

Ron accepted Dr Harrison's offer of a seat and, politely although nervously smiling, awaited his first question.

"Well," Dr. Harrison said with a forced smile marking his plump, round face, "what brings you to Lebanon?"

"I'm a teacher and I need a job," Ron answered honestly, trying to look Dr Harrison directly in the eye. But his hazel eyes were neither penetrating nor particularly attentive, making it hard for Ron to make contact. He felt as though he were responding more to an apparition than to a man in the flesh. Dr Harrison's lack of authentic interest, along with his inattentiveness, made Ron feel uncomfortable, and the superintendent's shiny bald head only contributed to his worldly and disinterested demeanor. In addition, his custom-tailored, brown suit, starched white shirt, and patterned, orange silk tie took Ron even further from his Tacoma, Catholic, smelter past— as did Dr Harrison's ashen white skin. Still, Ron managed to sit upright and confident in his straight-backed chair as he tried to look Dr Harrison in the eye while he awaited the superintendent's next question.

"Hummm, are you sure you can teach?" Dr Harrrison asked with a cynical, suspecting smirk on his face.

"Yes," Ron answered without hesitation. "I really think I can."

"What makes you so sure?" Dr Harrison asked, this time leaning across his desk with that same smirk on his face and with his bald head shining as if it were bathed in lotion.

"Well," Ron began to respond in the face of Dr Harrison's attack, "I'm sure I can teach because I proved it to myself during my student teaching experience."

"But student teaching isn't the real thing," Dr Harrison interrupted. "You've never had your own classroom," he added, still leaning threateningly across his desk, cynical smirk and all.

"I know it isn't the real thing," Ron said, "and I know I've never had my own classroom. But I know I can teach, and I look forward to having my own classroom and my own students. I know teaching isn't easy by any means, but I really feel that I was effective as a student teacher. And I see no reason not to expect that I can be just as effective as a real, full-time teacher. I've found something I can do and now I want to do it. I came to Lebanon because you have a job opening, and I'd like to get started without much delay."

"Do you have any idea of the kind of situation you'd be stepping into?"

"No, I don't. I only know that you have a position open at the high school."

"We have that position open," Dr Harrison continued with his cynical smirk frozen in place, "because we had to let the teacher go. She couldn't control the students and she took some liberties with them she shouldn't have. She embarrassed herself, the school, and this office. Do you understand?"

"I'm not sure, but I think so," Ron answered. "I can assure you that I never would do anything to embarrass the school or the district itself."

"How can I be sure?" Dr Harrison asked, still suspecting and still smirking. "As I said earlier, you're young and look even younger."

"I know I'm young," Ron replied, "and I know I look even younger. But I really don't think it will make any difference as long as I have confidence in myself as a teacher. I'm not interested in being anyone's friend. I'm only interested in being everyone's teacher. You don't have anything to worry about because I have great respect for the teaching profession."

"What about the young girls?" Dr Harrison asked with a leering smirk this time. "Some of them look as old as you do, and they can look awfully attractive."

"I know," Ron said, "but they're students and I'm a teacher. There's a difference and a necessary distance. Nothing embarrassing will happen because I won't do anything to encourage it. I really don't worry about the girls, and I really don't worry about discipline, either. I know I can do the job."

"Hummm," Dr Harrison responded, once again leaning back in his chair and cupping his right thumb and forefinger around his double chin. "Maybe you'll work out okay after all. I hesitate to admit it, but I am impressed by your confidence and belief in your ability. I don't think you're pretending."

"I'm not," Ron said. "I really think I can do the job and I'd like the chance."

"And you don't think you'll have any problems with the young girls?"

"No, I don't. I don't want to be a teacher because of the young girls or for any related reason."

"Why do you want to be a teacher?" Dr Harrison asked, leaning further back in his swivel chair.

"Because it's something I can do and It's something I'm suited for," Ron answered. "I look forward to accepting the responsibility."

"Well," Dr Harrison abruptly replied, returning his swivel chair to its upright position, "we do need a teacher, and we do need one now. You have an interview with Mr Polk at the high school at two o' clock. Isn't that right?"

"Yes, that's right," Ron answered.

"I'll talk to him in the meantime," Dr Harrison continued, "but I will say that if he wants you, as far as I'm concerned, you can have the job. I can't offer it to you without having you talk to Mr Polk first, but I don't think you'll embarrass anyone. I couldn't put up with any more of that after this semester."

"I don't think you would have anything to put up with. I'm only interested in being a teacher and nothing else."

"Well," Dr Harrison concluded, standing up from his swivel chair, "you must have learned something at Seattle University. Isn't that where you went to college?"

"Yes. All the information should be there in my placement file."

"That's right," Dr Harrison said, rummaging through the papers scattered on top of his desk. "I have that file someplace. But it doesn't matter. I've seen enough, and I'm satisfied. You're hired if Bill Polk is convinced you can do the job," he continued, extending his right hand as Ron stood up from his straight-backed chair.

"Thank you," he said, grasping Dr Harrison's hand once again as firmly as he had been taught.

"I'll have the contract ready for you to sign if Bill Polk wants you," Dr Harrison said, letting go of Ron's hand. "In the meantime, I hope you enjoy looking around Lebanon."

"I think I will. In fact, I already have."

"We have a nice little town here," Dr Harrison continued. "It's quiet and we expect our teachers to live accordingly."

"I don't think there would be any problem. I think I'd understand what was expected of me."

"That's good. That's what I'm looking for," Dr Harrison said. "I don't want any more trouble. Maybe I'll see you back here after you talk with Bill Polk," he added as Ron made his way to his closed office door.

"I hope so," Ron said as he grasped the doorknob and pulled open the door. "It was nice to meet you and thank you for your time."

"You're welcome, and it was nice to meet you, too," Dr Harrison replied, trying to smile as his bald head and round, ashen white face glistened in the light that filtered in through the open venetian blinds. "You can just leave the door open as you leave, if you don't mind."

"Okay," Ron said. "Thanks again for your time," he added as he stepped across the threshold into the secretary's office. He caught her smile and returned it as he turned to his right and walked out the door, down the hallway toward the main entrance, and out into the January mist—glad to be free from Dr Harrison's cynical, suspecting smirk that seemed permanently attached to his jowly, round face, complemented by his shiny bald head.

Once free of Dr Harrison's smirking countenance, Ron felt compelled to talk about the experience. He could have called his mother in Tacoma, but he knew she really wouldn't understand, never having met Dr Harrison. Ron felt that he had to be seen to be believed. He never had encountered anyone like him before and, as far as he knew, only the woman at the Gables Motel had shared his experience.

Knowing she would understand and knowing she would be genuinely interested in his observations, judging from her initial interest in him and in the vacant teaching job, he decided to drive back to the Gables in answer to his compelling need to talk about his first experience with a school superintendent. He hoped Dr Harrison was more atypical than typical, but he wasn't sure. Resolved in his decision, he stepped into his Malibu, backed out of the parking lot, found his way to Main Street, turned to the right, and wasted no time sightseeing as he headed south once again toward the Gables Motel.

# IV

Betty Williams, the woman from the Gables Motel, thought she might see Ron sometime before his scheduled interview with Bill Polk at the high school. Although she didn't know Dr Harrison personally, Lebanon was a small town, and the superintendent of its Union School District—that included even smaller towns in the immediate vicinity—was a prominent and important figure. She knew Ron would have a lot to say after his interview with him, and she couldn't help thinking of how he was reacting to Dr Harrison once the clock passed ten. She considered herself a fair judge of character because people were her main interest in life, and she never found Dr Harrison particularly likable. She wasn't sure anyone did for that matter, but she was convinced that some of the less than complimentary comments she had heard during his tenure would have been directed at any superintendent and not specifically to him. She considered such talk gossip and did her best to avoid it. She was more interested in the individual and thus she wasn't as close-minded as were the more idle gossips who made up a significant segment of Lebanon's population. Dr Harrison was right in that the residents of Lebanon had a nice little town, but their pleasant community left its less energetic residents with a decidedly narrow view of life and of people as well.

Like many Lebanon residents, Betty Williams had immigrated from another section of the country. But unlike the majority of them, she no longer had any direct church affiliation, although she was raised in a Catholic parish in Billings, Montana. She was a widow now after her husband, Jack, died of cancer in the summer of 1965, just one-and-a-half years before Ron Petrich arrived in Lebanon. She had been married to Jack Williams since 1942 and in 1955 they left Billings and headed farther west to Oregon and the Willamette Valley. Jack worked as a machinist in Billings, but when he arrived in Lebanon, he decided to leave that trade behind. He and Betty had begun to talk about running their own business of some kind, and an exploratory trip to Oregon had taken them to the Willamette Valley and Lebanon. There they discovered the available Gables Motel, at the time newly constructed and not quite firmly established on the Santiam Highway. After much consideration they decided they had found what they were looking for and made their move. Betty never actually regretted the decision, although sometimes she missed the open grandeur of the West's Treasure State and wished that Jack were still here to share in the continuing adventure of her life.

She was born and lived within the confines of the Catholic Church until the conclusion of Vatican II that coincided with Jack's death in 1965. She always took her religion seriously, which meant that she had to question her own faith in conjunction with the reforming direction of her church. The direction of reform, which seemed to embrace pulpit preaching more than she ever could remember, taught her that her individual belief was more centered in altar ritual and in the perennial celebration of the sacrificial life of Christ. She knew of the Church's pulpit rules and she did her best to obey them, but the sacrifice of the altar captured her imagination and awakened her curiosity. Vatican II's reform, that appeared to favor the pulpit at the expense of the altar, left her alienated from the Church but at the same time strengthened in her own faith in the affective altar message that she was convinced celebrated the creative potential of the individual human being. If she couldn't articulate this faith, she found comfort in it nonetheless. It helped her accept and affirm her husband's death because she knew a death that followed a sacrificial life was, in itself, life-renewing. After arriving in Lebanon, Ron didn't encounter a grieving widow in search of a savior. On the contrary, he encountered a woman of courage and conviction whom he knew would understand his reaction to having met and interviewed with Dr Harrison. And to Mrs Williams, Ron, with his Slavic name and youthful energy, represented the arrival of a new generation and a breath of fresh air in a confined community supported by lumberjack taverns and country Grange Halls. She knew he would be tested, but she welcomed his arrival and couldn't help speculating on the inevitable adventure of his life.

Ron pulled up to the Gables at about ten forty-five and Mrs Williams wasn't surprised when she noticed him walking toward the motel office door. She smiled in recognition and walked from her attached house to greet him as walked through the office door.

"You must want to talk about your experience with Dr Harrison," she said as Ron opened the door and stepped across the threshold.

"How did you know?" he asked, stopping just inside the door.

"I figured you'd want to talk to someone after such an experience. And as far as I know, I'm the only person in Lebanon you'd even consider talking to."

"But I wouldn't consider talking to you if I didn't think you'd understand," Ron said, walking toward the main desk.

"And what makes you think I'll understand?"

"Because you were genuinely interested in me and in the teaching position at the high school. Besides, I enjoyed talking to you when I first arrived in town."

"You're right," Mrs Williams answered. "I am interested and I enjoyed talking to you as well. But if we're going to talk further, you might as well come back here out of the office," she continued, motioning toward the living room of her house to the rear.

"Is it okay?' Ron asked, making no move to accept her invitation.

"Sure. It's all very proper. Besides, I'm certainly old enough to be your mother. So, come on," she continued, motioning with her head toward her living room. "It's more comfortable in here."

"All right," Ron said. "But how do I get back there?"

"I'm sorry," Mrs. Williams said, shaking her head. "This way," she added, lifting up the hinged portion of the counter top nearest the wall to Ron's left. "Just step on through and follow me."

"Thanks," Ron said as he stepped through the opening and followed her into the living room situated behind the outer office.

The room and the house itself was bigger than anyone would imagine after standing in the motel office. It wasn't as big as the living room in Ron's white frame house in Tacoma's Old Town district; but, nonetheless, it left him with the same warm, comfortable feeling. He welcomed the familiarity of the rust-colored shag carpet that covered the floor, wall to wall, and of the patterned couch and matching love seat as well. His own living room was decorated in a similar fashion, although his mother favored solid colors in her couch and matching love seat. Still, the quietly flowered design, embroidered in brown and orange, of Mrs Williams' matching pair tastefully complemented the rich shag carpet. The walls were painted in antique white, and off-white, barley-colored drapes hung gracefully on either side of the picture window that looked out toward the Santiam Highway to the west. A rust-colored rocking chair sat in one corner underneath what looked like an antique floor lamp. Its ornately designed golden base supported matching arms that stretched out to hold three individual light bulbs placed slightly underneath the glass enclosure that held the three-way reading light framed by a sloping white lamp shade.

The living room couch faced the fireplace on the north wall with the love seat placed to its right along the east wall. The fireplace mantle, painted the same antique white as the living room walls, held a decorative, green ivy plant and its polished, bronze planter. A framed charcoal drawing of a Willamette Valley country scene, faintly visible but complete with covered bridge, hung directly above the ivy. Ron sat down on the end of the couch closest to the love seat and somewhat nervously picked up the Newsweek magazine that was sitting on the antique oak coffee table in front of him and slightly to his left. He had turned around to look at the matching oak secretary standing behind him, also to his left, at the north end of the east wall when Mrs Williams sat down comfortably on the edge of the love seat directly across from him.

"Does it remind you of home?" she asked, smiling, as Ron put the copy of Newsweek back where he found it.

"Sort of," he answered. "Only my house is quite a bit older. I live in the North End of Tacoma near Commencement Bay in Old Town. It's not a fancy house like some of the North End mansions farther up the hill from the Bay, but it's old and homey. We can stand on our front porch and see the Bay and Brown's Point on the other side. Have you ever been to Tacoma?"

"No," Mrs Williams answered. "As a matter of fact, I've never been to Tacoma or Seattle."

"I went to Seattle University, but I didn't, and don't, have much to do with Seattle itself. I'm a Tacoman and Seattle thinks it's just a little superior to us."

"It's good to know who you are," Mrs Williams said. "It gives you something to live up to and to live for. It helps to make life an adventure."

"It sounds like you should be the teacher."

"Oh, not really," Mrs Williams replied, smiling, "but thanks for the compliment. That's just something I've learned from my own experience with life."

"So, maybe experience is the best teacher after all."

"I'm sure it is, but it's only what we make of it. I don't think it means much of anything unless we try to understand. If we take the time and if we try to understand, then I think experience has something to teach us. But we have to put forth the effort. We have to make the sacrifice."

"Your experience so far must have been pretty interesting," Ron said, continuing to look around the living room and at the same time studying the lady he still only knew as the motel woman. She had to be at least 45 years old, he thought, because she appeared to be close to his mother's age. And his mother was 47, having had Ron when she was 25. His motel woman, like his mother, was quietly attractive in the manner of a woman interested in dignity and its preservation. Neither his mother nor his motel woman seemed dedicated to the continuation of youth in the face of the natural advancement of time, and in both instances he felt secure in the presence of someone who wasn't afraid to stand up as an adult. His mother's hair was lighter than his motel woman's, but both women wore it curled with bangs that extended to the middle of their foreheads.

Where Ron's mother was fair-skinned, his motel woman was naturally darker, as though she somehow had more exposure to the sun. His motel woman's nose lacked the Slavic distinction of his mother's, but her eyes were every bit as alive and penetrating. Her cheeks were lightly rouged just like his mother's, and her lips were softly decorated with a slightly noticeable shade of red. His mother probably would use a lighter shade of lipstick because of her fairer skin, but she would be just as dignified in its application, relying on her own experiential judgment rather than on any socially popular expectations. In short, neither woman, in Ron's perception, appeared to lack the courage it takes to live a quiet, individual life. He wasn't ashamed to admit being inspired in the presence of either his mother or his motel woman.

Neither woman dressed loudly, as had become the fashion of the age, and neither had adopted the bell-bottomed style of slacks, although both had retired the traditional housedress associated with women of the recent, 20th century past. Ron's mother felt that bell-bottoms, if they were right for anyone, were right for the young but not for her. His motel woman must have felt the same way because she was wearing the same straight-legged slacks he knew his mother to wear. To complement the navy blue slacks, his motel woman was wearing a neatly pressed, white cotton blouse that couldn't be identified with any era. Neither his mother nor his motel woman could be categorized or typed. They were expressions of woman, plain and simple, who had followed—even if they and Ron didn't realize it—in the footsteps of Adam and Eve who had the courage to eat the apple when the serpent issued the call.

No wonder Ron felt comfortable talking to either woman. And for now, in Lebanon, Oregon, he couldn't help but see, even if he couldn't explain, the striking difference between his motel woman and Dr Harrison. Even at the relatively uninitiated age of 22, he could see that a person of the responsible countenance of his motel woman, male or female, should occupy the exalted and visible position of school superintendent.

"Well," Mrs Williams said, pausing briefly to reflect on Ron's inquiry into the nature of her experience with life, "I suppose it has been interesting at that. But I think everyone's experience with life should be interesting, each in its own unique way. I think it's more a matter of how honestly we reflect on that experience that really matters. Experience without honest reflection doesn't do anyone much good."

"That makes sense to me," Ron replied. "I like to think about what I've experienced. I like to try to figure out what it all means. I don't think I understand yet, but I know it has to mean something."

"I'm sure it does."

"Are you from Lebanon or did you come from somewhere else?" Ron asked, continuing his inquiry.

"I came here with my husband from Billings, Montana, in 1955."

"With your husband?" Ron asked surprised. "I'm sorry, but for some reason the fact that you were married never crossed my mind."

"Jack and I were married for 23 years," Mrs. Williams said wistfully. "But he died a year and a half ago in July of 1965."

"I'm sorry."

"That's okay. I had 23 good years with him, which is more than some people have. I wish Jack were still here, but I find a sense of strength in his death. As strange as it may sound, I find it life-renewing."

"And you didn't have any children?" Ron asked hesitatingly.

"No. We would have liked to have had children, but it just didn't work out that way."

"Have you ever thought of going back to Montana?"

"Yes, I have. Sometimes I miss the expanse of Montana and can feel confined in the Willamette Valley. But Lebanon has been my home almost as long as Billings was."

"I have relatives in Montana," Ron said, "in Butte."

"I've heard a lot about Butte, but strangely enough I've never been there. But from what I've heard, I can see the connection with your name. You must be Catholic then."

"Yes," Ron answered. "I went to a Catholic grade school, high school, and college."

"I never went to a Catholic grade school, and I didn't go to college, but I did go to Billings Central High School. So, I had some Catholic school experience. Have you ever been to Butte?"

"A couple of times," Ron answered.

"What did you think of it?" Mrs Williams asked.

"I found it interesting with all the copper mines and the steep hills, but I didn't spend enough time there to think too much about it one way or the other. I do know that almost everyone is Catholic in Butte and that it's a wide-open town in terms of drinking and related activities."

"Yes, that's putting it mildly," Mrs. Williams said with a smile. "I've heard many stories about the goings on in Butte. Sometimes I feel as though I've missed something by never having visited, even though I only lived 250 miles away. Billings is part of Montana, and I grew up Catholic, but my Billings experiences didn't always match the stories I heard about Butte. Still, Lebanon is a far cry from either experience. We do have a Catholic Church, however, St Edward's, close to Dr Harrison's office. You've driven by it several times already. But Lebanon, in relation to the stories I've heard about Butte and even in relation to my own experiences in Billings, isn't what you would call a Catholic town. It's a Protestant town if it's anything, and from what I can tell, the Catholic Church has decided to become more Protestant, even in its moral outlook. Things are changing and it's awfully confusing as a result. It'll be a challenge to teach the products of the confusion."

"I'm sure it will be, but I didn't get the impression that Dr Harrison cares very much about such a challenge. As you said, he mainly wants someone who won't embarrass the school or him."

"That's right. But I'm sorry. I almost forgot your reason for being here with all our talk about Billings and Butte, about being Catholic, and about Catholic and Protestant towns, and about confusing changes. What did you think of Dr Harrison?"

"I wasn't very impressed," Ron answered, "but I'm not used to commenting on adults. I think an adult should be respected, but I can't say I left Dr Harrison's office with much respect for him. I almost feel guilty."

"You have nothing to feel guilty about as long as you reacted honestly. Maybe Dr Harrison didn't prove himself worthy of your respect. If such is the case, you don't have to respect him. The trick, then, is to respect the role even if the individual occupying it isn't worthy of it. Do you see?"

"I think so, and I think I expected quite a bit from a superintendent."

"You probably didn't expect any more than what the role calls for."

"You know something," Ron said with a flash of insight, "it reminds me of something I remember from one of Shakespeare's plays, although I can't think of exactly which one."

"I don't know anything about Shakespeare," Mrs Williams said. "But what does it remind you of?

"Something one of his characters said about wearing a crown," Ron answered. "The words seemed interesting, but irrelevant, at the time because they referred to someone becoming king. And I've never known, and probably never will know, a king. But come to think of it, Dr Harrison is like a king in that he's a superintendent."

"It makes sense to me. Maybe whatever you remember from Shakespeare doesn't apply only to the role of king. Maybe it applies to any important role in society or to any role associated with responsibility of some kind. But I don't know. I may be getting way ahead of myself. Just what exactly do you remember?"

"I think the quotation says 'uneasy lies the head that wears the crown.' Dr Harrison wears a crown because he's the superintendent, but I'll wear a crown, too, if I teach here or anywhere else. It's something to think about."

"So, what do you think it means?" Mrs Williams asked.

"What does what mean?"

"The quotation. What do you think the quotation from Shakespeare means now that you've experienced it?"

"That's right," Ron answered with his eyes still alive. "I have experienced it. Now it's no longer irrelevant, even though it comes from a time as remote as Shakespeare's and even though it's spoken in reference to a person destined to become King of England. But it's not about becoming king at all."

"What's it about then?" Mrs Williams asked.

"It's about recognizing and accepting responsibility," Ron answered. "And I think it applies to all of us."

"And you think Dr Harrison is attracted to his superintendent role for reasons other than the responsibility involved. Is that right?"

"That's right. I think anyone can be attracted to a role, such as that of superintendent, for reasons that have nothing to do with responsibility."

"There are more than a few rewards as well," Mrs Williams added.

"That's for sure. I could tell that from sitting in his office."

"Can you describe it?"

"Yes, and it looked more like the palace of a king than the office of the superintendent. I mean I think any superintendent deserves an office that's equal to the status of his position. I can see where that makes sense. But I don't think a school superintendent should make such a huge distinction between himself and everyone else. It just makes him more aloof. As a man, as an individual, I don't think he can be any more important than anyone else. My dad works in a copper smelter, for example, but he can't be any less important as an individual than Dr Harrison, can he?"

"No, I don't think he can. As individuals we all have to be equal, but the roles we occupy in society aren't equal. Not everyone could become a school superintendent, for example. To think otherwise, I think, is to be awfully naive. I don't think it's easy to understand the idea of equality, especially when we appear unequal in so many ways."

"That's right. But maybe that's why we need literature and religion. Maybe they remind us of our equality as individuals. But I don't think Dr Harrison has much regard for equality. If he did, I don't think he'd have such elegant maroon-colored drapes decorating his windows. I thought they seemed awfully heavy for a superintendent's office, and the gold trim didn't help. I couldn't feel at ease. And all the books. I've never seen so many books."

"Maybe Dr Harrison is a learned man?" Mrs Williams inquired with a smile.

"I don't know," Ron answered, "but if he's an expression of that idea, he's sure let it go to his head. I don't think an authentic learned man would be so obviously attached to rewards. I think such a person, male or female, would be more inspired by responsibility and the fulfillment of it. Any rewards would be more of an embarrassment. They'd be secondary."

"Maybe that's what Shakespeare was trying to communicate. Maybe that's why the head that wears the crown is so uneasy. And maybe we shouldn't accept the crown if we aren't willing to accept that uneasiness. Maybe Shakespeare isn't so remote after all. His vision certainly isn't far removed from my experience or yours. Maybe this experience with Dr Harrison, and your recalling that quotation, will help you develop some focus for your teaching. Do you think so?"

"Maybe it will," Ron answered. "My interview with Dr Harrison wasn't much, and I couldn't take my eyes off his shiny, bald head and his pale, ashen skin. But he's convinced that I won't embarrass him. He told me I could have the job and that I could sign the contract today, if Mr Polk wants me. He left the final decision to him. I don't think Dr Harrison cares about me, but that's okay. I don't need him to care. I just need him to give me a job. More than ever, I know I can teach. I'm ready to accept the challenge."

"As an authentic learned man?" Mrs. Williams asked.

"As an authentic learned man," Ron answered without hesitation.

## V

Ron Petrich never held any social aspiration beyond that of being a baseball player or a smelter worker, which were the primary attractions of his childhood. But, eventually, he had to face the fact that being a baseball player lay beyond the reach of his physical prowess. He didn't find such a fact easy to accept because he wasn't without the gifts of the heart. But, it seemed, such individuals weren't automatically blessed with the necessary physical gifts. He had encountered a similar situation with regard to smelter work and other "manly" enterprises. Although he had great respect for his dad's work, he found out he didn't belong there—at least not in this day and age. So, when he reached college age, he concerned his parents. He seemed to lack the aspiration of someone who knew what he wanted to be. But Mrs Williams, perhaps inadvertently, had identified that to which he aspired. He wanted to be an authentic learned man—just like his mom and dad and motel woman.

He wasn't afraid of responsibility. On the contrary, he had begun to learn, as a result of his conversation with Mrs Williams, that he both searched for and was inspired by it. He knew that if he wanted to fulfill the responsibility of the teacher, he had to be an authentic learned man. As an expression of such an individual, in the person of a woman and a motel owner, Mrs Williams was far more alive than was Dr Harrison who, impressed with his extensive textbook library, hid from the authentic learned man's wisdom of experience. Ron had indeed discovered a focus for his teaching. As a teacher of literature, he was destined to be a teacher of the wisdom of experience and never again would he trust textbook wisdom that wasn't clearly born from that same experiential world.

"Well," Mrs. Williams said, taking up the conversation once again, "now you have to switch your attention to Bill Polk at the high school. As I said earlier, he'll be different than Dr Harrison. The high school is his school, and to apply what you said earlier about Shakespeare and crowns and the uneasiness that comes with wearing them, I think Bill Polk will prove to be a person more interested in responsibility."

"I hope so," Ron said. "I wouldn't want to be too closely associated with Dr Harrison. I wouldn't want him watching over me every day."

"I don't think you'll have to worry about that," Mrs Williams said, smiling. "I'm sure you'll never see him—unless you do something to embarrass him."

"I don't know what that could be."

"I don't either. But remember that you're young and Lebanon is far from being a Catholic town in its moral expectations. It certainly isn't the Butte, Montana, I've heard about. And it's not even Billings or Tacoma. Just be aware of that and conduct yourself accordingly without giving up your youth."

"Dr Harrison seemed to be worried about me getting involved somehow with my students, with the girls. Why would he think that?"

"Probably because that's how he thinks and probably because he would if he were your age and confronted with attractive young girls."

"But they're students and I'm their teacher. Doesn't that make a difference? There's no way I would ever be involved with a student in the manner Dr Harrison suggested. I'm interested in teaching and nothing else. It seems to me that I won't have any trouble if I can honestly give that impression."

"I think you're right," Mrs Williams said, "and I don't think you'll have any trouble. Still, Dr Harrison's fears have been realized more than once. But I don't think an authentic learned man determined to fulfill the responsibility of a teacher has realized them. I don't think it can happen with anyone aware of, and inspired by, the uneasiness that comes with the crown. And to your students, teaching is a role worthy of a crown. They won't respect you if you don't live up to its responsibility. You have to be everybody's teacher without worrying about being anyone's friend."

"You know something?" Ron asked, looking at his motel woman with admiration.

"What's that?" she asked in return.

"You just might be the best teacher I've ever had and you know something else?"

"What?"

"I don't even know your name."

"Thanks for the compliment, but I'm not a teacher. I just enjoy talking to you. And by the way my name is Betty Williams."

"Well, Mrs Williams, you've certainly made my stay here so far. If Dr Harrison were Lebanon, I don't think I could live and teach here. But if Lebanon has room for you, despite its Protestant moral expectations, I think it must have room for me to live and teach as well."

"It can get to me every now and then, and sometimes Billings looks awfully good. But, for now anyway, I think I'll stay here. It's still open enough and I still feel comfortable. But I know things are changing. I just want the freedom to quietly live my honest, individual life. If I can do that here, there's no reason to leave."

"I'm ready to start what you've been doing all along. And I guess Lebanon provides me with as good a place as any."

"There are worse places. You'll learn a lot in the high school. But if you're a baseball man, be prepared for the fact that football is king in Lebanon. The coach is more well known than Dr. Harrison."

"What's his name?" Ron asked.

"Judson Heath," Mrs Williams answered. "You won't have any trouble noticing him. You can't miss his authoritative presence."

"Sounds like our football coach at Bellarmine in Tacoma. I am a baseball man, but I don't know what Bellarmine would have been like without football and its colors and the fight song that goes with it all."

"I remember that, too, from my days at Billings Central. But without a doubt, things are changing. Neither my generation nor yours had to deal with problems like hair length, for example. All of a sudden the length of a person's hair has become a real issue. It's a little scary, I think. I don't know where it's leading and I don't know which side I'm on."

"I know I have a lot to learn," Ron said, shaking his head. "But I have to get the job first."

"Believe me, you'll get the job. Bill Polk certainly will recommend you. As a matter of fact, I think he'll consider himself lucky to find someone of your caliber and commitment this time of the year, or any time of the year for that matter."

"Thanks. I wish you were the principal."

"No, thanks," Mrs Williams replied, shaking her head. "I'm content to run the Gables Motel and observe life as it comes and goes. Besides, I think you'll find that Bill Polk is as good a man as you'll ever find in the role of principal. The two of you will get along well."

"After all you've said, I'm much more excited to interview with him than I was with Dr Harrison. I don't think I'll feel intimidated."

"You won't because Bill Polk will put you at ease. Appearances don't count with him and he'll be much more interested in you. He'll conduct a real interview, and when he learns who you are and sees what you have to offer, he'll call Dr Harrison. The next thing you know, you'll be on your way to his office to sign the contract he mentioned. I'm sure that'll happen, and now I'm going to make some lunch. How does some soup and a bologna sandwich sound?" Mrs Williams concluded, getting up from the love seat.

"It sounds just like home," Ron answered. "And I'm sure it'll even beat Bing's Kitchen," he added as Mrs Williams smiled and headed for the kitchen.

Ron did feel at home with Mrs Williams because he would have felt at home with any adult—male or female—in whom he could have faith. Dr Harrison hardly inspired such faith. As an individual aspiring to be an authentic learned man as a teacher of literature, someday Ron would encounter his fictional counterpart in the likes of Huckleberry Finn. But for now he was comfortable in his unconscious life, looking forward to his upcoming interview with Mr Polk. Only later, with the dawning of his conscious life, would he face a dilemma where he would have to choose "forever betwixt two things," in the manner of his still undiscovered fictional counterparts—that would turn out to include Adam and Eve and Christ as well as Huckleberry Finn.

During the course of his lunch with Mrs Williams, Ron learned of the location of the high school, and he ate his soup and sandwich in anticipation of his two o' clock interview with Mr Polk. Mrs Williams felt confident that he would be impressed with Ron, and when she said goodbye to him after lunch, he felt as though he already had the job. A much more relaxed and confident Ron Petrich left the Gables Motel for the second time that day and headed for Lebanon Union High School, Bill Polk's school, and the home of the Lebanon Warriors.

The five minute drive, at most, from the Gables Motel on the Santiam Highway to the high school on Fifth Street—built on the western edge of town looking toward Interstate 5, the new four-lane freeway that split the heart of the Willamette Valley and eventually would connect Seattle with Los Angeles—didn't leave Ron with much time to think. But with the time he did have he thought of Mrs Williams and of what she said about football being king in Lebanon. Given that image, he had to say that football was king at Bellarmine in Tacoma as well. He had to admit that football, accompanied by pep rallies that celebrated the blue and white school colors and the rousing fight song—a Bellarmine playing of the University of Notre Dame's fight song—served to unite the school. The football team carried the banner of the Bellarmine Lions, and the football coach commanded reverent, silent attention at the pep rallies. Ron remembered that high school world, and although baseball was king with him personally, he had no objections to football being given that status in the high school itself. He was sure he wouldn't have any objections with regards to Lebanon Union High School, either. In truth, he looked forward to being part of the festivities surrounding the standard-bearing football team.

But Mrs Williams had identified a growing problem Ron would have to confront. Football was king at Bellarmine High School in Tacoma, but during his years that ended in 1962, neither he nor anyone else seemed to equate it with morality that designated the coach as the moral standard bearer. To Ron as a high school student, football simply generated the enthusiasm and display of unity that helped make his high school experience an adventure. But in the five years that had passed since his graduation and arrival in Lebanon, the well-ordered world he remembered, and still identified with, was in the process of disintegrating. In the midst of this disintegration, reflected in the hair-length controversy Mrs Williams had identified, football had become the short hair bastion with the coach celebrated as the defender of so-called traditional values. At 22 Ron, sporting his standard, quiet hair style, certainly identified with the traditional values camp. But he never had thought about sport in association with morality. He never had thought about anything, for that matter, from the teacher's side of the desk. In time he would discover himself to be a creative, individual thinker; but for now he wasn't part of any revolution—social or otherwise. He was a rookie teacher, alive with inspiration, on his way to his scheduled interview with his prospective principal. With regards to the growing problem that Mrs Williams had identified, he remained more curious than convinced.

When he pulled into the parking lot, he found a school built in the architectural style reflected in Tacoma's Woodrow Wilson High School. He imagined that Lebanon's new school opened with the same optimistic and futuristic fanfare that accompanied the opening of Wilson in celebration of unquestioning faith in technology and the progress it represents. Such one-story, campus-style schools—emphasizing open glass, steel, and straight angles—were welcomed as improvements over the standard school structure—emphasizing multistories, paned windows, red brick, and rounded archways. Lebanon Union High School couldn't have been more than ten years old. It was clean and the surrounding grass remained green in the January mist. But in terms of architectural majesty, it couldn't match the red-bricked and arched grandeur of Ron's Bellarmine High School. That past wouldn't die easily with him in the face of the antiseptic cleanliness of modern high school architecture. But he had to start someplace. And why not begin in a building that accurately reflected the space needle promise he associated with the Seattle World's Fair of 1962?

As he stepped out of his car, he could see a row of classrooms that extended toward the west from the northside entrance to the school. With the main structure facing east and rows of classrooms extending behind it to the west, the school more closely resembled an airport than it did the traditional high school building. Ron never liked Woodrow Wilson High School in Tacoma in comparison to Bellarmine and its sense of antiquity, and as he stood outside the northern entrance to Lebanon Union High School, he couldn't help wishing he could start in a school that at least looked the part. Lebanon's radical departure from sacred school architecture proved a little disconcerting. But he had to teach in the present as an English teacher whose job, in part, involved keeping the experiential voice of antiquity alive if, in fact, it ever had been fully heard. He stood outside the northside entrance to the high school and concluded that if Mr Polk came so highly recommended from Mrs

Williams, his school couldn't be all bad, despite its less than inspiring design. With five minutes to spare before his two o'clock interview, he pulled open the steel and glass door and stepped across the threshold.

# V I

Marked by its cleanliness, the school lacked the familiar musty smell of antiquity that characterized the Bellarmine of his high school experience, and the corridor's waxed, tile floor bore no resemblance to the hardwood that decorated Bellarmine's hallways. As he walked down the corridor and listened for his footsteps, Ron acknowledged that he missed the telling squeak he associated with both Bellarmine and Lincoln High School in Tacoma, where he did his student teaching. Lincoln was an athletic rival during his Bellarmine days, but as a student teacher he came to feel a part of that school and its storied past as one of the two oldest public high schools in the city. With its landmark clock tower reaching toward the sky and standing guard over the school itself, Lincoln High School stood in direct contrast to what Lebanon, Oregon, had to offer. But then Mr Polk's school belonged to a different era. Continuing his quiet walk down the spotless, tiled corridor, Ron passed the faculty room and the room reserved for student government. In a matter of seconds, he reached the bright and open expanse of the main office area occupying the very center of the school.

    Standing next to the benches sitting in the middle of the open area itself, anyone could see in either direction to the north and south as well as down the wide corridor that stretched to the west. This open, central location housed the trophy cases that celebrated the athletic triumphs of Lebanon Union High School, past and present, as well as its triumphs in the less glamorous, but still competitive, fields of debate, speech, and drama. The athletic trophies, of course, were displayed most prominently, with the football trophies being displayed most prominently of all. But football or debate, baseball or speech, basketball or drama, Ron felt comfortable amidst the trophies as reflective of the school's heritage that was supposed to provide the generations of students with something to work for and live up to. He didn't know what magic, if any, lived in those trophies, but he did know it was two o' clock and time for his interview with Mr Polk.

"May I help you?" the secretary asked from behind her desk as Ron approached the office counter that stretched from north to south the entire length of the office.

"Yes," Ron answered. "My name is Ron Petrich, and I have an appointment with Mr Polk at two o' clock."

"Oh, yes," the secretary replied. "Mr Polk is expecting you. I'll tell him you're here," she added, getting up from her desk and walking toward the office to her right and behind her desk.

"Thank you," Ron said as he watched her reach Mr Polk's office and notify him of his arrival.

"You can come back now," the secretary said, pointing to the way around the square pillar standing to Ron's left at the end of the office counter. "Mr Polk is waiting for you."

"Thank you," Ron said once again as he made his way around the pillar. "Do I just walk in?" he asked, pointing toward Mr Polk's office.

"Yes, go ahead," the secretary answered with a smile. "He'll be waiting for you."

"Okay, thanks again," he said, walking towards Mr Polk's open door.

As Ron approached the door, Mr Polk stood up from his desk chair and walked around to the front of his desk where he was standing when Ron got close enough to knock. He wasn't an imposing figure, as Mrs Williams said the football coach, Judson Heath, would be, but in direct contrast to the uninspiring and pretentious Dr Harrison, Mr Polk was inspiring and dignified. He was six feet tall and moderately built, weighing approximately 170 pounds with graying hair traditionally cut around his ears and neck and parted neatly in the middle. His blue eyes were honest and penetrating and his nose and mouth comfortably fit the contours of his slightly weathered, at least 50-year-old, face. He was standing confidently straight dressed in his solid gray suit, white shirt, and red and black striped tie as Ron reached his open door.

"Come in, Mr Petrich," he said warmly, getting the short 'e' right the first time and extending his right hand in Ron's direction as he walked toward him. "I've been expecting you."

"Thank you," Ron said, grasping Mr Polk's hand as firmly as he felt Mr Polk grasping his. "I hope I'm not late," he added nervously as he stepped further into the office.

"Not at all," Mr. Polk replied. "You're right on time, as a matter of fact. Have a seat," he added, pointing toward the cushioned chair to Ron's right and at the same time sitting in his own desk chair and sliding it more toward his left and away from behind his desk.

"Thank you," Ron said again as he took the seat offered.

"Well," Mr. Polk began, leaning slightly toward Ron with his arms resting on his thighs and his hands clasped slightly in front of his knees, "what brings you to the Willamette Valley and Lebanon?"

"To be honest," Ron answered, catching Mr Polk's eye and sitting straight in his cushioned chair with his hands resting on his knees, "I need a job and I learned of the opening you have here at the high school."

"You mean you aren't out to change the world or anything like that?" Mr Polk asked with a smile.

"I don't know about that. I don't know about changing the world. I think I just want to teach English as best I can and see what happens from there."

"You wouldn't consider yourself a youthful idealist then?"

"I think I believe in ideals," Ron answered. "If I didn't, I don't think I'd have any business being a teacher. But I don't think I'm an idealist, although I have to admit that I haven't really thought about what I am in that sense," he added, already feeling more comfortable with Mr Polk than he did with Dr Harrison. He could tell Mr Polk was interested in him as an individual and, more importantly, Ron recognized his sense of humor. He could see why Mr Polk was far less aloof than was Dr Harrison. The crown fit him, and he seemed aware, and unafraid, of its responsibility. He was, perhaps, an authentic learned man set in the role of principal.

"I don't think I'd consider myself an idealist, either. A high school is death on idealists. Young teachers often see themselves as such and their enthusiasm is just as idealistic. That's why I asked you the question. I don't like to see the idealistic flame extinguished because it's never lit again. We don't need any more burned-out teachers just playing out the string until retirement. And we don't need any more of them turning to other jobs for which they aren't suited. We need teachers who will endure and prevail as well."

"I'm not exactly sure what an idealist is," Ron said in response, "but even though I'm young and look even younger, I don't think I'm unaware or naive. I don't think I carry an idealistic torch into teaching, and I think I have a fairly solid idea of how hard it is, although I know I have much to learn. I look forward to teaching and to learning."

"You are young and you do look young," Mr Polk said, leaning back in his chair, "but it's nice to hear you have your feet more on the ground than in the clouds. Tell me," he added, "how did you find out about our opening for a senior English teacher?"

"It's an interesting story. I found out about it through a teacher placement agency in Seattle, but I didn't exactly work through them."

"You didn't want to pay the fee. Is that right?" Mr Polk asked with a knowing smile.

"I guess that's right. I did talk to Dr Harrison on the phone from their office, but I didn't work through them after that. I told them I wasn't interested in the job and had Seattle University send my placement file to Dr Harrison. So, I guess I'm here more through Seattle

University than through the placement agency. It's a little dishonst, I suppose, but I have to admit that I don't feel guilty."

"It is an interesting story," Mr Polk said, "and I don't think I'd feel guilty either, although I'm sure some people would. But then those same people would easily be dishonest in less obvious ways. Anyway, I'm glad you found out about us. Tell me a little bit about Tacoma and how you grew up."

"Well, my mother always has been a housewife, and my dad always has worked at the Asarco copper smelter not too far from our house in Old Town, just up the street from the southern shore of Commencement Bay. Excuse me, but have you ever been to Tacoma?"

"I've only driven by it on my way to Seattle. But I've heard about it and its pulp mills."

"That means you've heard about its alleged aroma."

"Yes, I'm familiar with the 'aroma of Tacoma'."

"I guess it's real," Ron continued, "but it's not fair to think that the aroma is Tacoma. At least it's not my Tacoma," he added, glancing around Mr Polk's office that looked unashamedly like a principal's office in a high school and nothing else. Ron saw no fancy curtains and no pretentious display of books and academic wisdom. But he did see a metal desk, in keeping with the modernity of the school, cluttered with official papers and memos dealing with the day-to-day operations of a high school. There was no pretense about the office or about the man who worked at its desk. Venetian blinds neatly hung from the window directly behind Mr Polk's desk with Fifth Street in the background, and file cabinets took the place of Dr Harrison's bookshelves. Mr Polk's office never would be confused with a library; and the white walls, though neatly painted, lacked decoration except for a framed portrait of a baseball player, whom Ron recognized to be Stan 'The Man' Musial, that hung in the center of the south wall just to the right of Mr Polk's desk.

"And just what is your Tacoma?" Mr Polk asked with interest.

"For me it's a town of solid character and personality and a town without pretense, unlike Seattle that delights in exaggerating its own importance. And Tacoma is Point Defiance Park and the North End and Commencement Bay, and especially Old Town where I grew up, and where the city itself emerged in the early days of the late 19th century. Seattle may be the Queen City, but Tacoma's the City of Destiny," Ron concluded emphatically and confidently in the manner of a person aware, and proud, of his identity.

"I'll have to visit Tacoma beyond the aroma one of these days. Do you think you'll ever go back?"

"I don't know. Right now I'm just glad it's my hometown. I wouldn't want to be from anywhere else."

"And you went to Seattle University and majored in English with minors in history and philosophy?"

"Yes. All Seattle U graduates had to minor in philosophy."

"Even Elgin Baylor?" Mr Polk asked with an understanding laugh.

"I don't know about that," Ron answered, smiling. "But technically he would have had to."

"Are you a basketball fan?" Mr Polk asked.

"I like basketball," Ron answered, "but I can't say that I'm an authentic fan in the sense that I believe in it."

"But you are, as you say, an authentic fan of some sport?"

"Yes, I think so."

"And what's the sport?"

"Baseball," Ron answered, embarrassingly looking at the portrait of Stan Musial.

"Don't be embarrassed," Mr Polk said, noticing Ron's glance. "I know you aren't interested in telling me what you think I'd like to hear. You've impressed me as being an honest man so far, and being such a man, as well as a baseball fan, just works doubly in your favor. Are you a Cardinal?" he asked, turning his head toward his portrait of Stan The Man.

"No," Ron answered. "I'm a Yankee."

"A Yankee!" Mr Polk exclaimed. "What happened in the '64 Series, and what's happened since? First you steal the Cardinals' manager, and then you end up in last place."

"Bob Gibson just got lucky in the '64 Series, that's all. And Johnny Keane should have stayed with the Cardinals. I think Mickey Mantle was too much for him. But the Yankees will come back. Still, it doesn't matter because I'll always be a Yankee. It's like being in love and being married. It's forever and it's for better or for worse."

"I have to agree with that," Mr Polk said. "I used to coach football in my younger days before I became a principal, but baseball always has been my first love. Baseball and the St Louis Cardinals and Stan The Man. I think baseball is eternal and increasingly important these days where we seem to be obsessed with change. I think we should be just as interested in the eternal, don't you?" he asked, sitting in his chair with his blue eyes alive and looking directly at Ron.

"I haven't really thought about it like that, but it makes sense to me. Maybe that's why I'm interested in literature. Maybe it's because I seem to have feelings about it that are as strong as the feelings I have about baseball, even though I can't explain any of them as I'd like to just yet."

"These are tough times, that might even leave me in their wake. Do you think you can handle them? Do you think you can handle students, some of whom will look older than you and some of whom undoubtedly will fall in love with you?"

"I honestly think I can on all counts. And I'm anxious to get on with it. I really think I can do the job. I'm ready to give it all I have to give. I know I can teach, and I want to teach."

"You'd be teaching seniors who are only four years younger than you are."

"I know, but those four years are big. And I'm not looking for friends. I'm looking to be a teacher, and I don't think I would bring dishonor to that role. I think I've learned that the relationship between teacher and student is sacred. It's a relationship of equals, not one of peers, where a teacher should treat all the students with love and respect. You don't do that if you grant them peer status before they've earned it. I don't think I could have it any other way."

"Spoken like a true veteran," Mr Polk said admiringly.

"I believe it," Ron said. "And I learned it from my student teaching experience when a couple of students tried to get too close to me, as if we were friends and peers. I wasn't comfortable with the situation."

"What happened?"

"Nothing. I could see what they were doing and I could see why. But when I didn't give them any reinforcement, they didn't pursue their course any longer. I was confused at first, but I just did what seemed natural to me. I could see the right and wrong of the situation, and I tried to do what I saw as right. I'd do the same thing here in your high school."

"I'm sure you would," Mr Polk said with conviction. "I'm sure you would," he repeated. "Now, what about teaching senior English. How well prepared are you?"

"I probably feel more confident about teaching writing right now than I do about teaching literature. I think I understand writing better. I know literature must give expression to the eternal, but I'm not really sure I know how to explain it just yet. But even though I don't understand literature right now as I want to, I know I understand it better than a high school senior. Besides, I think my understanding will improve now that I have to teach it. You can't teach something you don't understand. I think that's the essence of teaching."

"What's that?" Mr Polk asked.

"Explaining what you understand, with love and compassion, to those who don't understand it," Ron answered. "In that sense I don't think teaching ever will change, no matter what may change around it. And the more you understand, the more you can teach. I don't think anyone should place limits on what a person can understand. As a teacher I know I'll do all I can to encourage understanding with no boundaries whatsoever."

"Well," Mr Polk said, placing his hands on his knees with his elbows slightly crooked, "I think Lebanon Union High School will be lucky to have you on the faculty. Do you want the job?"

"I sure do," Ron answered immediately.

"Then it's yours," Mr Polk said, reaching for the telephone sitting on his desk and dialing a number that Ron thought had to be Dr. Harrison's. "Hello," Mr Polk said as the party answered at the other end of the line. "This is Bill Polk at the high school. Is Dr Harrison available? Thanks," he added as Dr Harrison's secretary rang his office. "George," Mr Polk said as he heard Dr Harrison's hello at the other end, "I think we've found our teacher. I know he's young and I know some of the girls will fall in love with him, but I know he'll be able to handle it. Believe me, he won't embarrass any of us. He's going to be an authentic teacher and we're lucky to have him. Do you have that contract ready? Okay, he's already accepted my offer, and I'll send him back to you to make it official. Thanks, George. I know we won't regret it. Goodbye."

Mr Polk smiled and shook his head as he looked at Ron now sitting much more relaxed in his cushioned chair. "Dr Harrison's not as bad as he can appear. He's a little afraid of being embarrassed, and if you were to get involved with a student, he knows it wouldn't be the first time. So, don't take his skepticism personally. Sometimes I think he's a little too wrapped up in the trappings of his office, but then anyone would at least be tempted if he had the chance. Anyway, as long as you teach as you say you will and as I know you will, you won't have any trouble with superintendents along the way. They all probably feel a little social superiority to the rest of us, but I'll let you in on a secret about how to handle it."

"What's that?" Ron asked, sitting on the edge of his cushioned chair.

"Grant them the superiority they at least think they deserve because, in the end, social superiority is of little or no consequence. Grant them the superiority, and do your job with honesty and sincerity and most of all with compassion for all who are as willing to learn as you are to teach."

"I'll do the best I can," Ron said, inspired by Mr Polk's own sincerity.

"I know you will, Ron, and I'll leave you alone to teach. I won't invade your classroom, but I'll know what's going on. It's my school and it's my job to know. Now, can you start at the beginning of the second semester next week?"

"Sure. I just have to go back home, pick up my clothes, and come back here to find a place to live."

"If you need a place in the meantime," Mr Polk offered, "you can stay at the Gables Motel. Mrs Williams, the owner, would be glad to have you."

"I know. I stayed there last night and I've already talked to Mrs Williams. In fact, she made me lunch today after I talked to Dr Harrison this morning. She's a nice woman who has a solid understanding of life as far as I can tell. I think she'd make a good teacher."

"She's faced death," Mr Polk said, getting up from his chair, "and no one can understand life until he has faced, and affirmed, death in some way. Any understanding of life has to start with an affirmation of the reality and necessity of death. How's that for philosophy from a principal?" he asked with a smile.

"Sounds existential to me and inspiring at the same time," Ron answered. "Maybe that's what the eternal is."

"Maybe," Mr Polk replied. "Maybe that's what baseball is," he added wistfully, glancing at his framed portrait of Stan The Man. "But that's enough for now, before I get carried away with myself and forget my job as principal, which I still have to work at today. Dr Harrison will be waiting for you with the contract and I'll be looking forward to seeing you bright and early a week from today at the beginning of the second semester," he concluded, extending his right hand.

"I'll be there," Ron said, grasping Mr Polk's hand in a firm handshake. "Lebanon's as good a place as any to start."

"It certainly is," Mr Polk said, "and probably better than some. Have a nice trip home to Tacoma and we'll see you back here in a week. And by the way," he added as Ron made his way to his office door at the same time as Mr Polk moved to the front of his desk, "say hello to Mrs Williams for me. She's a fixture in Lebanon."

"I will. I told her I'd see her after my interview with you. I'll drive to Dr Harrison's office now and then stop by the Gables before I head home."

"Drive carefully in the rain and welcome to Lebanon and to the high school."

"Thank you," Ron said with a proud smile as he walked through the open doorway, past the office area to his left, and down the tiled corridor to his right toward his Chevy Malibu waiting where it now belonged—in the faculty parking lot at the north end of Lebanon Union High School.

# VII

Ron didn't waste any time finding his way back to Dr Harrison's office. He was impressed with Mr Polk who had proven to be nothing like his superintendent. And from his interview with him, Ron had learned how to get along with the likes of Dr. Harrison whom Mr Polk had suggested was more typical than atypical in his attitude toward his job and toward his teachers. On his way back to the superintendent's office to sign his first professional teaching contract, Ron couldn't help feeling relieved by the fact that Dr Harrison was just the superintendent, necessarily aloof and just as necessarily removed from the day-to-day operation of a high school.

In a matter of minutes he found his way back to the parking lot he had left earlier in the day, and taking even less time to park his car, he stepped out and found his way to Dr Harrison's office. He walked through the doorway into the superintendent's office, and the smile that graced the experienced and attractive face of Dr Harrison's secretary greeted his own.

"Welcome to Lebanon, Mr Petrich," she said with the proper short 'e' as Ron approached her desk. "Dr Harrison is waiting for you in his office. Can you find your way?"

"Thank you," Ron said. "I'm happy to be here and I think I can find my way. Can I just walk back there now?"

"Sure. There's no need to announce you. The door's open. Just knock on the doorway. Dr Harrison has the contract all ready for your signature."

"Okay," Ron said as he walked past the secretary's desk toward Dr Harrison's office. Looking as dignified as possible, he stopped just outside his doorway and knocked politely.

"Oh, it's you, Mr Petrich," Dr Harrison said, pronouncing the long 'e' once again and looking up from his desk. "Come in," he added, standing up out of his desk chair and moving to the front of the desk.

"Thank you," Ron said as he stepped across the threshold.

"Welcome to Lebanon," Dr Harrison said, extending his ashen right hand toward Ron as the two met at a point equidistant from the doorway and Dr Harrison's desk.

"It feels good to be here," Ron said, grasping Dr Harrison's hand with his own right hand and almost recoiling at the limpness that accompanied the ashen whiteness. "I can't wait to get started."

"I like to see that enthusiasm," Dr Harrison replied, relinquishing his less than firm grip on Ron's hand and walking back behind his desk. "Teaching requires enthusiasm," he added once he safely arrived.

"I know. I don't think there's any substitute for honest enthusiasm."

"Well, we'll see how long it lasts once you get started with the job," Dr Harrison said as he found Ron's teaching contract sitting alone on top of his desk. "High school students have a way of puncturing a beginning teacher's enthusiasm in a hurry. Do you think that will happen to you?" he asked as a sly smile crossed his face.

"I want to be a teacher because I know I belong in the profession. And I can honestly say that I don't think I ever will lose my enthusiasm for teaching. If anything, I think it will increase as I come to understand my subject matter better."

"Well, we'll see, I suppose," Dr Harrison said with his head down as his oily skin shined in the electric light of his office. "I have your contract here," he continued. "Take a seat in this chair in front of my desk, look it over, and sign it in the space provided at the lower right."

"Okay," Ron said, sitting in the chair and accepting the contract from Dr Harrison. He looked at it and read it, but he didn't even notice the

4,800 dollar yearly salary, reduced to cover the second semester, and the added duties of senior class advisor as well as assistant advisor to the Key Club. He found the lower right-hand corner and signed his name, making him an official member of the Lebanon Union High School faculty.

"That makes it official," Dr Harrison said as he watched Ron sign his name. "You're a full-time teacher now and you can't make the mistake of forgetting your responsibilities. We expect our teachers to live up to our community's values and not to do anything to embarrass us."

"I'll do my best not to embarrass anyone," Ron said, looking up at Dr Harrison.

"Fine," he replied, still looking downward with his bald head shining in the electric light. "You start the first day of the second semester and be aware of the fact that Mr Polk will keep a sharp eye on you. Young teachers have to be watched."

"I'll be there ready to teach," Ron said in response as he stood up from his chair.

"Here's your copy of the contract," Dr Harrison said, handing it to Ron across his desk and finally catching his eye.

"Thank you," Ron said, accepting the contract.

"You can go now," Dr Harrison said, "and, once again, mind your business and welcome to Lebanon."

"I will and thanks again," Ron said, walking toward the doorway and the secretary's office.

"I'll know how you're doing," Dr Harrison added as a parting remark as Ron reached the doorway.

"I know," he said, stopping at the doorway before he stepped across the threshold into the secretary's office where he caught her smile with one of his own and continued on his way to the parking lot and his waiting Chevy Malibu.

He pulled out of the parking lot a little after three o' clock and headed for the Gables Motel to tell Mrs Williams of his good fortune.

He felt he would have been hired regardless of who he was, given the time of year and Lebanon's need for a teacher, but he felt good knowing Mrs Williams knew he was an individual who would get the job mainly on the basis of his merit. He realized Dr Harrison had no interest in the individual, being blinded by his own fear and preoccupation with himself, but he knew Mr Polk was different. As he headed toward the Gables, he knew Lebanon simply needed an English teacher, but he felt proud knowing Mr Polk had hired him as an individual, just as Mrs Williams said he would. He knew he had earned the position and wouldn't have felt inspired if he had been given the position out of simple necessity or by default.

When he left the parking lot of the old high school this time, he took particular notice of what Mrs Williams had identified as St Edward's Catholic Church, which sat off to his right just across the street from the administrative building. It was a modest church housed in a white frame building complete with the appropriate welcoming spire reaching toward the sky and with stained glass windows decorating either side. The church belonged in a town the size of Lebanon, and Ron even felt that it would fit comfortably in his Old Town neighborhood in Tacoma. The sight of the church comforted him because he saw the Catholic Church as a second home, and his identity with it was strong. He took religion seriously and, for him, attending church had nothing to do with habit, tradition, or social expedience. The church's atmosphere impressed him and captured his imagination. He was fascinated by the altar and the tabernacle and the Blessed Sacrament and the priestly vestments and the votive candles and the statues and the Stations of the Cross and probably most of all by the crucifix that hung behind and above the altar. If Christ as the Incarnation of God proved hard to understand, Christ as the Incarnation of the courageous individual did not. Ron Petrich was such an inspired individual, but as yet he had no conscious recognition of his atonement with Christ and thus of his atonement with God. He had not been born, yet, from the womb of the established Holy Mother Church. Entertaining his still comforting, but increasingly curious, thoughts about the nature of church and religion, Ron pulled up to the stop sign at the intersection of Tangent and Main Street, turned right, and headed south through town and toward the Gables Motel.

He felt almost like a Lebanon veteran on this trip through town as he tried to take more particular notice of what this Willamette Valley community had to offer, now that it was going to become his home. As a teacher in a small town where the high school provided the primary social identity, he knew that he'd be living in a fishbowl environment, always under the scrutiny of the public whose children he was to teach. Part of him would have preferred anonymity, but he had to start somewhere. San Francisco or Lebanon wouldn't make any difference. He still was Ron Petrich. He had nothing to be ashamed of and nothing to hide. He was quiet, honest, and inspired by the thoughts of the responsibility that accompanied his justly earned crown. He hadn't deceived anyone and he was an honest product of the most expansive education Western civilization had to offer. To him nothing surpassed the unbounded adventure of learning.

He had no qualms about being part of the Lebanon community now that it, in the person of Mr Polk, had seemed to accept him without applying any pressure on him to adapt to it. He could bring his identity to Lebanon without worrying about having to allow the town to define him in its own image. He wanted to be in charge of his own life, and he would have resisted any attempt by anyone to deprive him of that responsibility. Due to the altar influence he didn't yet understand, he couldn't surrender his individual identity for that of any group or community. To Ron the strength of any community was determined by the nature of the strength of the individuals who comprised it. Thus the ideal community would be that which fostered individual development and not community indoctrination and social adaptation. He would bring his individual identity to Lebanon and to its high school and take his chances. He had ample room to develop because, at 22, he still remained more curious than convinced.

He was even more curious about Bing's Kitchen as he drove past it on his way to the Gables. Now that he was going to a part of Lebanon, he was going to have to pay more attention to such places. Bing's, for example, would be his restaurant now as well as Lebanon's, and he had to give himself a chance to be as proud of it as Mrs Williams proved to be. He already felt a strong identity with the Gables because of her, and he felt as though he were coming home when he turned left off the Santiam Highway and into the parking lot of Mrs Williams' motel. He pulled into his usual parking space, turned off the ignition, opened the door, and walked, once again, up the steps that led to the motel office.

"I can tell you signed the contract," Mrs Williams said as she saw Ron coming and greeted him at the door. "Come back here into the living room and tell me all about it."

"Is it that obvious?" Ron asked, following her behind the counter and into the living room.

"I can see it in your eyes," she answered, sitting down in the love seat once again and motioning for Ron to sit in his place on the couch. "They're alive with the spirit of adventure."

"Really?" Ron asked as he took his seat on the couch.

"Really," Mrs Williams answered, smiling.

"I guess I just can't hide my excitement. I can't believe I'm actually a real teacher."

"You are and you shouldn't try to hide your excitement. We shouldn't hide anything that's honest. And you're an honest man."

"I hope so, but I still can't believe it. I never was afraid of entering the adult world. In fact, I always looked forward to it. But I worried about finding a place in it. Do you see what I mean?"

"Yes, I do," Mrs Williams answered.

"I welcomed college because it gave me four more years and now here I am."

"But college did more for you than just give you for more years. It provided you with more adventure."

"I know," Ron said. "That adventure attracted me to college in the first place. I had no idea of what I was going to be. Now I can't wait to get on with the adventure of teaching."

"I know you'll be a credit to your profession. What did you think of Mr Polk?"

"He was everything you said he would be. I think he's an authentic learned man occupying the role of principal. Does he know you?"

"Only casually. He knows more of me, I suppose. Lebanon is a small town, you know."

"Anyway, he said to say hello to you and that you were a real fixture in Lebanon."

"I suppose I am," Mrs Williams said, smiling. "Sometimes I feel as though I've been here forever."

"Still," Ron said, "whether he knows you or knows more of you, he thinks a lot of you. I told him I thought you had a solid understanding of life, and he said that you'd faced death and that all understanding of life has to result from an affirmation of the necessity of death. And that makes us think of the eternal, which makes him think of his portrait of Stan Musial and baseball. He sounded like an existential philosopher."

"I don't know about that term," Mrs Williams said, "but if he said that about life and death and understanding, I guess I'm the same kind of philosopher interested in what you called the eternal. Did he ask you about baseball?"

"Yes. And when I told him I was a Yankee fan, he asked me what happened in the '64 Series and what's happened since. I think he's as much a Cardinal as I am a Yankee."

"Did you mention baseball as The One True sport as your dad refers to it?"

"No, I didn't, but I think he feels the same way. Football was king at Bellarmine just as you say it is here, but in the long run baseball grows on you the most. If I had to make a choice, I'd choose baseball. I think it has something to do with the eternal, just like literature. I think I have to discover and teach literature as an expression of the eternal. We have to find something permanent to hold on to these days."

"I think you're right, in the face of change that surrounds us," Mrs Williams said.

"It's funny, but I think I'm learning more right now that I ever did in college."

"You realize you have something to teach. I think you'll be teaching in a very interesting time. I don't know what's going to come of it. From what I can see, we don't seem to be especially interested in anything eternal, as you say. However, we do seem to be especially interested in change."

"I know. And even I wanted change—or maybe thought I did. I know I welcomed the Mass being said in English, for example. I was anxious for that change."

"What do you think now?" Mrs Williams asked, looking Ron directly in the eye.

"I don't quite know what to think. But I think I liked the Mass better in Latin."

"I know I liked it better in Latin, although I probably thought saying it in English would make it easier to understand. But Latin, now that I've thought about it, definitely sounded better. I miss it. It represented something that I don't understand."

"The eternal?" Ron asked.

"Maybe, but I don't know. I think I miss everything associated with the days of the Latin Mass, but I still realize the need for reform. We do live in a time of impressive scientific exploration and discovery. Maybe we've yet to discover the eternal."

"Maybe," Ron said. "But I think we have to."

"I suppose we have to keep exploring," Mrs Williams said.

"We're exploring space just as Columbus and the others explored the earth. Maybe we have to explore the likes of baseball and literature just to keep pace."

"And religion?" Mrs Williams asked tentatively.

"I think so," Ron answered just as tentatively. "I think we have to explore religion as well."

"It should be exciting for you. But be careful. Don't jump to any conclusions."

"I don't think I will, but we have to be curious. We have to keep up with science and all that we discover as a result of our exploration."

"You're going to be quite a teacher," Mrs Williams said, smiling and looking directly at Ron. "I wish I would have had such teachers when I was in school."

"I'm just going to teach what literature has to say," Ron replied. "I don't have any right to teach anything else."

"True," Mrs Williams said, "but literature probably has a lot to teach, if we pay attention to it."

"I know I'm ready to get started."

"When do you start?"

"Next week. The first week of the second semester."

"It's not the easiest way to being teaching," Mrs Williams said. "At the beginning of the second semester, I mean."

"I know, but I have to start sometime. And I'd rather not wait."

"You'll have to find a place to live first. Don't forget that."

"I won't. I should be able to find a furnished apartment in the Lebanon paper, don't you think?"

"I think so," Mrs Williams answered. "You can always stay here until you find a place."

"Thanks," Ron replied. "Hopefully, I won't have to. I think I'll come back Thursday or Friday and start to look."

"Stop in here first and maybe I can help get you started in the right direction."

"Sounds good to me," Ron said, sitting comfortably on the couch. "Are you spending the night here tonight?"

"No, I'm going home. The rain's not bad, and I don't have that far to go. Besides, I can think while I drive."

"Well," Mrs Williams said, standing up from the love seat, "I'm not trying to get rid of you, but you'd better get started before dark. You don't want your mom and dad to worry about you."

"You're right. If it weren't for you, I would have left right after I signed the contract. But I had to come and tell you."

"I'm glad you did. It's been an exciting day for me, too. I knew Bill Polk would like you, and I guess I knew you'd be hired even if he didn't. But you're not simply another teacher, even if that might appear to be the case. Dr Harrison hired another teacher as he would have with anyone. But Bill Polk hired you. There's a difference."

"I know," Ron said, getting up from the couch. "That's what I liked about Mr Polk. I could tell he was interested in me where Dr Harrison could have cared less. I hope I bring something to Lebanon and to teaching."

"Don't worry about that. I don't think many teachers bring what you do. For your sake, I hope you don't bring too much."

"How could anyone bring too much to teaching?"

"If schools are open wide enough, you can't bring too much. But I'm not sure of the direction they're taking these days. I guess we'll just have to wait and see."

"I suppose so. But I just hope I bring enough."

"That's the least of your worries," Mrs Williams said, smiling and moving toward the outer office. "But I think you'd better get started home. It's going on four, and darkness still comes early this time of year."

"I guess I'd better go," Ron said, following her out into the outer office. "I feel as though I've known you forever and I only met you yesterday. You've made me feel at home, and I can't tell you how much I appreciate it," he added, extending his right hand.

"I saw something about you that interested me," Mrs Williams said, taking Ron's hand in her own. "I felt like you belonged. As I said before," she continued, letting go of his hand, "Lebanon's lucky to have you. I'll be looking forward to your return and to your settling in."

"I'll come back here first thing," Ron said, moving toward the door. "Thanks for everything."

"You're more than welcome. Have a safe trip home," Mrs Williams added as Ron opened the door and stepped across the threshold onto the office porch.

"I will," he said as we walked down the steps toward his waiting Malibu. "See you in a couple of days," he concluded with a wave as he opened his driver's side door.

"See you then," Mrs Williams said as he closed the door, started the car, shifted into reverse, backed out of the parking space, and found the Santiam Highway— where he turned right and headed north toward Tacoma and home.

## VIII

The five-hour drive from Lebanon to Tacoma, with most of it following Interstate 5, gave Ron ample time to think. Lumber towns like Albany and the state capital of Salem, and even a cosmopolitan city like Portland, were no more than dots on the Santiam Highway and Interstate 5 as he was preoccupied with thoughts of the eternal. Having been raised in the Catholic Church in the mid-20th century, he was brought up in the face of an institution that seemed eternal, if ever there were such a thing. And that Church provided the foundation for his life. If anything, his own immediate, historical family followed the lead of Holy Mother Church and obediently sought to build its foundation on that which the Church had provided. A solid foundation created stability, and Ron liked the security and clarity his life with his family and the Church had established.

Still, he had to face change with the convening of the Church's Second Vatican Council that ran from 1962 to 1965. Like most Catholics, Ron was very susceptible to the popular thinking that saw the Church, in all its antiquity, as being out of date in the Space Age. It had to be reformed to be brought into the 20th century. Catholics found it easy to think, for example, that the Mass said in the vernacular, rather than in the established Latin, would be a creative step in the right direction. They even found it easy to think that increased, visible participation on the part of the congregation would be an improvement as well. As an authentic believer Ron anticipated these changes and more with the convening of Vatican II under the direction of Pope John XXIII. His experience with the Church had been more creative than destructive, and the majesty—as well as the love story it supported—captured his living imagination. He was growing up individually as the Church was growing up institutionally in the 20th century with America, and the human race, now firmly committed to a voyage to the moon. In the face of manned celestial exploration, the Church certainly had to reexamine its structural foundation.

With the conclusion of Vatican II and its implementation of immediate liturgical reforms, Ron and other authentic believers, such as Mrs Williams, found it impossible not to compare the old with the new—the Latin Mass with the English Mass, for example. Although he eagerly awaited and immediately welcomed the new English Mass and the reforms that accompanied it, Ron soon found himself questioning the affect of receiving the Blessed Sacrament as guitar-playing fellow students played and sang the popular folk song 'Blowin' in the Wind.' Such a song was catchy but melancholy and shallow in comparison to the quiet, celebrative majesty of the Gregorian chant that no one had to understand. For him, receiving communion to the strains of 'Blowin' in the Wind' had come to represent the desecration of something sacred. The path of institutional reform ran contrary to Ron's path of individual reform. He was growing into the majesty and its love story just as the Church was authorizing its dilution.

He acknowledged that the new seemed easier to understand in the face of the old, but he worried about it not being a match for the affect power of the old. And most of all he thought of the diluted majesty of the story of Christ. The old Christ, associated with the Gregorian chant, was an individual of courageous sacrifice and convicted promise, whereas the new Christ was more an individual of melancholic sadness and resigned despair. The old Christ was the central figure in a dramatic love story, and while the new Christ played that same role in a love story of his own, he seemed despairingly disappointed in mans' continued failure to love his fellow man. The old Christ, on the other hand, seemed to steadfastly and courageously hold out hope that individuals would discover their own capacity for sacrificial love that wasn't indiscriminately directed toward everyone. Ironically, in comparing the two Christs, Ron couldn't help thinking, contrary to the Church's direction, that the old Christ seemed more human, more admirable, and more heroic. The new Christ seemed burned out and doomed to melancholic despair.

Thus the supposedly creative reforms initiated by his church contributed to Ron's preoccupation with the eternal as he drove north on Interstate 5 in the January twilight. He followed the Willamette Valley to Portland and the mouth of the Willamette River that emptied into the mighty Columbia that eventually emptied into the Pacific Ocean at Astoria on the Oregon coast, marking the western terminus of the exploration of Lewis and Clark at the beginning of the 19th century. Like both Merriwether Lewis and William Clark, Ron Petrich was an explorer, but he was exploring the terrain reflected in the likes of religion and literature and baseball which led him to think about his philosophy classes at Seattle University. At the time philosophy seemed remote, although he managed to learn what different philosophers had to say to achieve the grades required to graduate. But his interview with Mr Polk and his conversations with Mrs Williams shed new light on his study of philosophy. Mr Polk was a principal and Mrs Williams ran a motel, but both of them were philosophers, even if they didn't see themselves as such. Their philosophy sounded existential as Ron remembered some of his learned terminology, and the talk about the eternal called back to his mind something he learned about Soren Kierkegaard, an authorized philosopher, who said something to the effect of having to discover the eternal if we were to have any hope of conquering the future. He was still thinking of the eternal when he crossed the Columbia River Bridge just north of Portland and drove into his home state of Washington, stopping in Vancouver, just across the river, to buy a hamburger and a root beer at one of the local A and

W stands close to the freeway access before continuing his journey north to Tacoma and Old Town.

    Back on the road and now fully enveloped in the January night, Ron thought about the future promise reflected in Seattle's space needle, the landmark of the 1962 World's Fair whose opening, perhaps coincidentally, coincided with the opening of the Second Vatican Council in Rome. The Seattle World's Fair put the city and the entire Northwest on the map. But for Ron and his thoughts, the Fair was most important for its celebration of future promise to be delivered by the magic of technology. In the five years since the Fair, the Queen City had its Seattle Center, complete with Food Circus and Science Center and Coliseum and Memorial Stadium and Opera House and Fun Land and Fountain of Nations. But, still, only one mile of monorail ran from the Center to downtown. As far as he could tell, that one mile would serve as a lasting symbol of the false promise associated with a technologically delivered, monorailed, utopian future. He couldn't help thinking, given the events of the last couple of days, that the promised future of the 1962 Seattle World's Fair represented the very future that Kierkegaard, the authorized philosopher, had in mind. Ron didn't oppose or condemn continuing scientific inquiry and discovery, but he couldn't help recognizing that science promised anything but the eternal. That left the world encompasing religion, literature, and baseball which always had been—and would continue to be—Ron Petrich's world.

    And now he was going to teach that world, as reflected in literature especially. As he thought about literature, he thought about religion and the story of Christ. If the story of Christ really were a story, then the story of Christ's religion had to be part of literature and not separate from it. Literature, then, was—in part—a reflection of religion as defined and expressed by the individual artist. Thus Ron couldn't be a teacher of literature without being a teacher of religion at the same time. But he had to be careful. The Lebanon School District saw a clear distinction between literature and religion, with religion being the province of authorized ministers and priests who taught religion as expressed and dictated by their respective institutions. But what if religion as expressed by the individual artist doesn't reinforce that expressed by the various institutions? Ron entertained such questions on his drive back to Tacoma and Old Town and could see no easy resolutions to them. He couldn't freely embrace the new interpretation of religion expressed by his church because it diluted the majesty of Christ. Still, he couldn't easily reject such authoritative teaching. He wished the reforms of Vatican II reflected the direction his own thoughts and experiences were taking.

Time passed quickly as he continued on his journey home. He liked to think and although he never was a memorable student in terms of achievement, he did have a knack for asking penetrating questions for which he seldom received an equally penetrating answer. His favorite question concerned the Mass and the transubstantiation. The idea of bread and wine becoming the Body and Blood of Christ always intrigued him, and finally, one day in an upper-division theology class at Seattle University, he asked publicly for the first time what he had asked privately countless times. He asked Father Martin, the teacher, if the bread and wine really became the Body and Blood of Christ and received no explanation of any kind. The transubstantiation was a mystery that had to be accepted as a matter of faith and that was the end of that.

Ron suspected that the bread and wine couldn't transubstantiate scientifically, but even if they couldn't really become the Body and Blood of Christ, he wouldn't lose his faith, although he couldn't explain why. He had tasted both consecrated bread and consecrated wine but neither tasted any different than the unconsecrated versions. He knew the difference didn't involve taste. If there was magic to the transubstantiation, he knew it wasn't scientific magic. The mystery wasn't scientific, and he wished his church, through the person of

Father Martin, would unequivocally acknowledge the same. The magic he associated with the Gregorian chant had worked on him, but he felt no magic associated with 'Blowin' in the Wind.' He and the likes of Mrs Williams missed that magic—even if they couldn't explain the emptiness.

Ron sensed that literature gave expression to the magic he had experienced with the consecration of the Mass. Now that he was going to be a teacher himself, and available to such questions as he asked Father Martin, he knew he had to provide answers equally as penetrating. He had nothing against the Father Martins of the world, but he never considered them authentic teachers, either. Ron couldn't become the very teacher that he, as a student, couldn't respect as an authentic learned man. He didn't attend Seattle University to become a teacher, but once he embarked on that path, and now that he had officially signed a teaching contract, he was invested with a profound responsibility that he sought to embrace rather than to escape.

The time and the miles passed, and Interstate 5 took him past Kelso, Chehalis, Centralia, Olympia, and finally to McChord Air Force Base and Fort Lewis just south of Tacoma. Preoccupied with his thoughts, Ron paid little attention to anything but the highway and the comforting hum of the Malibu's tires as they welcomed contact with the smooth blacktop. Had he noticed, he would have discovered that the trip from Lebanon to the Washington state capital at Olympia revealed what looked like an extension or western Oregon's Willamette Valley, even though the Willamette River had converged with the Columbia at Portland. The daylight hours would reveal a lush, green fertility and the urbanization of western Washington wasn't visible until the Capitol Dome appeared in Olympia. The Puget Sound of the Pacific Ocean stretched from Bellingham near the Canadian border to the north all the way to Olympia, 25 miles south of Tacoma. But by 1967 the 65 mile stretch from the capital to Seattle had begun to take shape as one, continuous urban center lined by the blacktop of Interstate 5. And the encroaching military compounds of McChord and Fort Lewis stood as reminders of a fragile world order maintained by power and the threat of its use. The peaceful, extended valley of the Willamette River and beyond had given way to the more frightening reality of a deceptive, scientifically ordered world.

Just a few miles past McChord and Fort Lewis, Ron spotted the exit sign for Tacoma's city center which would eventually lead him to the North End and home. Because the freeway planners, whoever they were, considered Tacoma a second-class city at best, its city center exit was more of an afterthought than anything else. A city of its size—Washington's third largest city at over 160,000 behind only Seattle and Spokane in the Inland Empire 300 miles to the east across the Cascade Mountains—certainly deserved a freeway exit acknowledging its position. Instead, it was given an almost indistinguishable exit that led the driver down the industrial darkness of A Street, past railroad tracks and the Brown and Haley candy factory, before depositing him amidst the neon brightness of Pacific Avenue and downtown Tacoma.

The main artery of any city comparable in size to Tacoma attracted its share of vice. But Ron's City of Destiny appeared to have attracted more than its share—all of which contributed to Tacoma's reputation as a decadent and second-class city represeenting more blight than jewel on the map of Washington state. The strip of Pacific Avenue covering the vicinity of the Greyhound Bus Depot, just a few blocks east of the financial center of the city, openly displayed every vice known to the human race, thereby keeping the nearby Tacoma Rescue Mission in business. Ron had made more than one trip to lower Pacific Avenue in his life, but he never was one to linger amongst the variety of drunks, pimps, and prostitutes that frequented its taverns and pawn shops. He couldn't help sympathizing with its population, however—except for the pimps—and he was convinced that those who campaigned the loudest for the strip's closure represented a vice far worse than that visible on Pacific Avenue any night of the week. He also couldn't help thinking that efforts to stamp out vice in general only contributed to its emergent decadence. Pacific Avenue wasn't a showcase for any city, but the righteous zeal of the crusaders who loudly complained of its blight, led Ron to develop a competing sense of pride in the Strip as being a necessary part of Tacoma. The Strip had decayed over the years, he thought, only because civilization itself had decayed. And besides, the virtue visible in his city's North End and Old Town easily could balance out Pacific Avenue's vice.

Ron continued on his adventurous drive through the vice of prostitution and the virtue of finance on his way to Old Town and home. He never tired of driving past Union Station, identifying the eastern edge of the Pacific Strip, because he never tired of seeing any reminder of the majesty of the past when the train, rather than the airplane, was king. With its magnificent copper dome and majestic, red brick expanse, Union Station was built to last, and its architectural beauty celebrated an aspect of life lost amidst the utilitarian appeal of airports. It belonged to Ron's world of literature, religion, and baseball. If it stood as a remnant of the majesty that was, it also stood as a reminder of the majesty that could be. A sense of magic surrounded Union Station and its elegant, copper-domed presence. And, like the transubstantiation of the Mass, it had nothing to do with science.

Beyond Union Station and the Lower Strip, Pacific Avenue continued on toward the Old City Hall, marking its western boundary, and Ron drove past the likes of People's Department Store and the Doric-columned Bank of California. He liked downtown and he liked to walk up its steep hills that led southward from Pacific to the more expansive retail area of Commerce, Market, and Broadway. Change was in the wind, however, with the recent opening of the Tacoma Mall on the open brush land of South Tacoma. But Ron couldn't help thinking that any search for authenticity had to lead the explorer through the architectural majesty that the welcomed convenience of the shopping mall couldn't match. He continued his journey through the antiquity of

Pacific Avenue until he reached the Old City Hall that sat across the street from the original Northern Pacific Railroad Depot, turreted front and all. At the City Hall he turned left and headed up the hill toward Stadium Way that would lead him to Tacoma Avenue and the final leg of his journey to Old Town and home.

One block up the hill in front of the east entrance to the City Hall and its steepled clock tower that watched over Pacific Avenue and downtown, he turned right and began the gradual ascent up Stadium Way that followed the bluff marking the southern shore of Commencement Bay. The road was named, Ron supposed, in honor of Stadium High School and its amphitheater of a football stadium carved out of that same bluff and open at its north end, offering any spectators a spectacular view of the Bay as well as of Northeast Tacoma and Brown's Point, visible across its expanse on its northern shore. The high school itself, originally built on the bedrock bluff in the late 19th century as a railroad hotel, was affectionately known as The Castle. The solid concrete and brick structure, complete with its turrets and parapets, seemed to be more appropriate for the European continent than for the bluff overlooking Commencement Bay in Tacoma, Washington, USA. Ron had no desire to attend a public school, but he wouldn't have complained if somehow Bellarmine Prep High School were housed in the Stadium building. He always felt that a person had to be made out of bedrock himself not to be touched by the grandeur that was Stadium Bowl and its accompanying high school. The bowl itself sat in disrepair and the days when it played host to presidents, big time football, and John Philip Sousa's marching band were long gone, but the magic remained for anyone interested in such things.

Whether or not he realized it wasn't important, but Ron Petrich was one of those interested in magic. And he never ceased to feel the inspirational power of Stadium High School illuminated at night in all its proud majesty, standing sentinel over Commence Bay and the eastern boundary of Tacoma's North End whose residential grandeur rivaled that of its castled high school solidly built on its bedrock bluff. If Stadium High School marked the eastern edge of Tacoma's North End, so did Rankos Rexall Drug Store located at the intersection of Tacoma Avenue North and Stadium Way where it became North 1st Street, aptly named because the streets west of Division, whether numbered or formally named, carried the north, rather than the south, distinction. At the corner overlooked by the familiar orange and blue Rexall sign comfortingly identifying Rankos, Ron turned right onto Tacoma Avenue North that would eventually lead to North McCarver Street and Old Town, built along the slope of the bluff that descended from Tacoma Avenue.

Money can buy residential grandeur, whether aged or modern, and the exclusivity that comes with it. Tacoma's North End, with its more aged grandeur, was no exception. And North End snobbery was a disease particularly offensive to Tacoma residents unable to buy either the grandeur or the exclusivity. The residents of Tacoma proper who were offended by North End snobbery were just as offensive in their resultant envy; but Old Towners—though certainly not immune—remained visibly unaffected by the pride and envy that could divide the City of Destiny. Though built on Tacoma's north end and the southern shore of Commencement Bay, Old Town wasn't the North End in that it naturally emerged from the working lumber mills and shipping docks that once lined the shores of the Bay. The workers built their frame homes close to the shore where they worked and left the high ground of the bluff above the Bay for those who owned the mills and the ships. Old Town developed as a community onto itself, more inclusive than exclusive, but dominated by immigrant, working class families held together by a common heritage and by the expansiveness of the Catholic Church.

Ron followed Tacoma Avenue North as it headed west past established apartment houses rich in architectural grandeur and built with the solid brick of the earlier decades of the 30s and 40s—before

World War II and before any economic boom helped lead to the emergence of the more modern phenomenon of fake-rich, prefabricated, instant housing developments. He drove past the Tacoma Lawn and Tennis Club, securely hidden behind its tall, thick laurel hedge, and past Victorian, Tudor, and Georgian styled residences enhanced by manicured, green lawns that sloped toward the tennis club and toward the just as exclusive Annie Wright Boarding School. Dressed in its ivy-covered, Eastern prep school majesty, the Protestant Annie Wright School seemed to stretch almost half the length of Tacoma Avenue North from the tennis club to McCarver Street that ran down the hill toward the landmark Old Town dock. The beauty and antiquity of it all, and not the exclusivity, from Tacoma Avenue's residences to its tennis club and its Annie Wright School, both attracted and inspired Ron as he continued on his way west to McCarver Street where he turned right and headed toward Old Town and his own modest, white-frame house waiting for him on North 28th Street.

# SETTLING IN

# IX

Leaving home wasn't easy for Ron, but then it's never easy to leave any place that's inspired love. His parents did all they could to prepare him to leave their home with the psychological independence he would need to guarantee his freedom. They labored within the shadow of their church, and as strong individuals themselves, they were more attuned to that church's altar than to its pulpit. They were obedient to the Church, but they recognized a difference between practicing religion and engaging in social action. As a result, they never quite grasped the post-Vatican II idea that equated such engagement, as well as obedience to social rules, with religion. Ron believed in obedience as a liberating virtue and his mom and dad, given their own regard for it, impressed him as being liberated and free.

By Thursday, two days after his return from Lebanon, he was ready to leave, but his mom and dad thought he should wait until Friday morning. On Thursday night his mom made his favorite dinner of scalloped potatoes and ham, followed by apple strudel—the likes of which he never tasted anywhere else in the course of his 22 years or, he thought, would taste in the course of all his years, however many that may be. Like the Church where celebrating the Mass took precedence over delivering the sermon, his home was more altar-centered than pulpit-centered and, therefore, more evocative than coercive. His mom and dad—equally—commanded, more than demanded, respect; and fear played no role in his home built around the preparation and serving of food. His mother prepared the food more out of celebration than resignation, and if magic marked the preparation and serving of food at the altar in church, it also marked the preparation and serving of food at that table in Ron Petrich's home. Supported by authentic love, the magic of ritual worked in both cases, and if Ron hated to leave home, he still felt prepared. His leaving represented both the beginning and ending of something. And without such natural beginnings and endings, there would be no anguish and rapture—and thus no authentic life.

Friday morning came and it was time to leave. Besides breakfast, there were no more celebrative meals to prepare. There was only the leaving. Not to delay that fact but to further acknowledge it, Ron's mother prepared him a breakfast of poached eggs, and, as usual, the eggs stood up straight on the crisp, white toast. Ron punctured each yoke with his fork and lightly mashed the whites, softening the crispness of the fresh toast. The perfect poached egg was a thing of beauty, and no restaurant, not even Bing's Kitchen, could match the perfection of the eggs poached at his home on North 28th Street in Tacoma's Old Town. After he finished breakfast, Ron packed his Malibu, stacking his clothes, and teaching vestments, neatly in the back seat, and stood, one more time, on his front porch —with its picketed railing and four-pillared support—and looked through the rare January sunlight across Commencement Bay to Brown's Point on the northern shore.

Although he only was driving five hours south along the connecting link of Interstate 5, he still found it hard to leave. He stood in contemplative silence on his front porch with his mom and dad waiting, it seemed, for the appropriate time to say goodbye. Finally, his mom said that he had better get started so that he'd have plenty of time to look for a place to live. She felt encouraged because Ron had told her about Mrs Williams and the Gables Motel, and while he and his mother were saying goodbye, his dad walked into the house only to return in a few minutes carrying a baseball glove. He had played baseball in Tacoma's City League for 22 years, ending in 1955 when he turned 40, and the glove he carried was his last and Ron's first. Having kissed his mother goodbye, Ron turned and grasped his dad's outstretched hand as firmly and as solidly as he could, at the same time accepting the baseball glove with his left hand. Then he smiled in recognition, released his dad's hand, turned and walked down the porch steps onto the front sidewalk and toward his waiting Malibu. With one last wave he started the car, jockeyed a U-turn on North 28th, and headed toward McCarver Street where he would turn left toward Tacoma Avenue North, Stadium Way, Pacific Avenue and, finally, to Interstate 5 southbound for Lebanon, Oregon.

He followed the same route to the freeway as he followed two days earlier, only this time he drove in the daylight, accompanied by the rare winter sunlight that seemed to celebrate his leaving home to begin the creation of his own home. In late January the threat of winter snow had eased and the bulk of the winter rain had fallen. Once more the sun did not set forever, and it was time to look forward again in commemoration of an ageless cycle. Commencement Bay glistened in the January sunlight, and anyone who looked closely at the flower beds surrounding the houses on McCarver Street and Tacoma Avenue North could see sprouting crocuses tentatively emerging from the soggy ground to test the state of the late January air. They were harbingers of spring, and with its coming the promise of blossoming and fulfillment returned to be followed once again, after summer and fall, by the silent—and always wet, if only occasionally frozen—repose of winter. And so it went in celebration, not in resignation, of the timelessness of life. Ron had been taught, as had any individual born in the shadow of Christianity, that the individual human being was more apart from nature than a part of it, but the older he grew, the less sense such teaching made. He may not have realized it, but he had begun to seriously doubt the truth of the fundamental Augustinian and Christian doctrine of original sin. And without that sin Augustinian Christianity made little sense.

Ron followed the familiar route to the freeway from McCarver Street to Tacoma Avenue to Rankos and Stadium Way and the Old City Hall to Pacific Avenue, but on this sunlit, January day the picture wasn't dominated by the architectural majesty of the Annie Wright School or Stadium High School or the Northern Pacific Depot or even by Union Station. Instead, it was dominated by the natural majesty of Mt Rainier rising above the Cascade Range to the east. During the gray Northwest winter, fog and low-hanging storm clouds obscure the mountain. But when the sun manages to penetrate the layers of overcast, Mt Rainier, more fittingly once known as Mt Tacoma, bursts forth with the power to inspire reverence. But given the Christian understanding of nature as being separate from the divinity, in contrast to the Northwest Indian interpretation of the union of divinity and nature, Mt Rainier didn't enjoy such status. It towered above the Cascade Mountain Range in all its quiet majesty but more as a comforting recreational site than as an awe-inspiring religious site. Ron Petrich wasn't much for participating in Northwest mountain recreation nor was he much for pretending to be a Northwest Indian. He was a Christian who had begun to think that maybe individual human beings were more a part of nature that apart from it. Such a thought wasn't always comforting, but, nonetheless, it was one from which he couldn't escape.

As he drove down Pacific Avenue past the Doric columns of the bank of California, past the solid brick architecture of People's Department Store, past the neon glitter of Pacific Avenue's vice dens, and finally past the copper dome of Union Station, he couldn't help thinking that at least the architectural majesty of his railroad station could match the natural majesty of Mt Rainier. He would miss the mountain and Union Station most of all because if you wondered and if you believed, you could find magic in that snow-capped peak and in that copper dome. That same magic worked in the transubstantiation and had nothing to do with science. Scientific magic, no matter how wondrous, couldn't touch the soul. The magic of snow-capped peaks, copper domes, and transubstantiations formed an integral part of Ron's world. He sought to understand it and would be just as willing to explain it, in case he ever was asked.

Once past Union Station he had little left to notice that would distinguish Tacoma from other industrial cities struggling to find another economic identity more consistent with the age of technology. The City of Destiny had Brown and Haley, which used to sponsor 'Amos n' Andy' on television, but Ron never identified with almond roca to any significant extent. As a result of his first visit, he knew that Lebanon, Oregon, had its plywood industry. But he also knew it had no Union station, no Old City Hall, no Stadium High School, no lawn and tennis club, no Annie Wright School, no Commencement Bay, and no Mt Rainier standing watch over it all from what appeared to be the back yard. Still, Lebanon had its high school with its principal, Bill Polk, who actually wanted Ron Petrich, and not just anyone, to teach senior English. In spite of what he was leaving behind, such a thought inspired Ron as he followed Pacific Avenue to its junction with Interstate 5, where he picked up the sign pointing toward Portland and eased his Malibu into the traffic heading for points south of his City of Destiny.

# X

The January sunlight followed him all the way to Lebanon, and he only stopped in Vancouver, on the Washington side of the Columbia River, to buy a hamburger and a root beer at the A and W where he had stopped on his way home a couple of days earlier. He was anxious to get to Lebanon to begin his teaching career as part of the continuing adventure of his life. In 1962 when he enrolled at Seattle University, he had no idea he was going to be a teacher and thus didn't go to college specifically to prepare for the profession. He went, in part, because it offered him four more years of indecisive youth. But most of all he went because of the promise of adventure. Ron had learned the importance of being honest and responsible above all things, and whereas the majority of his college contemporaries were open to the inspiration of marriage, he was mostly alone in his openness to the inspiration of love.

His adventurous spirit illustrated the difference between the pulpit religion and the altar religion of his Christianity and the difference between the pulpit-centered Protestant Church and the altar-centered Catholic Church where delivering the sermon took second place to celebrating the Mass. The pulpit religion spoke of marriage as the noble end, or purpose, of human life, with the emphasis placed on the individual as an obedient child of God who was to populate His Kingdom. But the altar religion, in unconscious opposition to the pulpit message, spoke more quietly of love as identifying the noble purpose, or end, of human life with the emphasis placed on the individual as being an obedient child of God set free to populate his own kingdom. And Ron Petrich was nothing if he wasn't obedient.

When his eyes and heart were in agreement, he was obedient in his pursuit of love, and more than once he appeared foolish in the process. He believed in True Love, and his adventure had taught him that such love was born only when the beloved shared the adventure and believed the same. And now, with his role of teacher secure, as once was his role of college student, he was free to think of the promise of discovering love in Lebanon, Oregon. Such thoughts always made him smile, just as they always made his heart beat faster in promised anticipation.

So, with a heart alive with the promise of adventure Ron arrived in Lebanon, this time not as a visitor, in the waning afternoon hours in late January of 1967, just three-and-one-half days removed from the beginning of his teaching career. The town seemed more familiar now as he drove past its identifying sign sitting in front of St Edward's Catholic Church, just down the street from the old high school and Dr Harrison's office. Although he had begun to question the post-Vatican II direction of his church, in conflict with his own direction, he still attended church and looked forward to testing what St Edward's had to offer. He never would be ashamed of his Roman Catholic heritage, even if he felt alienated from the still emerging, post-Vatican II church with its reformed emphasis on the pulpit and supporting liturgy that most often celebrated the character of the local parish or community more than it did that of anything truly universal or "catholic." By January of 1967 Ron's separation from the Roman Catholic orthodoxy had begun, but it was far from complete.

Lebanon looked increasingly familiar as he drove through downtown, this time having to stop at its one stop light that allowed pedestrians to cross the street freely in pursuit of their retail venture. As he sat at the red light, he thought of his anonymity that soon would be no more. In a short time, perhaps even a few months or a few weeks, he would be recognized as Mr Petrich, high school English teacher; and being stopped at that same light, he would be acknowledged as such. He felt comfortable in his anonymity, but he wasn't afraid of his coming notoriety, either. He didn't fear responsibility, and he felt confident in the fact that his promised notoriety would be more complimentary than derisive. But for now he remained anonymous, and when the light turned green, he accelerated gently and continued on his way to the comforting familiarity of the Gables Motel.

He smiled in recognition as he drove past Bing's Kitchen, and a half-mile later he turned left off the Santiam Highway and into the parking lot of Mrs Williams' motel. More cars occupied the spaces than he remembered from his previous visit, but he had to admit that he paid little attention then. Lebanon sat off the beaten path, and a good portion of the southbound travelers had to drive by it completely on Interstate 5 with the bigger city of Eugene, the home of the University of Oregon, just 45 miles down the road. He felt good to see that some travelers still came to Lebanon and the Gables as he found his familiar parking spot in front of the main office. The sign in front showed a vacancy as he parked his Malibu, stepped out of the car, and walked up the steps leading to the motel office.

"Welcome back," Mrs Williams said from her position behind the counter as Ron walked in the front door. "I saw you pull off the highway, so I thought I'd come out front to greet you. Did you have a nice drive from Tacoma?"

"Yes," Ron answered, stepping across the threshold once again. "It was exciting, to be honest, and the sunlight followed me all the way. Maybe that's a good omen."

"I'm sure it is," Mrs Williams said with a smile. "You're one of us now, you know. You aren't anonymous anymore."

"I know. I thought about that when I stopped at the light in town. But I'm not afraid to lose my anonymity. I'm just going to be myself so that I'll have nothing to hide. I'm ready to accept the responsibility of teacher."

"'Uneasy lies the head that wears the crown,' remember," Mrs Williams said as Ron smiled in recognition of the now familiar reference to Shakespeare.

"I know, but there'd be no adventure without responsibility. And I like adventure."

"That's the way it should be. Let's take the adventure to the living room, shall we?" Mrs Williams asked as she lifted up the hinged counter top.

"Okay. Sounds good to me," Ron answered as he walked through the opening and followed her into the living room.

"Well," she said, settling in to her familiar position on the couch, "I suppose you should try to find a place to live, first of all. What are you looking for?"

"I don't know, exactly. I've never looked for a place to live before, but I don't need anything fancy. I only have my clothes, towels, bedding, kitchen gear and my clock radio."

"What else do you need?" Mrs Williams asked, laughing.

"Nothing, I guess. I just need a place with furniture and a kitchen where I can cook."

"You mean you don't plan on eating your meals at Bing's?"

"No way. I'm going to cook. I think I can make enough meals to sustain me. I wouldn't want to eat out all the time. I'd rather try to make myself a home, and I think preparing and serving food, even if for yourself, is important. I'm not a fanatic or anything, but I actually look forward to cooking for myself. I don't mean anything fancy, but I want my place to smell like a home, at least. I'll never forget the smells of my home in Tacoma. I think my mother cooked more in celebration than in anything else."

"In celebration of what?" Mrs Williams asked.

"I don't know," Ron answered. "In celebration of life, I suppose. She didn't laugh or sing as she was cooking, but I could tell she cooked in celebration. I think she's like you. Mr Polk said you had confronted death. My mother has, too, and I think she has affirmed its existence and necessity. I think she and my dad are more noble than they realize. I know they've made me proud to be a Petrich, and they've given me a solid foundation to build my life on. But now it's up to me, isn't it?"

"Yes, I suppose it is. But it sounds like they've done their job. Now you're free to build your own life. I'd like to meet your mom and dad."

"I know they'd like you. I told them about you and the Gables, and they felt better knowing you were in Lebanon."

"But you don't need me."

"I know, but it's helped to have you so far."

"Well," Mrs Williams said, picking up the local newspaper that was lying on the coffee table in front of the couch, "I did take the liberty of looking in the paper for furnished apartments you might be interested in. Lebanon's a far cry from Tacoma or Seattle, you know, but I think you might be interested in a couple I've circled. How soon would you like to move in?"

"Today, if I could. I can't think of any reason to wait if I can find a place I like."

"We'd better not waste any time then," Mrs Williams said, opening the paper to the classified section. "What do you think of this?" she asked, moving to a seat closer to him on the couch.

"Sounds promising to me," Ron answered after he read the ad mentioning a one-bedroom, furnished apartment with kitchen facilities for 50 dollars a month. "Isn't the high school on Fifth Street?"

"Yes," Mrs Williams answered, "and this apartment is on Second Street just a few blocks away. Do you think it might be too close?"

"It won't make any difference. Do you think it's a separate place or do you think it's the upstairs of a house?"

"I think it's probably an upstairs. But if it is, I'm sure it will have its own private entrance. I think it'll be a decent place. I've driven by there many times and it's a nice neighborhood. But remember, you are in Lebanon, Oregon."

"I know, but there's nothing to worry about. I'm ready to earn my status as a teacher and I can't wait to get started. Finding a place to live is just the beginning, and I think I'll go check out this place. I just drive like I'm going to the high school, only I turn on Second Street instead of on Fifth. Isn't that right?" Ron asked, standing up from the couch.

"Yes, that's right," Mrs Williams answered, standing up herself. "It's an even-numbered address, which means you'll find it on the right side of the street as you're heading north. It won't be hard to find, not in Lebanon."

"You're a great help," Ron said as he walked toward the outer office. "If I take the place, I'll let you know right away," he added as he made his way to the office door.

"I'll be waiting," Mrs Williams said as he opened the door and stepped outside onto the porch. "I hope it's what you need."

"So do I," Ron said. "I'll let you know," he concluded as he closed the door and walked down the steps to his parked Malibu.

He remembered the route to the high school from the Gables and had no trouble finding the white house on the 300 block of Second Street just three blocks northeast of the high school. If need be, he easily could walk to work from the upstairs apartment with its private stairway and entrance attached to the south side of the frame house that looked as if it belonged in Tacoma's Old town. Ron parked his car in what seemed like familiar territory and walked up the sidewalk to the front door. He rang the doorbell and looked around the house and yard as he waited for the answer to his ring.

If the house looked as though it belonged in Ron's Old Town neighborhood, its owner, who shortly answered the door, did not. An Old Town resident appeared more comforting than did the man who answered Ron's ring, and the Old Town resident appeared more tolerant as well. Ron's potential landlord appeared anything but tolerant standing in the doorway wearing a scowl on his face and dressed in a pair of brown slacks, held up by soiled suspenders, over which hung a protruding belly covered only with a white, sleeveless undershirt. The man who answered the door didn't fit the image the house awakened in Ron's imagination, and he momentarily was taken aback by the owner's unexpected appearance. But he recovered in a few awkward seconds and identified himself as Ron Petrich, who was to begin teaching at the high school come Monday, and who would like to look at the available apartment.

At Ron's mentioning of teacher, the man at the door, who identified himself as Leroy V H Brands, smiled, hitched up his slacks, sucked in his belly, and said he'd be happy to show Ron the apartment. He said it would be a pleasure to have a teacher as a tenant because nothing was more important than the education of our youth. Ron wasn't sure he and Mr Brands embraced the same understanding of education, but he couldn't disagree with him. He never had known a man named Leroy, but he had to smile to himself as he thought that if anyone should be so named, his prospective landlord would be the one. People come in all shapes and sizes, he thought, as Mr Brands came back to the front door carrying the apartment keys and motioned Ron to follow him up the stairs. Ron nodded okay and followed Mr Brands, who had combed his thick and bushy red hair but who walked out into the January chill dressed as he was when he first answered the doorbell.

Ron wasn't laughing at his prospective landlord as much as he was laughing at the fact of how different individual people could be. He was sure Mr Brands lacked the more expansive tolerance that identified the men and women of his Old Town neighborhood, but he realized he couldn't expect Mr Brands to be any different than he appeared to be. He represented Ron's first contact with Lebanon's more Protestant, pulpit-centered morality that had a strong tendency to confuse temperance with abstinence. Ron sensed the difference between Mr. Brands and himself, along with the residents of his Catholic Old Town neighborhood, but he didn't feel superior. He realized he wouldn't be any different had the circumstances of his life been the same as those of

Mr. Brands'. Still more curious than convinced, Ron followed him up the stairs along the south side of the house and into the apartment that he hoped to call home.

Mr. Brands reached the top of the stairs and, almost out of breath, opened the door to a pleasant, if not spacious, living room decorated with white, laced curtains that adorned the windows overlooking Second Street below. A maroon and gold, patterned throw rug lay in front of a dark maroon, early American couch that sat underneath the window sills. Ron thought the couch was very early American, indeed, as his eyes scanned the airy, immaculately clean room. Mr. Brands showed him the bathroom, equipped with a shower, off to the right of the living room and just in front of the kitchen area that came complete with an electric stove and oven and a small, half-size refrigerator next to which sat a medium-sized, formica-topped table with two straight-backed wooden chairs. Behind the kitchen area at the far north end of the living room, beige, floor-length curtains marked the entrance to the bedroom with the headboard of its double bed set against the west wall and with its walk-in closet occupying the east wall. The bedroom's paned window looked over Mr Brands' lawn below and over what looked like a duplex rental that sat behind the house.

Strangely enough, Ron was taken by the place. He hardly expected an executive suite, and 50 dollars a month, now that he had to start thinking about money and how far it would go in relation to his teaching salary, seemed fair enough. He didn't hesitate to take it, and Mr Brands said he could move in immediately for the first month's rent and a 75 dollar cleaning deposit. Ron had the money, partly in savings from his days as a smelter worker and partly because of what his mom and dad had given him to help him get started. He didn't have a checking account yet, but he gave Mr Brands 125 dollars in cash. His first landlord shook his hand, welcoming him to Lebanon, and that was that. He had a place to live. Mr Brands gave him a key, keeping one for himself, told him never to hesitate to call him if he ever needed anything, and left him alone to move his clothes, bedding, clock radio, and kitchen utensils into his new home. Ron was free to settle in.

He didn't waste any time transferring his belongings from his car to his new apartment. He brought along a few boxes of books, but even though his new home lacked the storage space for them, he thought he'd eventually be able to locate some bookshelves. For now he was happy to have found a place to live, and he was determined to make a home for himself. He shook his head in recognition of Mr Brands and thought he would make a good character in a novel someday. Ron saw him more as an individual to understand and appreciate than as one to disregard and judge. And now he was his landlord. After he finished moving in, he looked around, decided everything was in order for now, stepped outside, locked the door, and headed down the stairs toward his Malibu that Mr Brands said he could park in the back behind the house. He was ready, now, to head back to the Gables Motel.

Mrs Williams had to laugh at his description of what he called his Woodrow Wilson couch, but she was pleased to know that Ron was going to be comfortable and that he was excited about the prospects of living and teaching in Lebanon. She still hoped, for his sake, that he didn't bring too much to teaching, but then she thought that both the profession and her town could use some fresh blood. Times were changing, she knew, and she hoped they would change Ron's way. His sense of adventure reminded her of her own. That common spirit united the two of them and could, in time, unite mankind as well. As far as she could tell, mankind was nothing more than a collection of individuals in need of unity.

Ron was anxious to get back to his new home and after briefly describing the rest of his apartment, he left to get something to eat at Bing's Kitchen, deciding to wait until he was more moved in to fix his first meal. He never would be far from the Gables, and he knew he had found an ally in Mrs Williams. She know who she was, and her individual identity helped give her life a sense of purpose. She entertained no thoughts of clinging to Ron. He was now a welcomed addition to her adventurous life, but she realized he had to develop a life separate from her now that he had found his place to begin. She didn't know how often she would see him, but before he left to return to his new home, he did accept her dinner invitation for Sunday night—the night before he was to officially begin his teaching career.

By Sunday afternoon Ron had comfortably moved into his apartment and had fixed his first meal of steak, green salad, and french fries Saturday night and had attended his first Mass at St Edward's Sunday morning. But he didn't know what to expect on Monday morning and couldn't help wishing he was starting at the beginning of the year with everyone else. He knew nothing about the nature of his teaching curriculum and thus had no idea of where, or with what, he was expected to start teaching. Burdened with the subsequent apprehension, he left home early Sunday evening and headed for the Gables and dinner with Mrs Williams. He felt settled in his apartment, and he was anxious to begin teaching Monday. But he was afraid of not being prepared. To be prepared in front of a hostile audience could be intimidating enough, but to be unprepared in front of that same audience could be devastating. He might as well show up naked.

# XI

Mrs Williams had prepared a Sunday dinner of roast beef, mashed potatoes, gravy, and green salad dressed with vinegar and oil, all of which made Ron feel as though he'd never left home. In fact, dinner with Mrs Williams proved to be an extension of his home and he responded accordingly. Just as his mother would have, Mrs Williams could tell something occupied Ron's mind, and just as his mother would have, she asked him about it after they had sat down to eat. Ron didn't associate the dinner table with frivolity, and for anyone who lived in celebration of time, dinner conversation could take on the importance of ritual. He'd already decided that he'd rather sit in silence than participate in meaningless conversation and had grown protective of revealing himself to those not genuinely interested. But when Mrs Williams asked what he had on his mind, he didn't hesitate to tell her the truth—just as he wouldn't have hesitated to tell his mother or father the same.

In between bites of roast beef, mashed potatoes, and salad, he told her that he was worried about being unprepared to meet his classes on Monday. Neither Dr Harrison nor Mr Polk had told him where he was supposed to begin, and he had learned from student teaching just how much time a teacher had to face in each class period. In fact, from the teacher's side of the desk, as opposed to the students' side, facing all that time seemed overwhelming at first. Ron discovered that he couldn't sit behind his teacher's desk and do nothing while his students sat at their desks and worked on time consuming assignments that he would have to correct on his time. Being faced with time presented him with a dilemma he had to resolve, and he quickly learned, in his student teaching experience, that he couldn't simply waste time behind his desk and ask students to consume time behind theirs.

Mrs Williams couldn't speak from experience as a teacher, but she could speak from experience with time. She told Ron that he should treat the students' time as being as valuable to them as his time was to him and that, as a result, he never should assign anything that simply served the purpose of consuming time. But he said he was afraid of having to do exactly that, which would mean he'd feel guilty for not teaching and for unjustifiably taking students' time as well. Then Mrs Williams said he had to make sure he understood what he was supposed to teach to avoid that situation in the future. It seemed to her, she said, that teaching consisted of explaining what you understood to those who didn't understand it. The more Ron understood, she continued, the more he would have to teach and authentic teaching involved celebrating time and not merely consuming it. He said he knew what she was saying but that he worried about being able to give students something worthy of their time tomorrow when he didn't even know what they were supposed to study.

She told him that he had his youthful good looks on his side in that regard. She was convinced that his mere presence, initially, would work to his advantage. In the beginning, she said, whatever he said wouldn't make much difference, but that as the year progressed, he'd have to prove himself. For tomorrow, she said, he just had to be prepared to teach, in general, about literature and writing to lay a solid foundation on which he could build the rest of the year. He said it wasn't going to be easy, and she asked him if it was supposed to be. He had to say no, it wasn't and that was that. After dinner he had to go home and prepare his presentation to five different classes the next day. He knew he had to speak with conviction, as if he genuinely understood what he was talking about.

Ron didn't receive any sympathy from Mrs Williams, but he did get the truth which, she said, never hurt. Deception hurt while truth only hurt those who were afraid of it. She told Ron the truth about time and about how a teacher should seek to use his students' time. As long as he gave students something worthy of it, he had a right to expect that they listen and give him the time he asked for. And he understood that he had no right to expect students to give what he didn't offer himself as a teacher. Ron's anxiety over tomorrow was natural, Mrs Williams said, and he had to stand up to it to defeat it. He had to work as hard as he could to understand as much as he could. He just needed a shot of confidence—along with his roast beef, mashed potatoes, gravy, and green salad dressed in vinegar and oil. Mrs Williams gave him all he needed, and he went home that night knowing what he had to do and knowing that no one would, or should, feel sorry for him. He was ready to face the next day with new resolve, and when his alarm rang at seven o' clock the next morning, he was prepared to meet the challenge.

When he arrived at the high school at seven thirty-five, dressed in the vestments of his role and imbued with the responsibility they awakened, he realized he had no idea where to go. He was a member of the faculty, but he didn't feel right about going to the faculty room where no one had the slightest idea of his presence. Furthermore, he had no idea which classroom belonged to him. For the first time he realized that no one had prepared him for these eventualities and he felt lost. If it weren't for the fact that he knew Mr Polk would understand, he may have turned around and headed back to the safety of Old Town and the smelter. But, luckily, he had Mr Polk, and when he entered Lebanon Union High School for the first time as a teacher, he went straight to the principal's office for the last time.

Mr Polk smiled when he saw Ron because, through no fault of his own, he knew he'd be unprepared. He hadn't thought of showing Ron his classroom, and he hadn't thought of telling him where he was supposed to begin with his senior English classes. He apologized for his oversight and took Ron to his mailbox, located in the copy room in front of and to the left of the main office. There Ron found a copy of the senior English curriculum, and Mr Polk told him he could look it over to see where he was expected to start with his classes the second semester. Ron discovered that senior English consisted of a survey of English literature starting, in September, thank goodness, with 'Beowulf' that he remembered from his own high school days. Although he had little faith in his understanding of English literature, he felt better when he noticed that the curriculum saved January and February for a study of Shakespeare's 'Macbeth.' Of all the courses he had taken in college to meet his degree requirements, Shakespeare's comedies and tragedies were his most affective. He didn't necessarily understand either, but at least he felt relatively comfortable with both and confident in the fact that even his limited understanding exceeded that of his senior students for whom immediate concerns, as they should be, were paramount.

Thrown into the breach in the middle of the year, Ron's first day as a professional teacher was bizarre to say the least. Luckily, he had Mr Polk who had decided to personally introduce him to all five of his senior English classes and who had eased Ron's anxiety somewhat when he reminded him that his situation could be worse. He could be replacing a teacher exceedingly popular with the students. As it was, Ron was replacing someone who didn't enjoy that popularity despite the fact that the students, rather than the teacher, controlled the classroom. Ron couldn't allow students to control the classroom and still live up to his responsibility, but, on the other hand, he couldn't simply demand that he assume control. Under less than ideal circumstances on the first day of the second semester, the bell still rang at eight o' clock. And with that first bell, Ron's teaching career began.

If anything, he proved himself to be a natural and required little assistance after Mr Polk's initial introduction of him to each class. The classroom was his arena, and the students sensed as much once he established his presence. He wasn't interested in making friends. He was interested only in teaching, and even if he hadn't mastered his subject matter, he was accomplished at creating the illusion that he had. He knew teaching consisted of explaining what he understood to those who didn't understand, and he worked as hard as he could to understand both literature and writing. He never referred to notes—but only because he always memorized what he had to say.

He couldn't think quickly on his feet, but his self-directed study taught him that he could interpret literature better than he thought. He never liked the overly intellectual exercise of literary interpretation and thought Shakespeare would be more at home in a bar than in a library. Ron thought Shakespearean literature, and any other literature worthy of comparison, had to be grounded more in individual human experience than in collective academic study. Thus any such study had to be geared to identifying and understanding this truth of experience. He he was as much a student as he was a teacher, but his interest in literature and writing, along with his commitment to the communication of their inspiration, earned him the respect of his senior students. To be young, athletic, humorous, and handsome didn't hurt. But he knew his youthful charm couldn't last.

His hostile audience tested him for his fairness because, above all, a teacher should treat every student as a special student without identifying any student, or any type of student, as the special student. If all men were created equal, Ron quickly learned that such equality didn't extend to the realm of intellectual skill. He also discovered that genuine hard work didn't automatically produce skilled work worthy of the grade reflected in the effort. Furthermore, he quickly learned that students blessed with an abundance of intellectual skill often saw themselves as special students who were treated as such by the school itself. These students, whether male or female, sought to impress their teachers. And one such attempt established Ron's reputation for fairness and earned him lasting respect for being an authentic teacher who honestly practiced what he preached.

Lebanon's senior English curriculum required that students study vocabulary development, and every Friday was given over to such study and the accompanying testing. Ron soon learned that a significant number of his students, whom he respected because of their willingness to seek to understand, could not—no matter how hard they tried—remember enough words and definitions to achieve 60 percent and a passing grade. His observation made him question the usefulness of the Friday vocabulary study, but he was obedient, which meant he did what the curriculum expected. The intellectually skilled and righteous students sailed through the vocabulary study. Those less skilled struggled and even failed. And the intellectually skilled and enterprising students cheated.

The occasion to cheat was obvious with the temptation being even more so. Ron couldn't permit and condone cheating, but at the same time he couldn't remove the occasion and the temptation and still obey the vocabulary requirement in which he had little faith. Under the circumstances, cheating on the vocabulary tests, while certainly improper, constituted a venial sin at best, and he knew such sins didn't earn anyone a trip to Hell, no matter its definition. Although he hadn't caught anyone cheating, he knew the occasion had been created, the temptation had been awakened, and no doubt the act had been perpetrated. In all honesty he couldn't say he wouldn't have cheated himself, given the same set of circumstances, which explained his sense of humor with regard to the more enterprising students in his classes. His test came midway through his first semester when one of the intellectually skilled, righteous students—and a noted student leader and a girl—informed on one of the intellectually skilled, enterprising students—and a noted student prankster and a boy.

"Mr Petrich?" Traci Warren asked, raising her hand.

"Yes," Ron answered, standing, as he always did on vocabulary Friday, in front of his desk at the head of the classroom.

"Do you know Tom is cheating?"

"Really?" Ron asked in return.

"Yes," Traci answered. "I've been watching him all period. And I don't think it's the first time. He always cheats on vocabulary tests," she added with a smile, convinced she had done her duty.

"Do you always watch that closely?" Ron asked as he turned his eyes toward Tom Bell seated in the second to last desk in the last row nearest the windows overlooking the school courtyard.

"Maybe not always," Traci answered, still smiling with satisfaction. "But I have been this period."

"Well, thanks for your vigilance, Traci," Ron said, turning his eyes back toward her. With her shoulder length, natural blonde hair, alluring blue eyes, and noticeably mature figure—all of which she was more than aware—she represented all the girls Dr Harrison had in mind when he questioned Ron about his commitment to teaching. If he were more vulnerable to teenage flattery, he wouldn't have been the first young male teacher to disregard the sanctity of his social role. As it was, Traci Warren, regardless of her position as noted student leader, had much to learn about her current senior English teacher. "You have to watch certain guys," he added. "Isn't that right, Tom?"

"I don't know," Tom answered as the blood rushed to his cheeks, turning his face the color of his hair. Flustered, he squirmed in his seat and sneaked a glare at Traci across the room as Ron walked toward his desk.

"What's your technique?" Ron asked, suppressing his smile as he reached Tom's desk and stood to his immediate left.

"It's nothing, Mr Petrich," Tom answered, slinking further down into his desk chair completely hiding his six foot frame.

"Traci's right, isn't she? You were cheating, weren't you?" Ron asked, somewhat delighting in Tom's embarrassment.

"Yes," Tom answered sheepishly but truthfully.

"Well, then, how did you do it?"

"Like this," Tom answered, holding out his right hand for inspection.

"Traci's right," Ron said, examining the palm of Tom's hand as Traci basked in her expected glory. "All the answers are there, in ink, on the flesh. Not very original but still effective. Until you're caught."

"I guess so," Tom said, still slouched in his desk and not looking at Ron.

"You know what I have to do, don't you?"

"Yes," he answered, reaching for and then handing Ron his test paper. "You have to tear this up," he said, finally sitting up and looking at Ron.

"You'd only do the same," Ron said, accepting the test paper and tearing it in half as Tom looked on. "Maybe next time you can be more creative."

"Maybe there won't be a next time," Tom said as Ron, holding the torn fragments of Tom's paper in his right hand, walked over to Traci's desk on the other side of the room.

"I hope not," Ron said as he stopped at her desk and reached for her paper.

"What are you doing, Mr Petrich?" she asked in astonishment.

"I don't like stool pigeons, either," Ron answered, tearing her paper in half as well.

If the students had been a crowd, they would have cheered as Ron, carrying the fragments of both papers wadded up in his right hand, walked back to his desk—triumphant in his defense of the fundamental premise that says every student is a special student and no student is the special student.

Immediately following such an experience the Traci Warrens, both male and female, of Lebanon Union High School—and especially Traci Warren herself—weren't impressed with Ron and remained closed to whatever he had to teach. The skilled and enterprising and the not-so-skilled but committed just as immediately were impressed. Ron had established himself, in their eyes, as an authority who could be trusted. As a result, they decided both he and literature were worth listening to. In the presence of such an authority, operating out of a sense of genuine fairness that singles out no individual or type of individual, even Traci Warren and her allies couldn't remain closed for long without recognizing that they were responsible for their alienation and isolation. After a short time, then, marked by anger and simmering resentment, Traci and her followers recognized the folly of their own making. An aura of discipline, built more on mutual awareness of responsibility, rather than on imposed obedience to a set of rules, settled over Ron's classes. He recognized early that a classroom was sacred. And as long as he respected its sanctity, he had every right to expect the same from his students, all of whom—skilled or unskilled—were capable of responding in kind.

# XII

Ron respected the sanctity of the faculty room as well, but he didn't enjoy instant acceptance among the faculty members. They were friendly and acknowledged his presence, but no one went out of his or her way to make him feel welcome or at home. He learned from the faculty's reaction to him that he would have to earn peer status in their eyes. If such status wasn't immediately forthcoming, it did come as word spread of his handling of the Traci Warren incident and as word spread of the disciplined nature of his classes. Ron felt proud of the way he handled the cheating situation with his action being more inspired than calculated. He proved to himself, to his students, and to his fellow teachers that he could command, rather than demand, respect. To demand respect a teacher had to be someone to fear. But to command respect a teacher had to be someone to love.

Still, no instant friendships developed between Ron and any members of the faculty, male or female, although he did come to share coffee with Judith Griswold, a fellow English teacher, every morning before the first bell summoned him to his classroom. Judith was five years older than Ron, and she was teaching while her husband, Ken, attended Oregon State University in Corvallis just 18 miles west of Lebanon across Interstate 5. Ron came to count on her coffee, never making his own in the morning before he left home, and, eventually, Judith decided to bring an extra cup along with her thermos to accommodate him. She smoked filter-tipped Kools while he smoked straight Lucky Strikes, and over morning coffee and cigarettes a sense of mutual respect, that led to solid friendship, developed between the two of them. If Ron had to identify his chief ally on the faculty after those first few months, he would have chosen Judith whose mysterious husband quietly arrived each day at three-fifteen to take her home.

Mrs Williams had told him about the football coach, and Ron had little trouble identifying him. She was right. Judson Heath's presence demanded attention. He looked like the incarnation of a younger Bud Wilkinson, the legendary University of Oklahoma coach, with his closely cropped crew cut and steely eyes that glared at whatever they saw. He had to be close to 40, and standing lean and trim at six feet four inches, he looked like he still could block and tackle and catch passes with the best of them. A thick, black beard accompanied his prominent, bulbous nose and round face marked by its thin-lipped mouth. Ron easily could picture him barking commands in support of his coaching motto that celebrated "all for one and one for all." Unlike his faculty room ally, Judith Griswold, Judson Heath didn't drink coffee and he didn't smoke cigarettes. But he did cuss. He was a man surrounded by the majesty, fading but still seductive, of the institution of sport for which football provided the foundation. And upon hearing of Ron's disciplined classroom, he wasted no time in taking him under his wing and introducing him to the coaches' room where the authentic men held forth.

In the coaches' room men could cuss, tell dirty jokes, talk about women faculty members they'd like to bed, walk around naked, and pass gas to their heart's content. Ron couldn't say that the coaches' room brought out the best in men, but he couldn't say he didn't like being included in their fraternity, either. He could move freely between the faculty room and the coaches' room where his colleagues in either simply stayed put. The time would come when he would have to choose "forever betwixt two things," but not yet. For now, he could move in both worlds. And all the time Mr Polk, who rarely appeared in either world, stood solidly in the background in careful and concerned observation.

Away from school Ron had been discovered by Rob Wesley, an Oregon State graduate and junior high math teacher, who happened to live in one of the duplexes behind Leroy Brands' house. Wesley, no one ever called him Rob, was two years older than Ron, but he was single. And even though his orgiastic approach to life contrasted with Ron's more ritualistic approach, he came to be a reliable friend whom Ron could trust. No moss grew on Rob Wesley, and if there wasn't a party brewing somewhere, he would make sure to correct the situation. Girls especially, and Wesley had several contacts at Oregon State, were taken in by his life of entertaining, non-stop adventure full of all the "sound and fury" anyone could ask for. Ron had a hard time keeping up, but he did his best.

Where Ron reached five feet ten inches, Wesley stood at six feet two inches, but where Ron was athletically coordinated, Wesley was athletically awkward. Their hair color matched the same shade of dark blonde or light brown with Ron's being of finer texture, and Wesley forever bushed back his tousled front, kept that way by his life lived on roller skates. Their eyes reflected the same blue-green color, but while Ron's appeared excitedly patient, Wesley's appeared just as excitedly impatient. Both were fair-skinned, but Wesley's weathered skin, marked by his thick, dark-shadowed beard, reflected his youthful years spent on the wind-swept southern Oregon coast. His nondescript nose contrasted with Ron's decidedly Eastern European sculptured look, but his mouth was noticeably wider and thicker-lipped as a result of many years given to playing the trumpet in his high school and college pep bands. Coming from a loosely connected Protestant background, Wesley saw both teaching and believing more in terms of convenience than conviction. He was a classic expression of the common mercenary heart who proved to be the most reliable, interesting, and entertaining expression of such a heart that Ron had ever come across.

As a result of his friendship with Wesley, Ron was introduced to Paul Sorenson, another Oregon State graduate and a Lebanon native who taught science at the junior high. In addition, he met Steve and Sue Carlson, six years Ron's senior, who were parents to three young boys and who knew Wesley through the junior high where Steve worked as a math teacher and counselor. Standing five feet eight inches and weighing 180 pounds—and struggling to stay there—Paul was no Ron Petrich any more than he was a Rob Wesley. His legs were thick but not fat, and his heavyset stature belied an athleticism that more than rivaled Ron's and dwarfed Wesley's. His hair, darker brown than either Ron's or Wesley's, was perceptively receding at the temples in reflection of his thoughtful, Scandinavian nature. His dark and penetrating eyes reflected Ron's patience more so than Wesley's impatience. Ironically, given his Scandinavian heritage, he was less fair-skinned than either Ron or Wesley, and his suntanned face befit his upbringing and work on a Lebanon farm. His beard darkened around his full chin and above his thin, upper lip, leaving him with a prominent five o' clock shadow while his thick, but handsomely sculptured, Scandinavian nose and narrow mouth completed the picture of the most unlikely female charmer Ron had ever seen. Although Paul had grown somewhat disenchanted with teaching and believing, for him they remained more a matter of conviction than of convenience. If he lived the way of the mercenary heart, at least he could claim default. He was a dreamer for whom magic had proven to be only scientific. As a friend he was as reliable as Wesley, and if Wesley was the most entertaining mercenary heart Ron had ever seen, Paul Sorenson proved to be the most challenging.

As the first established married couple he had met who fell roughly within the boundaries of his generation, Steve and Sue Carlson represented the fulfillment of Ron's romantic dream. His attraction to Sue was immediate and had she been younger and accessible, he would have welcomed the agreement his heart and eyes had forged. Sue didn't project the sensual voluptuousness of a Marilyn Monroe nor the sensual innocence of a Natalie Wood. Instead, she projected a more sensible balance between the two, and her smile could illuminate any room and touch any man's heart. Her blue eyes were alive with vitality and romance complementing her naturally blonde hair, cut short to match the contour of her exquisite face. Her inviting mouth and elegantly straight nose completed the picture of the most attractive woman Ron had ever seen. Their attraction was mutual, but Ron knew that her heart rested and belonged with Steve whom Ron considered to be the luckiest man alive.

Steve didn't exactly share his wife's interest in literature, which under different circumstances could have made him Ron's rival. He didn't trust anything made up, and he didn't trust religion under any circumstances. But he was amongst the most honest men Ron had ever met. He wasn't particularly athletic, but he was solidly built, bordering on the rugged. His thick, wavy hair grew darker than Sue's but still lighter than either Ron's or Wesley's. His alert, but cautious, sky-blue eyes sometimes seemed to hide under thick, brown eyebrows; and his skin and tough beard together contributed to the handsomely rugged features that reflected his basically outdoor life as a fisherman in western Oregon's streams and rivers. His noble nose may not have reflected any specific ethnic heritage, but it belonged with his rock-solid jaw and creased face that completed the picture of a masculine face that appeared far more experienced than its 28 years. He believed in anything solid that could be made. He was a natural man, committed to his job, who found religion—if there were such a phenomenon—in the likes of the swift current of the Santiam River. As a skilled fisherman and a solidly honest man, Steve commanded Ron's respect. He considered it an honor to experience the magic that can accompany drinking beer with such a man.

Save for Mrs Williams' decision, toward the end of the school year, to sell the Gables and return to Montana—this time to Butte which she thought would prove to be more interesting and more morally expansive than her native Billings—Ron's first semester at Lebanon Union High school proved to be uneventful. He had proven himself to be a committed teacher devoted to the unbounded adventure of learning and had established an alliance with Judith Griswold and her mysterious husband to accompany his friendships with Wesley, Paul Sorenson, and the Carlsons. But for all practical purposes he still belonged to Tacoma and Old Town which he still considered home. After one final summer of work at the Asarco copper smelter, his life in Lebanon and his identity with it wouldn't begin in earnest until the fall of 1967. Then he, Wesley, and Paul would join forces and move together into a three-bedroom house in the vicinity of the Carlsons and their self-built home, set in the heart of Lebanon's pasture and farm land several miles up River Road near the Lebanon Lumber Company and close by the banks of the Santiam River. From that house Ron would completely settle in Lebanon, and from that same house, which the three of them lovingly referred to as The River Road Athletic Club, he would make his decision "forever betwixt two things" in the manner of his still to be discovered fictional counterparts from Adam and Eve to Christ to Huckleberry Finn.

He knew Lebanon wouldn't be the same without Mrs Williams, and he didn't know what he would have done without her in the beginning. She made him feel comfortable and at home without stooping to condescension and accommodation. He found comfort in the thought that he didn't have to forget her simply because she had moved to Butte, Montana. He always could write to her, and he would have little trouble driving the 700 miles that separated the Mining City, as his uncle referred to it, from Lebanon. She had made his adjustment to his new surroundings easier than it would have been otherwise, but he understood her desire to leave the Gables and the lumber and farming community it served. Maybe the time would come when he would have to leave as well, but Ron didn't see that time in the near future as he said goodbye to Mrs Williams in Lebanon for the last time and headed north toward Tacoma and Old Town and one last summer spent working at the Asarco copper smelter.

## XIII

The summer of 1967 passed quickly, but then Ron had been looking south anyway. He wasn't an Oregonian by any stretch of the imagination, but he had established himself as a teacher in Lebanon and had won considerable respect among both the students and his fellow teachers. He had entered a new stage of his life in the social world, and in teaching he found a profession for which he was appropriately suited—almost as if he were born to be a teacher. Being a loyal Petrich from Old Town, he was inspired by the responsibility, and he understood that how he taught took precedence over being a teacher. He would earn rewards only by embracing the responsibility that accompanied his social role, with no particular role being superior to any other. Neither pride nor envy found a home in the Petrich family mythology.

Ron's final summer working at the Asarco smelter wasn't without conflict. He always respected the plant and its workers and didn't feel as though he were alone in his understanding. But by the summer of 1967 that general foundation of respect had crumbled, leaving the smelter itself and his dad's generation of workers separated from the younger generation that included Ron and anyone up to 30 years of age. Ron felt particularly uncomfortable because he didn't feel as though he belonged to either group. He found the division within the smelter to be similar to that which he saw within the Church and even within Lebanon Union High School—reflected in the gulf that separated the coaches' room from the faculty room. In any case he wasn't sure where he belonged, although he felt more closely aligned with the anachronistic smelter veteran than he did with its contemporary rookie.

Attending church all summer at St Patrick's presented him with a continuing conflict simply because he couldn't embrace the institution that had emerged out of the Second Vatican Council which concluded in 1965. The once pervasive magic had disappeared, leaving the consecration and transubstantiation meaningless exercises in habit and tradition. Also, the majesty Ron always associated with Christ and his sacrifice was missing and the post-Vatican II collective belief, built around the pulpit reference to social justice and community service, seemed empty and hollow. The altar had been turned to face the congregation, and, finally, everyone could see for themselves that the bread and wine of the Mass remained bread and wine with the consecration having no transubstantial affect at all. Ron sensed that religion had been diluted in the name of reform, as if the Church had deserted its magic of its own accord without realizing that it never had been scientific in the first place. For the first time since the conclusion of Vatican II and the implementation of its liturgical reforms, Ron found that he couldn't join in the congregation's participatory responses to the priest. A change he initially had welcomed in the name of greater participation in the Holy Sacrifice of the Mass had lost its charm. He no longer could recite the Creed, and he found himself longing for the quiet magic of the past when participation was greater than anyone ever seemed to have recognized.

The troublesome, private conflict that distinguished the summer of 1967 actually began in earnest in Lebanon the previous spring when, for the first time he could remember, Ron knowingly and willingly—with no excusable reason—decided to miss Sunday Mass. Rob Wesley had discovered him by then and they had become trusted companions, if not fast friends, but he couldn't blame Wesley, although Catholicism to him was of little consequence with any Sunday obligation being even less so. Wesley was reliable and trustworthy and he was an exciting companion, but unlike Ron, he wasn't rooted in the virtue of obedience. Thus he never could understand why Ron attended St Edward's every Sunday morning regardless of the weather. Spring Sundays in the Willamette Valley oftentimes dawned sunny and beckoning. On such Sundays anyone could feel the lure of the picturesque and rugged Oregon coast waiting only 50 miles to the west. Ron wasn't immune to that siren call, but the command of the Church proved to be every bit as strong—until one day when he decided to follow Wesley to the coast at the expense of Sunday Mass.

Mrs Williams accurately spoke of changing times and of how Ron would be teaching in an interesting era. Away from Seattle University, Tacoma, Old Town, and St Patrick's, Ron felt the change more strongly than before. But although he knew his decision to miss Mass and follow Wesley to the coast that spring Sunday constituted mortal sin as defined by the pre-Vatican II Church and collective belief, he couldn't see his decision as an act of disobedience. He couldn't help thinking that the Church relinquished its right to demand obedience if it failed to present something worthy of obedience in the first place. The convening of the Vatican Council in 1962 and the implementation of its reforms following its conclusion in 1965 forced Ron to confront the nature of his commitment to, as well as identity with, the collective belief of the Catholic Church and its drama of sin, redemption, and salvation.

He concluded that he probably wasn't much different than any other serious believer in that in the beginning fear inspired his belief more than anything else. And that fear resulted from the threat of Hell whose subterranean darkness more than matched the promise of Heaven and its celestial light. With or without any Vatican II his fear of the Hell of that collective belief, along with thoughts of its promise of Heaven, had abated. Heaven needed its dark counterpart to ensure its beatific existence, and if there was nothing to Heaven and Hell, there was nothing to religion. And if there was nothing to religion, life would be robbed of some, if not all, of its magic and adventure. So, Ron's belief, initially fear inspired, had given way to authentic love for the majesty and beauty he associated with the ritual of the altar and not with the doctrine of the pulpit. His belief had gone beyond anything inspired by fear. Such a belief lasted only as long as did the fear itself.

Ron found little, if any, evidence to prove the existence of Hell as defined by his pre-Vatican II collective faith. And the post-Vatican II vision conveniently skirted that central issue and shifted its emphasis to a spineless ecumenism that diluted Christ as God and, instead, preached a doctrine of social justice and social action conducted in the name of love. Such preaching, that decried the fear invoking retreat sermons describing the pain of Hell that awaited any disobedient soul cut off from the salvatory, sanctifying grace of the Church, fell on deaf ears for Ron. That pulpit message of love ran contrary to the message the altar magic had awakened in his heart, and he found that he couldn't live in obedience to the collective, pulpit faith offered by the post-Vatican II Church. In the absence of any majesty and magic, that Church proved itself unworthy of his obedience. But he didn't disobey in order to obey nothing, and he knew he couldn't return to the unreformed, collective belief of his pre-Vatican II past.

Rob Wesley didn't tempt him into sin in the spring of 1967. In Ron's eyes the Church had sinned when it proved itself to be disobedient to the all-inclusive majesty of love celebrated, unknowingly, on its altar and subsequently awakened in his noble heart. In effect, and independent of Wesley, Ron had disobeyed the collective belief of the Church to obey the individual belief of his noble heart awakened by the magic of the altar. And that magic had little to do with the pulpit message of indiscriminate social action masquerading as the fulfillment of the promise of love. On that fateful spring Sunday in 1967 an obedient Ron Petrich took his first tentative steps away from the safety and protection of a collective belief. At the same time an obedient Ron Petrich took his first conscious steps along the path illuminated by his mythological parents and fictional counterparts—Adam and Eve.

His first conscious steps had to be tentative because he faced the nagging thought that maybe the Church was right. Maybe its pulpit preaching, directed toward the celebration of a life dedicated to social activism, did represent the fulfillment of the promise of love. Ron never had thought about love in those terms before, but then no authority carrying the majesty of the Catholic Church had preached that understanding, either. He thought about his catechism that reminded him of his duty to know, love, and serve God in this world and to be with Him forever in the next. He took that admonition seriously and couldn't help thinking that in willfully deciding to miss Mass he had decided not to know, love, and serve God, with such a command granting any individual life a noble purpose. But then what if the Church is derelict in its duty? he thought. Maybe the Church wasn't knowing, loving, and serving God. If God is love, he continued, the love that is God would have to be all-inclusive. It couldn't be limited only to those individuals able to practice indiscriminate social action conducted in the name of love and thus in the name of God. Those individuals who benefited from such action couldn't practice the love themselves and, therefore, had to be excluded. And what did God mean anyway if it didn't describe inclusive love as a way of life knowing no social or economic distinction?

Ron had taken his first conscious steps along the path of individual belief, inspired by experience with the monstrous nature of life. He had disobeyed to obey, but the break with the collective belief and authority of his pre-Vatican II youth wasn't easy. He attended Mass at St Patrick's regularly during the summer of 1967 with the hope of discovering something that had, as yet, eluded him. Instead, he came up empty. He wouldn't ask about the transubstantiation these days, regardless of its interpretation, because he clearly recognized that it played an insignificant role in the post-Vatican II, pulpit-centered church. His mother and father continued to attend church, but he knew something was missing for them as well. They didn't discuss their feelings with him, but he knew they felt abandoned by the Church at the very time they needed it the most. The changing times placed inordinate emphasis on life as being primarily an economic venture. As a result, the likes of Ron's mom and dad, for whom life had unconsciously transcended economic promise, were left out in the cold and dark to discover the warmth and the light on their own. The obedient path of individual belief wasn't the well-traveled path, but someone honestly alienated from the collective authority, that once directed his individual life, had little choice. No responsible individual, male or female, interested in the noble majesty of love could choose a path of meaningless expedience punctuated by varying degrees of social and economic success supported by sporadic acts of indiscriminate social action accomplished in the name of justice and love.

In its split between the coaches' room and the faculty room Lebanon Union High School reflected the changing times Ron was experiencing, and those Mrs Williams mentioned in reference to his teaching career. He was welcomed into the coaches' room before he was welcomed into the faculty room, and Judson Heath had taken him under his authoritative wing. In Ron's mind Judson resembled a priest still ennobled by the majesty of his institution, and next to the institution of Church and its Pantheon of Heroes stood the institution of sport and its corresponding pantheon. Essentially, Ron's experience could be defined as being a matter of morality. By the summer of 1967 students and adults alike, now free from the constraints of fear, were challenging cherished moral standards. Order was giving way to chaos, and Ron Petrich, now a professional teacher aware of and inspired by the responsibility that accompanied his crown, knew he had to determine—once and for all—where he stood. The academic year of 1967-68, the year of The River Road Athletic Club, was destined to be the most adventurous year of his life.

In the spring of 1967 he bought his own car, a new Chevy Camaro, over his mother's objections. She preferred that he keep the Malibu she and his dad had provided him, but Ron was determined. Buying his own car, more reflective of his youth and station in life, represented a symbolic act of breaking away, although he never entertained thoughts of escaping his parents, his home, or his past. A person only seeks escape from that which is repressive and oppressive, and Ron knew he had been given nothing from which he could justify any escape. But he wanted to leave and fully intended to build his life on the solid foundation his parents, maybe more unconsciously than consciously, had given him. Understandably, his mother wanted to hold on, but his dad knew that if his son were ever to become the man he aspired to be, he would have to break away from his mother. He also knew that achieving the necessary break only could strengthen, not weaken, the love between the two of them. He knew, as did his wife—even though she wished otherwise—that they had to set Ron free. And he felt free— although not totally unattached from the womb of Holy Mother Church—as he loaded his belongings, which still consisted of nothing but clothing, bedding, and his clock radio, into his Bolero Red Camaro, sporting black, custom interior, said goodbye to his mother and father, and headed for Lebanon once again. But he knew that no matter where the adventure of his life may take him, whether to Lebanon, Oregon, or to New York City, he always would take Tacoma and its magic richness with him.

It was August 20, and Ron, Wesley, and Paul Sorenson were scheduled to gather at the Carlson's house that afternoon in preparation for their move into The River Road Athletic club that Wesley and Paul already had procured. Because Paul was a Lebanon native and because the three of them were teachers in the community, for 120 dollars a month the real estate agency was willing to rent them a brand-new house the agency rather would have sold. But the market was slow, and because of Paul's hometown connections they could rent The River Road Athletic Club. Wesley provided the stereo system, and he and Paul informed Ron that he had to bring more than his clock radio to the

Club. They assigned him the color television set, and he had to laugh when he thought of the arrangements. He could picture Wesley explaining his responsibility to him with the bravado and excitement only he could muster. Wesley boiled over with endless enthusiasm for excitement whether or not it signified anything, but he made it abundantly clear that he wasn't in teaching for the duration. Paul, on the other hand, conducted himself more quietly. He was more reticent and lived more in conflict with himself with regard to teaching. Ron, in further contrast, was as committed to teaching as anyone his age could be, and he never had met anyone quite like either Wesley or Paul Sorenson. But the three of them belonged together, at least for the 1967-68 school year, and Ron drove with purpose to Lebanon and the scheduled rendezvous with his River Road Athletic Club roommates.

He arrived in Lebanon around two o'clock in the afternoon and drove through the now familiar downtown toward the Lebanon Lumber Company and the turnoff to River Road that would lead to the Carlson's house that Steve and Wesley, given his carpentry background, had finished building during the summer. Ron preferred to avoid downtown because he no longer was a stranger in Lebanon, and he and his red Camaro were far from anonymous. He tried to drive through downtown as quickly as possible, hoping no one would notice.

He had proven to be a popular teacher amongst the class of 1967, and he knew that a good number of the members of the class of 1968 wanted to be in one of his coming senior English classes. But he wasn't fooled by the deception. He knew he was far from being an established teacher in terms of understanding literature, and he realized that his popularity, to some extent, resulted from his sense of humor and his youthful, attractive appearance. He'd rather be popular than not, but he knew his youthful charm would only take him so far before it naturally would fade. But his commitment to understanding and to communicating his discoveries would remain constant. He felt confident that his popularity among his past and prospective students had as much to do with their appreciative awareness of his honest commitment to the responsibility of teaching.

Luckily, he drove through town unrecognized, and in a matter of minutes he had driven past the familiar landmarks of Jerry's Market and Bing's Kitchen and finally to the Gables Motel, now under new management. But the Gables remained frozen in time for him as always belonging to Mrs Williams, who now operated the Rose Motel in Butte, Montana. The Rose didn't mean anything to him, although he had a vague idea of its location on Butte's South Montana Street near the base of what Butte residents called The Hill that Ron remembered as the home of the copper mines. He didn't stop in the Gables' parking lot this time, but he smiled in wonder as he thought of how something seemingly as insignificant as a motel can assume such importance in an individual life. He drove past the Gables and continued southward until he found the intersection of River Road and the Santiam Highway where he turned left at the Lebanon Lumber Company and headed for the Carlson's.

Nobody greeted him when he pulled into the driveway in front of Steve and Sue's just completed country home, but he noticed Wesley's blue Volkswagen and Paul's tan Plymouth Fury parked in front of the house. As a city boy used to neighborhoods and sidewalks, Ron had no desire to live in the country, away from those amenities, but the Carlson's country home, nestled amidst the tall firs and cleared pasture land of the Willamette Valley, represented the fulfillment of their dreams. In addition to being a skilled fisherman and outdoorsman, Steve Carlson was a master builder. He had reason to be quietly proud of his creations, and now that he could display it as a finished product, his house proved to be no exception. With Wesley's help, Steve had transformed a country hovel into a country home.

It stood in opposition to the two-storied, basemented frame houses that identified Ron's Old Town Tacoma neighborhood. But, with its weathered cedar siding and natural, shake roof, it fit in perfectly with the natural tall firs that shaded western Oregon's Willamette Valley. With its front entrance facing the driveway and River Road, the house reflected a sense of comfort, warmth, and unpretentious country elegance that almost persuaded Ron to abandon his own dream of neighborhoods and sidewalks. This country dream house suited the outdoor, naturally-ordered lifestyle that attracted both Steve and Sue. To the left of the front door Ron could recognize the living room with its identifying fireplace, and to the right he could see the expansive, sparsely furnished family, or "recreation," room. Studying the house that extended back into the protection of the Oregon firs, he remembered, from his image of the unfinished product, that the dining room sat behind the living room and in front of the kitchen. And he remembered Steve and Sue's bedroom, with proposed master bath, as being across the hallway to the right of the kitchen and behind the newly added family room. And he also remembered that the boys' bedrooms were supposed to be built behind the family room and off to the right of the master bedroom where a second bathroom fit in the hallway leading from there to the boys' rooms. Ron looked around the front of the house as he stepped out of his Camaro and decided that everyone had to be sitting out back, safely removed from any traffic sounds of River Road. He closed his car door and, not bothering to ring the front doorbell, walked toward the left, or east, corner of the house and the fence that connected it with the adjacent, cleared pasture land. He paused for a moment and then continued through the gate that opened to the back of the house and the still natural forest of tall firs.

He walked along the side of the house, parallel to the cleared pasture land, until he reached the back corner of the kitchen and, still undetected, found himself standing in the back yard. And there they were, Wesley and Paul and Steve and Sue wearing their summer shorts, comfortably seated on the newly constructed back deck that extended toward the back yard from the sliding glass doors that opened into and out of Steve and Sue's bedroom. Ron had to smile. In an uncertain world, he had discovered some certainty after all. He knew that if Wesley was around, beer had to accompany him. And sure enough in the August warmth there sat the four of them holding their wide-mouthed paper cups and drinking beer drawn from the pony keg that rested in its bucket of ice set in the center of their half-circle. Still smiling, Ron walked toward the deck to join his compatriots, undoubtedly continuing a celebration they had begun the night before.

# XIV

"Well," Wesley exclaimed, setting down his beer, springing to his feet, and holding his arms spread wide as he spotted Ron walking toward the deck, "here he is. The Legend in his own time has returned. Have a cool one, Petrich. It's running clear."

"Does it ever run any other way?" Ron asked, laughing, as Wesley filled his cup from the tap, threw his head back to get his sun-bleached hair out of his eyes, and ceremoniously presented Ron with his first beer of the new season.

"Here," Wesley said. "Have a drink and wash down some of that road dust. Here's to Greater Northwest Living," he added, raising his cup in a toast.

"Greater Northwest Living," Ron said as he raised his cup and took a long, soothing drink. "Best beer I ever had," he added, exhaling, as Sue and Paul and Steve now rose to greet him.

"Nice to see you, Ron," Sue said as she greeted him with a tentative hug. "We missed you around here this summer."

"I missed all of you, too, although I wouldn't have been much help on the house," Ron said, examining what Steve and Wesley had accomplished.

"You could have kept the beer flowing at least," Steve said, extending his right hand. "Welcome back."

"Thanks," Ron said, firmly grasping Steve's hand. "It's nice to be back, although I hated to leave the City of Destiny," he added, relinquishing his grip on Steve's hand.

"Welcome back to the Valley, Leg," Paul said in reference to Wesley's greeting Ron as being a Legend in his own time. The legendary status was a standing joke amongst the five of them, and Ron had earned it in reference to the fact that love, and never a girl, had a habit of making a fool out of him. In matters relating to the foolishness of love, Ron truly was a legend.

"I had to come back to give you guys something to laugh about," Ron said, shaking hands with Paul. "But I've been looking forward to coming back. It should be a good year."

"Well, hell, what do you expect?" Wesley asked, still standing with his arms stretched out again. "We're ready for Sunset Magazine. Now, why don't we sit down and work on the keg before it gets warm?"

"Sounds like a good plan to me," Steve said, sitting down as Ron found his chair at the end of the half-circle, nearest the back door that led to the hallway separating the rear half bath from the kitchen.

"Well, Ron," Sue said after all five of them had taken their places around the keg, "how was your summer?"

"Not bad," he answered, taking a drink of his beer. "I worked at the smelter as I said I was going to, made some money to get me back here, and ran around with some of my old high school buddies who still live in Tacoma. All in all, I had a good summer, but I wasn't necessarily sad to see it end. I'm anxious to get back to teaching. I'm ready."

"Did you keep up our established pace in your City of Destiny?" Wesley asked, hoisting his cup of beer.

"I did my best," Ron answered, laughing, "and I thought of you undoubtedly running ahead of me and the rest of the pack."

"You're right there, Leg," Paul said. "No moss grows on Wesley, no female goes unchased, and no keg goes untapped."

"Maybe, but look at the house," Wesley said. "It's finished, isn't it?"

"Yes," Sue answered, "but there were times when I had my doubts. I think the two of you drank as much beer as you pounded nails."

"But Sue," Wesley implored, "a man has to have a little fun."

"That's for sure," she replied, "and you and Steve managed to experience your share."

"Maybe, but you never were too far behind, you know," Steve said, smiling. "Besides, Wesley's right. We got it done and it makes the beer taste even better as far as I'm concerned. As a matter of fact, I think it's time for a refill. Anyone else?" he asked, standing up and moving toward the keg.

"It's still running clear," Wesley said as he followed Steve to the keg.

"I'm ready," Ron said, following suit.

"Me, too," Paul said, following Ron.

"So am I," Sue said, following Paul, and with full cups of beer the five of them settled back in their chairs to enjoy the August sunshine filtering through the boughs of the tall Oregon firs.

"The house looks pretty good. I like the deck," Ron said, looking around at its expanse that covered almost the entire back of the house.

"It's nice to have it finished," Sue said, "but I think it'll take me a while to get used to the space. I'm not used to all this room, and you know me. I've never been one to get too excited about cleaning house"

"We'll manage somehow," Steve said. "Besides, the house always was clean enough before. Nothing will change. Anyway, as long as the keg's running clear, I'm not going to worry about it. Isn't that right, Wesley?"

"Spoken like a true Northwest believer," he answered, hoisting his cup of beer. "You've got the right attitude. No one ever will accuse you and Sue of not living in your house. Vacuuming just wears out the carpet anyway."

"I'm not that bad," Sue said. "It's just that cleaning the house never has been the highlight of my life. But at least I admit it. At least I'm honest."

"I can't deny that," Paul said, laughing. "But whenever you get the chance, you can come and clean our house anytime. I'm sure it'll need it. I think we'll have to hire someone just to keep Wesley in check so that we'll get the deposit back one of these days."

"Maybe we should get Steve to build a separate cabin just for him," Ron said.

"Now wait a minute," Wesley said. "Let's go easy on the badmouthing. Who bought the stereo?"

"Who got the house?" Paul asked.

"I'm glad I live with Sue and the boys and not with you three," Steve said. "I don't know if any of you will survive life in The River Road Athletic Club."

"We'll survive," Wesley said, "as long as the Legend here springs for a color television set. That's the least he can do after watching my old black and white spinner all last spring. I thought my power bill was going to triple. Have you bought the set yet, Petrich?"

"Give me some time," Ron answered as he took a drink from his cup. "I just got to town. I have to shop around."

"Don't worry," Wesley said. "We have that all taken care of. Haven't we, Paul?"

"Yep," Paul answered, leaning back in his chair and taking a drink of beer. "We have the new Zenith all picked out. It has a great picture, and it's just what we need."

"You guys think of everything. Where would I be without you?"

"Still in your executive suite above Leroy V H Brands. That's where you'd be," Wesley answered. "And still going to church every Sunday."

"You're partly right," Ron said. "But even without you, I don't think I'd be going to church every Sunday. Still, even though you Protestants like to laugh, it dies hard."

"C'mon," Wesley said, "that Latin mumbo-jumbo wasn't that special."

"You only say that because you've bought the Protestant propaganda. But we didn't call it the magic show for nothing."

"You said didn't," Sue broke in. "I was always interested in that Latin mumbo-jumbo, coming from my Episcopalian background. But there's no more magic?"

"No," Ron answered. "Vatican II took care of that. There's much more sound and fury, I think, but there's no more magic."

"What's all this religious talk?" Steve asked. "I'd rather go fishing anyway. At least fishing's something real. I can cast and then watch the fish strike the fly. There's no magic involved. You learn the proper arm movement and lay the fly on the water. That's all. What the hell is Vatican II in the first place? And who cares about the Pope?"

"Vatican II was the Church Council called in 1962 to bring the Church into the 20th century," Ron answered. "It concluded in 1965, and since then nothing has been the same. For some reason magic accompanied that Latin mumbo-jumbo, but it's gone now. Maybe you're the luckiest one of all, Steve. If you've never experienced the magic, you can't miss it when it's gone. And there's probably a lot of religion in how you fish."

"Here we go again," Wesley said. "No wonder you're an English teacher. I used to say that anyone can teach English, and I still believe it. But no one teaches English the way you do."

"What do you think of this religion business, Paul?" Steve asked.

"I'm a science teacher, and I have to believe in science because it make sense. There's no mumbo-jumbo or magic to it. Science is rational and sensible."

"Maybe we're supposed to believe in both," Sue offered cautiously.

"Both what?" Steve asked.

"Both science and religion."

"What does all this have to do with Greater Northwest Living?" Wesley asked incredulously. "It's running clear and here we sit talking about science and religion. How in the hell do you believe in both?"

"Well," Ron answered, "I'll be the first to respond to the rallying cry of 'running clear,' but I think we have to discover a way to believe in both science and religion. And I think Steve just might be more religious than he realizes. Maybe he finds religion in fishing. It's possible because I can't guarantee anyone will find it in church. Going to church and being religious can be two different things. It's easy to attend church for reasons having nothing to do with religion."

"What do you mean?" Paul asked.

"Well," Ron answered, taking a sip of his beer, "going to church for the social experience has nothing to do with commitment to religion."

"And you think people go to church for that experience?" Wesley asked.

"I think it has a lot to do with it. And the new Catholic Church certainly has placed renewed emphasis on the social experience, now that it's junked the Latin mumbo-jumbo."

"And that's why you'd rather not go?" Sue asked.

"I think so," Ron answered.

"So, you want the Latin mumbo-jumbo back?" Steve asked.

"I think the situation's more complex than that. I'm just saying the experience used to be more than social when the mumbo-jumbo served as the language of the Mass."

"Maybe you should discover fishing," Steve said with a sly smile.

"Maybe I should," Ron said, returning his smile. "But right now I'd just like to sit back, relax, have another cup of beer, and then go move into The River Road Athletic Club. Today the Club, tomorrow the Zenith."

"Now that's Greater Northwest Living," Wesley exclaimed, tossing his head back to get the hair out of his eyes. "I'll drink to that."

"So will I," the rest of them echoed in unison as they hoisted their cups in tribute, perhaps unknowingly, to their communion.

"Running clear," indeed, became the rallying cry at The River Road Athletic Club, and very rarely did the Carlsons and Wesley and Paul and Ron fail to answer its call. Ron knew the week had ended when, on Friday afternoon, Wesley turned on the stereo, and the likes of 'The Mighty Quinn' blared out of the speakers. It was a far cry from Ricky Nelson's 'Hello, Mary Lou,' which remained Ron's anthem of Love, but nonetheless a welcomed sound that marked the end of a week's teaching. He always felt he'd earned the weekend because he worked as a tireless teacher who never allowed himself to be one of Wesley's "anyones" in reference to teaching English. And weekends at The River Road Athletic Club proved to be just as far removed from those associated with the executive suite resting atop the home of Leroy V H Brands.

Before Wesley discovered Ron, he even devoted, in some manner, most of his weekend time to teaching. He had countless papers to correct, and he treated every student composition as if it were a legitimate work of art, which meant that many times his comments proved to be as extensive as the students' papers themselves. In addition, he had to prepare for his classes, which meant that he had to memorize each day's presentation to help create the impression that he understood his subject matter and could teach without the aid of notes. He had discovered that students listened more attentively when he taught seemingly from his own understanding without referring to notes or books. His students wanted a teacher in charge of his subject matter. Ron never went to class unprepared, even if he had to stay up until two or three in the morning to commit that day's class to memory.

He knew he was creating the illusion of understanding and authoritative mastery, but the more he taught, the more he studied, and the more he learned, the more he felt himself developing an understanding of literature that would become second nature to him. The more he studied and the more he concentrated in his attempt to find a way to explain the significance of literature, the more he realized it revolved around the compatible concepts of hero and love—which just happened to be the very ideas that dominated his experiential life. Maybe he didn't understand either concept in great depth as yet, but he knew that without hero and without love, life degenerated to the level of mere economic venture full of "sound and fury" but "signifying nothing."

Ron rarely was separated from teaching, but by the time Wesley discovered him, about two months into the spring semester of 1967, he was more settled in than he was when he first arrived in Lebanon to begin the semester. He required less time to prepare for class because he had begun to rely less on memory and more on his own emerging understanding with his teaching being as much a revelation to him as it was to his students. He found that he could understand literature after all, even if he still didn't feel comfortable with any strictly academic discussion of it. And he was beginning to understand that reducing literature to the level of mere academic exercise meant removing it from the realm of everyday experience where it properly belonged. He already had experienced the magic of the Mass, and now, as he was teaching, he was experiencing that same affect with literature. His commitment to duty compelled him to attempt to explain literature in such a way that allowed hero and love the chance to work their magic. Wesley's "anyone," unfortunately, didn't understand magic.

With his growing confidence Ron felt more comfortable in his role and in living up to its responsibility. Thus he welcomed Wesley's discovery of him and didn't balk when he took him out of Lebanon and introduced him to Corvallis and Oregon State University. And, finally, when the weather cooperated and when he thought he had found a suitable sorority sister for him, Wesley introduced him to the Oregon coast.

Ron's legendary foolishness in obedience to love didn't materialize with Marcia Peters from the timber city and southern coastal town of Coos Bay. Several times during that first semester in Lebanon he and Marcia found themselves together either at the coast or at the Beaver Hut, the tavern that catered to Oregon State's population and chose the name of its adopted mascot. But those times never became anything more than pleasurable moments devoid of the enchantment that lives when the eyes and the heart agree. So far, despite Wesley's intervention and despite Ron's compatible moments with Marcia, love proved elusive in Lebanon.

Paul was primarily responsible for procuring the house while Wesley provided the stereo that blasted out the sounds of 'The Mighty Quinn' so that the Carlsons could hear them a half mile and three pastures away. And Ron lived up to his responsibility, agreeing to buy the 21 inch Zenith that Wesley and Paul had picked out. They already had moved into the house, and Ron wasted little time following suit once the keg on the Carlson's deck was drained of the remnants of the previous night's festivities. It was an appropriate beginning to a year when the cry of "running clear" echoed far beyond the boundaries of The River Road Athletic Club.

The Club itself was a brand new, soft brown and yellow, three bedroom, ranch-style house that came complete with a spacious living room covered, wall-to-wall, with light green pile carpeting. It sported a fully equipped kitchen with a dishwasher and garbage disposal as well as a family room distinguished by its stone-hearth fireplace and sliding glass doors that opened up onto a green-grassed back yard and a lazy irrigation canal that fed the surrounding pasture land. A prospective buyer would have to think that no realtor in his right mind would rent such a house to three red-blooded bachelors not afraid to respond to the clarion call of 'The Mighty Quinn.' Because Paul assumed primary responsibility for renting the house in the first place, he rewarded himself by laying claim to the master bedroom that came complete with its master bath and wall-to-wall carpeting which matched that of the living room. Because Wesley had moved in before Ron and because he had provided the stereo sounds, he claimed the double bedroom just across from the master bedroom. And because Ron had arrived last and had provided only the color television, he was left with what amounted to a spare bedroom, with space for only a single bed, just across the hall from the recreation room. Each bedroom came equipped with an accommodating walk-in closet, although, once again, Ron's proved to be the least accommodating. And where Paul claimed sole use of the master bath, Ron and Wesley were left to share the remaining bath off to the left of the hallway that led to the two rear bedrooms. Because the house had no specific dining area, its one major flaw, the three of them had to place their dining table and chairs along the wall just outside the kitchen entry way and in front of the recreation room opposite the elevated, stone-hearth fireplace.

Other than its one flaw, that Wesley said accounted for its failure to sell, the house was perfectly suited for any purposes the three of them had in mind. Paul's mom and dad donated a couch and a couple of living room chairs from their home in Lebanon, and Wesley managed to scare up a bed for Ron so that the Athletic Club looked completely furnished with few open spaces. The sliding glass doors didn't open out onto an expansive, wood deck as did those at the Carlson's dream house, but they did open onto a smooth concrete patio. The beer kegs, that never ceased to run clear, never had to rest on the uneven grass of the back yard. Neither Ron's previous executive suite nor Wesley's duplex could match The River Road Athletic Club that had nothing to do with expectations of abstinence and that, sometimes, stretched the boundaries of temperance. Wesley, Paul, and Ron were distinct individuals, each with his own past, present, and future. But for that one year they belonged together, and for that year the promise of "running clear" provided more than one individual with a welcomed respite from the teaching wars.

Thursday nights at the Athletic Club were given over to men's poker nights, and never did a woman even attempt to be invited for any reason. Sue Carlson, for one, said she wouldn't be caught dead at The River Road Athletic Club on poker night, beer or no beer, because she wouldn't be caught dead in a men's locker room, either. She said she preferred men and not little boys masquerading as such. Judith Griswold, from the high school English faculty, felt the same. For her, being present at a Thursday poker night would be equivalent to frequenting the coaches' room at the high school. And nothing repulsed her more than the manly behavior associated with that bastion of masculine zeal. So, the segregated poker nights continued without any protest from the excluded females, and the men who attended did so faithfully as a way to measure time and the passing of the weeks. Thursday nights took on the quality of ritual more associated with the celebration of time rather than with the fearful consumption of it.

Two junior high schools, as well as the high school, were included in the Lebanon Union District, and because Wesley taught band along with math and had to split his time between the two junior highs, he had connections with the faculty and administrations of both. Thus the Thursday poker nights included men from all three schools. The River Road Athletic Club served as a unifying force where, for at least one night a week, teachers and administrators could forget the hierarchical distinctions that identified their social roles and confront one another as individuals and equals. Ron found it all very interesting and was especially fascinated by the fact that when Thursday ended and the school day began once again on Friday, the social distinctions slipped back into place, upsetting the equality that prevailed the night before. He always invited Mr Polk to the Athletic Club for poker, but he always respectfully and honorably declined. Ron was disappointed at first, but the more he thought about it, the more he realized he was glad Mr Polk declined his invitations. Although Mr Polk always was the principal and he always was the teacher, Ron knew he considered them equal as individuals. As an authentic learned man, Mr Polk was more inspired by responsibility than attracted by rewards. And if Ron couldn't be Mr Polk, he certainly could be a Mr Polk and another incarnation of hero.

Friday nights at The River Road Athletic Club differed, completely, from Thursday poker nights. If those poker nights were destined to be exclusively male, Friday nights were just as destined to be inclusively male and female. On Friday nights the beer ran clear and plentiful, and the attendant crowd reflected every individual distinction possible, even if the various school administrators, who looked forward to Thursday nights, never showed any particular interest in attending. But the teachers, accompanied by their wives and husbands, showed up in droves because the Athletic Club was "safe" from any moralizing eyes. After laboring for a week in the teaching trenches, something had to give. Wesley always made it home first on Friday afternoons, and when Ron drove into the driveway between three and three-thirty, he could hear—loud and clear—either the seductive strains of Manfred Mann and 'The Mighty Quinn' or the rasping sounds of Kenny Rogers and The First Edition's 'Just Dropped In (to see what condition your condition was in)' or, sometimes best of all, the pulsating sounds of The Beatles and 'Lady Madonna.' Wesley's stereo sounds had to reach every corner of Lebanon's Willamette Valley pasture land and sidewalked neighborhoods because by eight o' clock the crowd began to arrive for The River Road Athletic Club's Friday night festival.

The keg always sat in all its aluminum glory on the concrete patio just outside the sliding glass doors. "Running clear" was the rallying cry, and Wesley led the chorus. No one could surpass his act, and no Friday night was official without his proclamation. Once he announced the Budweiser as running clear, the festival began, setting in motion another manifestation of collective and individual humanity's capacity for merriment that shattered any rules of the morality of abstinence and sorely tested those of the morality of temperance. Wesley's "nectar of the gods" flowed freely and clear. And the unrestrained celebrant responded—in Wesley's words—by "letting it all hang out" to whatever extent that individual desired, male or female, without distinction or discrimination. Without fear of judgment or condemnation and safely removed from the scrutinizing eyes of the proper Lebanon community, everyone was left to his own individual judgment and sense of propriety.

Of the three charter members of The River Road Athletic Club, Wesley's Friday night behavior probably commanded the most attention. He remained in a class by himself and proved to be well worth the price of admission, as he might say along with proclaiming that every keg was the best he'd ever had and that every Friday night festival represented "the greatest thing since night baseball." If any individual celebrant were reluctant to "go to the keg," in his words, Wesley managed to fill up his cup until the particular individual felt free to find his own way to the concrete patio. Anyone who failed to enjoy a good time at the Athletic Club, he said, only had himself to blame. And he practiced what he preached, oftentimes to Ron's amazement, although he participated as much as he observed.

Wesley wasn't known for his discretion any more than he was for his sense of discrimination. And whenever a female companion from Oregon State joined him for one of the Friday night festivals, he showed a tendency to be conspicuous by his absence as the evening wore on. Paul was more discriminate and more discreet as well while Ron, although susceptible even to Wesley's degree of indiscrimination and indiscretion, didn't trust love that blossomed as a result of sharing in Wesley's "nectar of the gods." He tried to keep his eyes open for the love that first blossomed in the heart. Then with such blossoming any "nectar" that might be shared with the beloved carried the power of a magic potion. Paul, more so than Wesley, showed interest in such love, but more often than not, Ron, rather than either of his roommates, found himself without female companionship. On a Friday night that proved otherwise, the experience always proved to be of the unsatisfying variety.

Most of the time he was content to attend the festivals on his own, which allowed him to observe as well as to actively participate. Steve and Sue were regulars, along with Judith Griswold and her mysterious husband, Ken, whom Ron knew, primarily, from is daily appearance in the faculty room where he would slink inside the door and wait for Judith to notice him. Ron had to appreciate anyone interested in such unobtrusive entry into a world in which he thought he didn't belong.

The alliance that had developed between Judith and Ron in the high school faculty room blossomed into a solid friendship at The River Road Athletic Club, and at the same time he was able to develop a similar friendship with Steve and Sue independent of Wesley and Paul. Although Ken Griswold, with his black hair and dark, penetrating eyes set in a sculptured, European face framed by his straight-angled nose and solid chin, lived in contrast to Steve's fair, more rugged appearance, he proved to be his equal in the natural worlds of fishing and hunting. But despite their equal physical stature at roughly six feet and 160 pounds, Ken faded when it came to matching Steve beer for beer. Steve liked his beer, and he could put it away with the best of them. Ken was more methodical in his consumption, and Ron felt honored to experience the company of either or both of them. In their own ways both were religious men, although neither realized the connection.

Ron and Judith approached teaching differently, but their friendship still was built on a foundation of mutual commitment to the profession. Judith was quietly attractive and kept her short, frosted hair neatly combed around her face identified by its piercing blue eyes, straight, definitive nose, and complimentary chin. Her smooth, but not delicate, complexion supported the soft red shade of lipstick that always decorated her thinly contoured lips. Slightly built, but far from fragile, at five feet one inch, she lived and worked with an intensity that drove her to correct and return papers to students the next day to reinforce the learning experience. As a result, she accumulated a wealth of paper work that often overwhelmed her. But she was serious. In her classroom she meant business. She had her life with Ken, and at the Friday night festivals her piercing eyes would relax. She'd bring her guitar and sip her brandy, allowing Ken to circulate as mysteriously as he pleased in quiet observation of the human behavior on display.

Sue Carlson, too, was a teacher, although she wasn't employed at any school during the year of The River Road Athletic Club. But Ron's friendship with her, as far as he could tell and independent of his friendship with and respect for Steve, went beyond any mutual commitment to teaching. For some reason Ron's heart agreed with his eyes, and more than once he confided in Ken Griswold that he feared he had overstepped the boundaries with regard to his friendship with Sue. But Ken, in his quiet and interested observation, always reassured him that his actions, no matter how intimate they appeared to him, always fell safely within the bounds of friendly and temperate propriety. Ron needed Ken's reassurance. Given his respect for Steve and his honest manhood, he couldn't violate the sanctity of his union with Sue. Once again the object of his awakened love proved to be inaccessible. But this time he regularly found himself in the company of such a beloved. Only the appearance of another beloved, this time unmarried and accessible, could ease the pain.

## XV

Debbie Wright entered Ron's life in the classic manner reserved for Medieval tales of courtly love, and it all began about three-and-one-half months into the year of The River Road Athletic Club. Paul already had settled in with a steady girlfriend from Oregon State while Wesley continued to make his presence felt among a seemingly endless supply of female companions. Ron's eyes remained alert as scouts for the heart, but the three never seemed to reach agreement, no matter how much he desired the accord. He even tried to talk himself into it, but he failed miserably in the art of self-deception. Thus Ron's lot remained basically that of the agonized lover who all too often found himself in the company of an inaccessible beloved. But all that changed in early December of 1967, and he couldn't wait to get home from school to tell Wesley and Paul of the adventure. As usual, he was the last one home, and on this Monday night he didn't even bother to say hello as he walked through the front door and into the recreation room, where he found his roommates sitting quietly on the stone hearth in front of the fireplace.

"It happened," he said, standing in the middle of the room with a smile on his face and holding his arms outstretched in proclamation.

"What do you mean?" Paul asked.

"What happened?" Wesley asked next.

"I found her," Ron answered, arms still outstretched.

"Who did you find?" Wesley asked, tossing back his head to get his blonde hair out of his eyes.

"My true love," Ron answered seriously.

"Your true love?" Wesley asked incredulously, still sitting on the stone hearth. "Just like that? You found your true love just like that? You sound like the guy you described in your stories about the love chains you'd string up in your dorm room and letters you'd write every day. Are those stories true after all?"

"Of course they're true," Ron answered, lowering his hands to his side and finding a seat on the couch sitting against the wall next to his bedroom. "It's all part of the magic of love, but then you don't believe in magic."

"Not in that kind of magic," Wesley said. "It sounds suspect to me."

"Still," Ron said, "I've found her, and it's driving me crazy because I don't know what to do about it."

"How did you find her?" Paul asked. "Weren't you at school all day?"

"I found her at school, in the library."

"You've got to be kidding," Wesley said, shaking his head and then burying it in his hands. "Don't tell me you've fallen for some high school student. This is too much."

"C'mon, Wesley. You know I'd never 'fall' for any high school girl. I'm a teacher, remember."

"I remember. Go on. Tell us what happened."

"Sure," Paul said. "How'd you come across her."

"Well," Ron began to answer, sitting on the edge of the couch and not even bothering to take off his top coat, "I was in the library with my fifth period class while they did some research for their term paper that's due sometime in March. And there she was, working behind the desk."

"Hadn't you seen her before?" Wesley asked.

"No. That's just it. I don't know where she came from. I've been in the library many times, especially during the last couple of weeks, and I've never seen her before today. I still can't believe it. I walked in the door with my class and there she was. The thunderbolt hit and I wasn't expecting it in the least. But this is it. This is the real thing. I know. I've been here before."

"Am I looking at the Legend all those stories refer to?" Wesley asked. "Is this how you earned such status?"

"I guess so. But it's the truth. I saw her and my heart leapt to my throat and began to beat at least a thousand times a minute. If I had seen her during first period, I never would have made it through the day. Luckily, I only had one more period to go. And it wasn't scheduled for the library."

"So," Paul said, moving up to the edge of the stone hearth, "what does she look like?"

"She's a vision of delight," Ron answered as Wesley groaned and cast his eyes toward the ceiling.

"Now you sound like one of those poets you're always talking about," he said. "They're always referring to visions of delight. It's funny that I've never come across one—attractive, maybe—but never a 'vision of delight.'"

"Well," Ron continued, "this girl is such a vision. I don't know another way to describe her."

"I bet she's blonde, like Sue Carlson," Paul said, smiling. "Besides, aren't 'visions of delight' supposed to be blonde?"

"She is blonde, but I don't think she has anything to do with Sue. And I don't think a 'vision of delight' has to be blonde, although I have to say that it seems to help in my case. She's blonde like Sue, but she's a lighter shade. Her hair looked soft and welcoming, just like her eyes and face."

"This is too much," Wesley said, shaking his head and running his hands through his thick, dark blonde hair. "How can hair be soft and welcoming like someone's eyes and face? Did you see a vision or an individual human being?"

"I saw an individual human being," Ron answered immediately. "And her beauty triggered my heart. It doesn't happen all the time, but this is legitimate. I can tell."

"Did she see you?" Paul asked.

"Yes, but I don't know how her heart reacted, although I'm sure she saw me with more than just a passing glance. But I don't know about her heart. And even if it acted similar to mine, I can't guarantee that she'll obey it. Not all of us respond to the call of adventure"

"Tell us more about her," Paul said, resting his arms on his thighs and folding his hands together in front of his knees. "Be more exact. Besides being a 'vision of delight,' what does she look like?"

"As I said, her hair is lighter than Sue's, and she has the smoothest skin I've ever seen. It's natural and free from any heavy makeup. And she has sparkling blue eyes. What can I say? She's naturally youthful and vibrant. She's not a mature-looking woman like Sue, but then I'm not a mature-looking man like Steve, either. If I didn't wear a tie to school every day, I easily could pass for a student. But this girl in the library is absolutely gorgeous. No other word can describe her," Ron concluded as his eyes sparkled with the promise of love.

"What happens now?" Paul asked.

"I don't know. It's only Monday. I have to face this agony of rapture all week."

"I've heard it all," Wesley groaned. "What about this vision's body. What's it like?"

"It's as gorgeous as her face. She had to leave her desk a couple of times and I watched her walk across the room. I couldn't handle it. It's going to drive me crazy, and I have to visit the library every day this week."

"Sounds pretty foolish to me," Wesley said. "It's beyond my experience. But I enjoy watching the Legend in action, finally."

"I know it's foolish," Ron said, "but that's the way it goes."

"The way what goes?" Wesley asked.

"The way love goes," Paul answered.

"That's right," Ron added. "Love makes fools out of us. Maybe that's what Shakespeare meant when he said 'the fool doth think he is wise, the wise man knows himself to be a fool.' Maybe we're supposed to be foolish. Or maybe we're supposed to allow ourselves to be foolish. Maybe it's not so immature after all. Aren't we supposed to remain as children to enter the Kingdom of Heaven?"

"This is getting to be too much for me," Wesley said, getting up from his position on the hearth. "I think I'll head to the Elks for a beer before I eat. Anyone care to come along?"

"No thanks, Wes," Ron answered. "I think I'll stay home and try to figure out my next move," he added, settling back into the couch still dressed in his top coat. "I wonder where she came from so suddenly?"

"You go ahead, Wes," Paul said. "I'll stay here and keep the Legend company. Maybe we can figure out where his 'vision of delight' came from. Maybe we're missing out on some magic land somewhere."

"You two deserve each other," Wesley said, laughing. "I'll be back soon, and let's have dinner all figured out by then. In fact, I took some steaks out of the freezer this morning before school. We can whip up a salad and broil the steaks, that is if our legendary roommate can bring himself to eat"

"It won't be easy," Ron said, catching Wesley's smile. "But I am hungry. Enjoy the Elks and stay out of trouble."

"I will," Wesley said as he walked down the hallway to his bedroom closet to get his coat. "Catch you later," he added as he walked toward the front door, putting on his coat at the same time. "Keep your eye on the Legend," he said to Paul as he walked through the doorway toward his waiting blue Volkswagen.

"Don't worry about him," Paul said, moving to close the door behind Wesley. "I think I understand him."

"Later," Wesley said, starting up his Volkswagen.

"Later," Paul replied, closing the front door and returning to the recreation room where Ron still sat in his top coat leaning back, entranced, into the soft comfort of the couch.

Wesley returned after a short stay at the Elks Club in downtown Lebanon and the three of them enjoyed their dinner of steak and salad, with the steaks being taken from the side of beef they bought from Paul's father at the beginning of the year and stored in one of Lebanon's meat lockers. They took turns cooking, and if their meals lacked variety, they didn't suffer from lack of preparation. They liked to cook fish periodically, and Ron enjoyed fixing his mother's spaghetti as well. But beef, whether in the form of hamburger or steak, dominated their diet. They rarely ate out, and when they did, Bing's Kitchen was their choice. All three of them welcomed the relative seclusion The River Road Athletic Club offered, and they preferred to be seen in Lebanon proper as little as possible. The three of them approached teaching differently, but, unanimously, they felt most at home in their rented Athletic Club not far removed from the sloping banks of the Santiam River.

Ron still had to survive that first, trying week, and he didn't expect an easy time. He couldn't avoid the library, but he didn't know what to do about his "vision of delight" once he arrived. He knew he couldn't talk to her beyond exchanging the normal greetings associated with any library worker because, among other things, his students were watching his every move. His "vision's" beauty didn't escape their eyes nor did Ron's initial reaction to it. He wanted to avoid adding any more fuel to the fire, but he couldn't call his "vision" on the telephone because he didn't know her name. She knew his name, but wanting to be discreet as possible, he hesitated to inquire about her identity. Wesley and Paul delighted in his nightly pangs of anguish as he struggled with his dilemma. He had lost his heart once again, but this time the circumstances made his adventure even more painful.

The week did pass, however, and by Friday Ron had made no progress with regard to his "vision of delight." Every day he took at least one class to the library to work on its term paper assignment, and every day he said hello to his "vision" working at the main desk. Every day he resolved to talk to her, but every day he feigned disinterest in order to keep the snickers and whispers from his students to a minimum. Judith Griswold didn't know the girl's name, but she suspected she was a local girl home from school for the Christmas holidays. Unwilling to totally tip his hand, Ron faced dim prospects of learning her name before the scheduled Friday night festival. Once again he found himself without the promise of female companionship and headed home to the Athletic Club, bearing a burden he hadn't carried since his arrival in Lebanon almost a year ago.

Before he pulled his Camaro into the driveway, he could hear the strains of 'The Mighty Quinn' blasting from Wesley's stereo speakers. He didn't know the 'Quinn' from the song, but he did know that he didn't feel mighty at the moment. And he knew he couldn't handle another one of Wesley's arranged dates. If he couldn't attend the festival with his "vision of delight," he'd rather be alone. For the first time since he arrived and settled in Lebanon, he wished he had other plans for a Friday night. He wished he had never seen Lebanon Union High School, and he wished he had never seen any "vision of delight" in any library. The clarion call of 'The Mighty Quinn' didn't inspire him, but he parked his Camaro anyway and walked through the front door of The River Road Athletic Club, carrying his books in the crook of his left arm.

"You still don't know her name, do you?" Wesley asked, standing in the middle of the recreation room in front of the fireplace and greeting Ron with a bottle of Budweiser.

"No, I don't," Ron answered, setting his books on the couch resting against the wall outside his bedroom and throwing his top coat across them. "But how did you know?"

"How did I know?" Wesley asked in return. "Do you think I'm blind. I've lived with you long enough to know what's going on. If you had found out her name, your smiling eyes would have given you away. Here, have a little Budweiser and forget about it for a while. Besides, we have a festival scheduled for tonight. Let Paul and I take care of you."

"Not another one of those," Ron said, removing the cap from his bottle of Budweiser. "I don't want anything to do with one of your groupies tonight. I'd rather be alone."

"Don't be so harsh on my followers," Wesley said, smiling. "Some of them think you're pretty sharp, you know."

"Maybe so," Ron said, sitting on the couch, "but none of them particularly excite the eyes and the heart."

"Maybe you pay too much attention to the eyes and the heart. Maybe you ought to forget about them for one night," Wesley said as both of them heard the front door open and close.

"Oh, oh," Paul said as he walked into the recreation room and immediately looked at Ron, sitting on the couch gripping his beer in his right hand. "You still haven't found out her name, have you?"

"No. I don't know any more about her today than I did on Monday. And I probably never will."

"Did you ask Judith?" Paul asked, setting his books on the dining table and laying his top coat across the back of one of the chairs.

"Yes, but she doesn't know anything about her. She thinks she might be a local girl filling in for the holidays. But that's all."

"And of course he won't ask anyone else, and he certainly won't ask his 'vision,'" Wesley said, turning down the stereo now that Manfred Mann had finished celebrating the exploits of 'The Mighty Quinn.'

"I can't ask anyone else, and I can't ask one of my students," Ron said. "Let's face it. I'm doomed," he added, taking a long swig of his Budweiser. "It's been the worst week of my life. Every day in the library has driven me crazy, and I can only say hello to her and smile and think of some excuse to walk up to the main desk. But I can't do that because all my students watch my every move. They could care less about their term paper under these circumstances."

"Would you if you were in their place?" Wesley asked.

"Probably not. But that doesn't make it any easier on me."

"I've got an idea," Paul said, pulling up one of the dining table chairs and sitting in it with his arms draped over the back in front of his chest. "Why don't we take the Legend here over to Corvallis and find him a date for tonight?"

"I already told Wesley I'd rather be alone," Ron said. "No blind date tonight. I can't take it."

"Paul and I have contacts we haven't even tapped yet. We'll come up with someone for tonight's festival. What do you say. Are you game?"

"I don't know. I'm not sure I can trust your taste."

"Then let Paul take charge. Do you think you can handle it?" Wesley asked, turning his eyes toward Paul seated as he was at the dining table.

"It won't be easy, but I'll see what I can do. What time do you have to pick up, uh, what's her name?"

"Polly," Wesley answered.

"Not her!" Ron exclaimed. "She's the groupie of all groupies."

"Maybe so," Wesley said. "But she's good for the glands."

"Would you let her use your toothbrush?" Ron asked as he laughed for the first time since he came home.

"That's one of my lines, you know. You'd be surprised how effective it is."

"I know," Ron said, still laughing. "I've seen its effects, and if you tell Polly that you'd let her use your toothbrush, you'll never get rid of her. Maybe she's the groupie who won't be discarded. Just keep her away from my toothbrush."

"Toothbrush or not," Paul said, "what time do you have to pick her up?"

"At seven," Wesley answered.

"It's almost four-thirty," Paul said, glancing at his watch, "and we have to get the keg, pick up the house a little, and get something to eat.

We don't have too much time. I'd better get on the horn and take care of the Legend. What do you think?"

"Sounds good to me. You can call Karen. How does that sound, Legend?"

"Do I have much choice?" Ron asked in response. "Go ahead, Paul. And I'll try to keep an open mind," he added, taking the final drink of his Budweiser.

"Great," Wesley said, tossing back his head to get the hair out of his eyes. "Get right on it, but first a couple more cool ones and let's hear from The Beatles and 'Lady Madonna.'

To Ron's relief he wouldn't have to deal with Wesley and his contacts tonight. Polly had a roommate, but Ron had no interest in spending the evening with the girl the three of them had nicknamed 'the Boomer.' Polly was okay, but she was desperate and thus vulnerable to Wesley's entertaining charm. Ron didn't exactly feel sorry for her because she had the age and the experience to know better, but sometimes he wished he could take her aside to tell her to at least play Wesley's game on his terms. She wasn't unattractive with her blonde hair, average features, and full figure, but she was too easy to seduce. And in the presence of an entertaining charmer like Wesley, more often than not she played the role of seducer. The Boomer wasn't unattractive either, but being of even fuller figure that Polly, she was more than willing to play the seducer if she thought someone to be even mildly interested in her. Ron knew he was no match for her desperation. The Boomer didn't figure in his plans for the Friday festival, leaving his fate in the hands of Paul and Karen.

Karen Wilson had come into Paul's life about a month earlier, tempering his behavior in the process. Being a charmer in his own right, he had little trouble keeping up with Wesley, but he was far more susceptible to being a one woman man. No one ever would mistake Karen for Polly or the Boomer, either in appearance or demeanor. Where Polly and her roommate were fully endowed, Karen was slim and demure almost to the point of being delicate. Her dark blonde hair reached her shoulders in soft curls, and her blue eyes, while shy and tentative, lacked the desperation reflected in Polly's and the Boomer's. Her delicate stature emphasized her vulnerability that contributed to her charm and not to any sense of sad desperation. Paul was a solid man who promised loyalty and security, and Karen looked at him with adoring eyes that, Ron thought, had marriage in mind. Karen didn't belong in the same league with Wesley's groupies, and although she didn't affect Ron as did Sue Carlson, he rested more easily knowing that she and Paul would be in charge of his Friday night fate. After eating their dinner of steak and salad, he felt free to accompany Wesley on his journey to the Town Tavern to procure the night's keg.

As usual the keg was waiting and within half an hour Ron and Wesley returned to The River Road Athletic Club to tap the keg on the concrete patio just outside the sliding glass doors opening to the irrigation canal and the back yard. Early December usually meant rain in the Willamette Valley and throughout the Northwest, but tonight promised clear skies and crisp, winter air. A full moon illuminated the back yard and its light reflected off the shining, aluminum keg. Ron remembered Mrs Williams talking about the oppressive rains of Northwest winters, but as a native he didn't notice the oppression. She said she sometimes missed the clear, crisp days and nights of Montana winters, and Ron had to think she would feel right at home tonight as he helped Wesley position the keg on the concrete patio. Wesley had tapped countless kegs in his life; and before Ron knew it, the spigot was open, the initial foam had run its course, and the Budweiser was running clear.

# XVI

"Got it tapped?" Paul asked, stepping onto the concrete patio and into the December moonlight.

"No problem," Wesley answered, filling three cups one at a time and giving one each to Paul and Ron. "And it's running clear. Here's to Greater Northwest Living," he said, raising his cup as if he were paying tribute to the moon.

"To Greater Northwest Living," Paul and Ron replied in unison as, simultaneously and ceremoniously, the three of them drank from their wide-mouthed paper cups.

"Well, Leg," Paul said as the three of them lowered their cups and stepped into the recreation room and out of the chilled moonlight, "you're all set. Karen and I have found you a date."

"I'm almost afraid to ask," Ron said, "although I know none of Wesley's groupies are involved," he added as Wesley groaned and shook his head.

"You're right there, and she's not the Boomer," Paul said, laughing.

"Well, then," Wesley said, spreading his arms for emphasis, "who the hell is she?"

"Karen's roommate," Paul answered.

"Karen's roommate?" Ron asked in surprise. "Do you know her?"

"No," Paul answered as they drank from their cups. "I've never met her."

"Why not?" Wesley asked. "You've seen Karen every night for a month."

"But her roommate never has been around. She's either been out with her boyfriend, with whom she recently broke up, or she's been at the library. I've never seen her, but Karen assures me she's 'pretty,' to use her description."

"But she must not be a sorority girl," Ron said. "Am I right?"

"Yes. She's independent, just like Karen."

"That counts in her favor. If she's not a sorority girl, she can't be all bad."

"Where's she from?" Wesley asked as the three of them continued to drink their Budweiser.

"I don't know," Paul answered. "I never bothered to ask. Sorry about that."

"It doesn't make any difference," Ron said. "What year is she? She does go to Oregon State, doesn't she?"

"Yes. She's a Beaver, and she's a junior."

"A junior," Ron said, thinking ahead. "That means she had to be there when you guys were. Wesley, get your senior yearbook. I've got to look her up. If I'm destined to keep this date, at least I'd like to look at her first. What's her name, Paul?" he asked as Wesley walked back into the recreation room carrying his yearbook.

"Debbie Wright."

"Let's see," Ron said, stepping over to the dining table and setting his beer down. "That must be W-r-i-g-h-t."

"Must be," Paul said as Ron turned the pages.

"Did you find her?" Wesley asked as Ron's eyes opened as big as targets, his cheeks flushed, and his heart jumped to his throat."

"What's wrong?" Paul asked with concern. "Are you okay?"

"I can't believe it," Ron said, gasping for breath.

"Can't believe what?" Wesley asked, moving closer to the dining table to have a look.

"It's her!" Ron exclaimed, setting the book down on the table in disbelief. "I can't believe it. It's her!"

"Who?" Wesley asked, looking at the page but not noticing Debbie Wright.

"It's her," Ron repeated, pointing to the picture of the striking blonde in the middle of the third row on the right hand page. "That's my 'vision of delight' from the library."

"You've got to be kidding," Wesley said. "There's no way."

"Really?" Paul asked, looking at the picture. "This is classic."

"Really. I can't believe it. Paul, you've fixed me up with my 'vision of delight.' I can't believe it. What time is it?" Ron asked, looking at his watch. "It's almost six-thirty," he answered in response to his own question. "What time are we supposed to be at Karen's?"

"I said around seven," Paul answered. "We have to pick up Polly first, remember."

"I remember," Ron said, but not paying any attention to his answer. "I have to get ready. I'm still wearing my teaching vestments. I'm going to change. Are you two ready?"

"Sure," Paul answered amidst his laughter.

"I just have to brush my teeth and comb my hair," Wesley said. "My followers know what to expect from me."

"Maybe," Ron said, finishing his Budweiser and swallowing his heart at the same time, "but Debbie Wright doesn't know what to expect from me. She'll never know what hit her."

"That's for sure," Paul said, finishing his beer. "I hope she can handle it."

"Well," Wesley said, moving toward the sliding glass doors, "I'm going to hoist another Budweiser and think about it. I can tell we're about to participate in a legendary experience. Anyone care to join me?" he asked, opening the doors.

"Not right now," Paul answered.

"Later," Ron answered. " I have to get ready," he added, walking into his bedroom. "I still can't believe it," he continued.

In a matter of minutes he walked out of his bedroom dressed in his tan, Levi cords, matching desert boots, and in a soft, cream-colored sport shirt covered by a burgundy V-neck sweater. He had shaved in the morning and could have shaved again, but given his light beard, he had no real need. He did rub some Mennen Afta into his skin, and he managed to brush his teeth and comb his hair that had grown noticeably longer since his arrival in Lebanon. A trace of sideburns sneaked down the sides of his face in front of each ear, and his hair, now more full on the sides and along the back of his neck, reached tentatively to the top of his shirt collar. No one could call him a hippie, but his hairstyle did reflect the times that Bob Dylan kept reminding everybody were changing.

"All set, Leg?" Paul asked as Ron presented himself in the recreation room, carrying his blue winter coat.

"You're wearing your campus costume again," Wesley said, finishing his second cup of Budweiser. "You must be ready."

"I'm ready. I just have to get my heart out of my throat. And I've been wearing these shoes, Levi cords, and V-necks since 1962. I don't see any reason to change now. Do I have to drive or are we taking the Fury?"

"We'll take the Fury," Paul answered. "I don't want you to drive in your condition. What do you think, Wes?"

"The Legend shouldn't have to do anything in his condition. I just hope this Debbie Wright is up to the task. I hope she listens to her eyes and heart, to quote our legendary roommate, as much he does. If she doesn't, someone's in for a real crash."

"You have to take the chance," Ron said. "I'm ready. Let's hit the road," he added, walking toward the front door.

"Off we go," Paul said as he and Wesley followed Ron out the front door and into the Fury waiting in the driveway.

Ron couldn't remain silent during the 20 mile drive to Corvallis. He had to talk about Debbie Wright and the significance of this occasion. Being an English teacher, he couldn't help recognizing the connection between his own experience and the Medieval tales of courtly love that he taught, although his students found it hard to understand, or even care about, something associated with such a remote time.

"This is incredible," he said as soon as Paul had backed the Fury out of the driveway and headed it onto the twisting, dirt road that led to River Road and eventually to the western outskirts of Lebanon and the intersection with the main road leading to Corvallis. "It's something out of a Medieval romance, and it's happening to me."

"What the hell's a Medieval romance?" Wesley asked as Paul laughed and concentrated on his driving.

"It's a story of love," Ron answered, "of what the troubadours, the Medieval poets, called Amor. It's a story of the eyes and the heart and the connection between them. The eyes are scouts for the heart and when all three are in agreement, true love is born."

"Yes," Wesley said, "but we don't live in Medieval times. We live in the 20th century."

"I know," Ron said as Paul turned in front of the Lebanon Lumber Company onto the Santiam Highway that led through Lebanon and to the truck route that met the main road to Corvallis. "But it's happening right now. I feel the same as a Medieval knight stricken by love. I'm living the Medieval romance."

"But you're not a knight," Wesley said. "You're just a 20th century English teacher, nothing more, nothing less."

"But that's not the point. Those stories aren't simply Medieval stories. They're stories of Love, of Amor, set in the Middle Ages. The setting of this unfolding story may be different, but the story's the same. The truth lies in Love and not in some Medieval costume."

"You're acting like a fool, if you ask me," Wesley said as Paul steered the Fury off the Santiam Highway and onto the truck route that would take them around the western edge of Lebanon and to the Corvallis highway leading farther west toward the Pacific Coast.

"I suppose I am," Ron said as he realized the stories he taught were made up. But they were made up from experience which made them ring true. "But I'm not a fool. Maybe I'm a wise man who knows himself to be a fool. And if I can know myself to be a fool, anyone can know the same about himself, given the chance. This is incredible, but it's really happening. Love makes fools out of us. Now I know what Shakespeare meant. I don't know why, but I must be a believer."

"A believer in what?" Wesley asked from his position in the front seat as he turned to look at Ron sitting in the back.

"A believer in religion," Ron answered. "A believer in the Religion of Love. I must be a believer in the Religion of Love, and it's making a fool out of me. And it's not the first time, even if it's the most incredible. I just hope my heart settles down before Debbie Wright gets in the car. If it doesn't, I'm done for. I'm going to be as calm as possible," he concluded as Paul guided the Fury onto the Corvallis highway, all the time smiling in recognition of, if not belief in, Ron's religion.

But it's hard to remain calm when your heart's beating at least a thousand times a minute and has jumped all the way to your throat. Visions such as Debbe Wright usually remain afar, but not this time. Ron could maintain some semblance of calm only if he kept talking, much to the delight of Paul who had the Fury well on its way to Corvallis and Ron's date with destiny. Wesley, finally witnessing the Legend in action, delighted in the spectacle as well.

"This is going to be different, Wesley," Ron continued as Paul steered the Fury through the sharp curves of the Corvallis highway west of Interstate 5.

"Different from what?"

"Different from the other times."

"Different from the times that sounded so unbelievable?"

"Yes."

"How different?" Wesley asked as Paul negotiated the final curve and headed the Fury in a straight line toward Corvallis.

"This time I'm going to be more careful. I'm going to be more cool about the situation. I'm going to enjoy tonight, but I'm not going to ask her out for any other night just yet. I'm going to control myself and go slower."

"I'll believe that when I see it," Wesley said, "and not until then."

"You'll see. Just wait."

"Well," Paul broke in, "we don't have to wait much longer," he added as the Fury climbed the hill and crossed over the bridge that deposited them in the city of Corvallis. Ron's watch read six-fifty, giving them about ten minutes to get to Karen's and Debbie's apartment close to the Oregon State campus, located only a few blocks up Main Street leading from east to west.

"Aren't we going to stop at Polly's first?" Ron asked as his heart uncontrollably leaped to his throat once again.

"I suppose we'd better," Wesley answered. "You know your way to the Alpha Phi house don't you, Paul?"

"I've been there more times than I'd like to remember," he answered, continuing to guide the Fury in a straight line.

"Now that you've discovered Karen, maybe you won't have to make any more trips on your own behalf," Wesley said as Paul drove on.

"Maybe not," he answered, smiling.

"Rice is nice, you know," Ron said as he tried, once again, to swallow his heart and return it to where it belonged.

"That's what I hear," Paul replied as he turned right and stopped across the street from the Alpha Phi house. "Do you think she'll be ready, Wes?"

"Aren't my followers always ready?" he asked in return, opening his passenger side door. "I'll be right back and you, Mr Legend, can move to the front seat for now. Can you handle it?"

"I think so," Ron answered, stepping out of the back seat. "I may be foolish, but I'm not helpless."

"Not even in the presence of Debbie Wright?" Wesley asked as he closed the front door after Ron and walked briskly and purposefully up the sidewalk to the Alpha Phi house.

"I guess that remains to be seen," Ron answered, looking at Paul who delighted in listening to their exchanges.

"I guess so," he replied, "and I don't think we'll have to wait too long. Polly must have been waiting at the front door," he added, nodding his head in the direction of her and Wesley as they stepped off the sorority house porch and headed down the sidewalk toward the Fury.

"Better sooner than later," Ron said. "The sooner I meet Debbie, the sooner my heart will find its way back to my chest. It might not stay there the rest of the evening, but I wouldn't mind getting it back there temporarily at least. I wonder if she's figured out who I am?"

"I don't know," Paul answered as Wesley and Polly approached the car, "but Karen knows where you teach. And I'm sure she's told Debbie. So, she probably knows who you are. But I don't know if she mentioned you to Karen, and if she did, I don't know how she described her initial reaction. Are you her 'vision of delight? I don't know. I suppose that, too, remains to be seen."

"I guess so," Ron said as Wesley opened the back door for Polly and followed her into the car.

"Hi, Polly," Ron said as she moved slightly across the back seat to give Wesley some room. "Did you bring your toothbrush?"

"What?" she asked in response, looking helplessly at Wesley.

"Don't mind him, Polly," Wesley said. "It's an insignificant private joke."

"How are you, Polly?" Paul asked, smothering his laughter.

"I'm fine, but would someone mind telling me what's going on?"

"Our legendary roommate, your friend and mine, Ron Petrich from Tacoma, Washington, is about to meet his 'vision of delight,'" Wesley answered. "That's what's going on, and we'd better get on with it or he'll be late."

"What?" Polly asked. "I don't understand."

"Don't worry about it," Wesley said. "Nobody understands," he added as Paul pulled away from the curb and steered the Fury in the direction of Karen's and Debbie's apartment.

Ron couldn't speak as Paul found his way to their apartment just a few blocks north of the Alpha Phi house along the eastern boundary of the Oregon State campus. Thoughts of Debbie Wright, and the incredibility surrounding their meeting, occupied his mind as he focused on the enchanted moment when he discovered her picture in Wesley's yearbook. That moment provided living testament to the power and rapture of Love when the beloved, seemingly destined to be forever afar, is presented as being inescapably near instead. The rapture—natural, honest, and consuming—only appeared foolish in the eyes of the nonbeliever. Its adventure held infinite promise until proven otherwise, and Ron embarked on its path without fear. He couldn't turn back now, and he tried his best to keep his heart out of his throat as Paul pulled the Fury to a stop directly in front of Karen's apartment.

"Here we are, Leg," he said, turning toward Ron.

"Leg?" Polly asked from the back seat. "I thought his name was Ron. Are you three playing some kind of a joke?"

"Leg is short for Legend, Polly," Wesley said. "His name is Ron, but sometimes no given name accurately describes his actions. Under those circumstances he needs another moniker. Right now he's acting in the manner of legendary lovers. So, we call him the Legend."

"He doesn't look any different to me," Polly said. "He still looks like Ron as far as I can see."

"That's okay," Wesley said, putting his arm around her as she snuggled closer to him in response. "The stuff of legends might not be immediately visible."

"Oh, I see," she said, laying her head on Wesley's left shoulder.

"Well," Paul said, shaking his head, "it's time. Are you ready?"

"I think so," Ron answered as his heart continued to beat in his throat.

"C'mon, you two," Wesley groaned from the back seat. "The keg's waiting and we have festival guests due to arrive pretty soon. Drag the Legend out of the car if you have to, Paul, and get to the door. Time's a wastin'."

"I'm ready," Ron said, opening the passenger side door and stepping out onto the curb just as Paul walked around the front of the Fury.

"Follow me," he said, and together they walked down the stairs to the lower level of the three-tiered apartment building.

Standing in front of Karen's and Debbie's apartment, Ron couldn't bring himself to ring their doorbell. He left that job to Paul as he stood motionless outside the door, gazing into the clear, moonlit sky. He heard the doorbell ring inside and in a matter of seconds the front door opened as Karen welcomed the both of them into the living room of the two bedroom apartment.

"Hi, Paul. Hi, Ron," she said, stepping aside from the open doorway. "Come in. Debbie will be ready in just a couple of minutes."

"Hi," Paul answered, stepping across the threshold.

"Hi, Karen," Ron said, following Paul into the middle of the small living room, all the time trying to gulp his heart back to his chest.

"Debbie's excited to meet you," Karen said. "She doesn't like blind dates, but when I told her who you were and where you taught, she realized that she knew you. That made a difference. It's quite a coincidence, don't you think?"

"It sure is," Paul answered. "But that's not the whole story. Right, Leg?" he asked, trying to hold back his laughter.

"Not exactly," Ron answered, trying to control the beating of his heart and the flush in his cheeks,

"What do you mean?" Karen asked.

"To make a long story short," Paul answered, "the Legend here, Ron Petrich to the average lay person, has been moaning all week over this 'vision of delight' working in the high school library. And it turns out that his 'vision' is none other than Debbie Wright. Mere coincidence, then, doesn't adequately describe this meeting. One rarely meets such a 'vision' under any circumstances, let alone these we're witnessing. Ron, therefore, has been living up to the legendary reputation we've heard so much about."

"He doesn't look any different to me."

"Maybe not, but you won't find his heart beating in his chest. Right, Leg?"

"I'm trying, but it's not easy," Ron answered as he turned to see Debbie appear out of the hallway that led to the two bedrooms located immediately behind the kitchen area.

"There you are," Karen said as Debbie walked tentatively into the living room to meet her date for the evening. "Paul, this is Debbie, and, Debbie, this is Paul."

"It's nice to meet you," Debbie said, smiling. "I've heard a lot about you this past month."

"I'm sure it's all been properly flattering," Paul said, returning her smile. "It's nice to meet you, too. I thought you must have been the phantom roommate," he added, knowing that Ron saw her as being much more substantial.

"Oh, I've been around, only not when you've been here."

"And, Debbie," Karen said, turning their attention to the knight without any shining armor standing perfectly still in the middle of the living room, "this is Ron and, Ron, this is Debbie."

"Hi, Debbie," Ron managed to say, still trying his best to look calm and composed as his heart beat faster in his throat.

"Hi, Ron," Debbie answered with an inviting smile that almost brought him to his knees. "I know you from the library at the high school in Lebanon. If I didn't, I don't think Karen could have talked me into our date tonight. This is quite a coincidence, isn't it?"

"It sure is. Events like this only happen in books, if they happen at all. And I'm glad that Karen talked you into coming tonight."

"I am, too," Debbie replied with the same inviting smile as Ron couldn't take his eyes off her. She was slightly taller than Karen, who stood about five feet two inches, and not quite as delicate, but, still, she was a college girl while Ron was less than one year away from being a college boy. In contrast to Karen's dark blonde hair that curled to her shoulders, Debbie's light blonde hair curled at the ends, turning inward toward her slender neck at a length half way between her ears and the top of her shoulders. She parted her hair on the left and combed her bangs back and up away from her face where a faint trace of hair spray held them in place. Her lightly rouged cheeks gave her a fresh, slightly blushed complexion, highlighting her shining blue eyes that moved from side to side, from Ron to Paul to Karen and back to Ron, whose own blue eyes remained fixed on his vision of delight. Soft, red lipstick covered her lips while her small, straight nose and perfect, slightly pointed chin completed the picture of the radiant face that had launched Ron's heart. Her red, pull-over sweater fit comfortably over the contour of her breasts while her gray skirt reached slightly above her knees, revealing exquisitely shaped legs that more than complemented her quietly dignified, female figure.

"Well," Karen said, breaking Ron's reverie for the moment, "I guess we'd better go. We'll get our coats and be right back."

"Okay," Paul said. "You're right. Wesley's in the car waiting with Polly," he added as Karen and Debbie disappeared around the corner and into the hallway that led to their bedrooms.

Karen was a college girl as well, but Ron didn't see her in Debbie's light. Although attractive and vulnerable, she wasn't strikingly radiant. She, too, wore a skirt and sweater combination, and she looked becoming and wholesome in her navy blue and off-white colors. Ron liked Karen and he could tell that she had discovered her heart's desire in Paul. But he didn't identify her with the mysterious allure of love that attracted him to Debbie. Karen didn't suffer in comparison, but Debbie's striking radiance and beckoning promise of adventure eclipsed her marriage-like wholesomeness and wifely appeal.

"How're you doing, Leg?" Paul asked, turning his attention to Ron as Karen and Debbie moved out of hearing range.

"I'm maintaining, but my heart keeps pounding. I have to control myself. I must look stupid."

"Not in the least," Paul assured him. "No one can hear your heart, although you can feel it. But, definitely, you are priceless. I hope Debbie's a match for you. She's a vision all right, but I don't know. I don't think she's ever come across anyone like you here at Oregon State. The average Beaver isn't susceptible to the rapture that can overcome you. It'll be a new experience for her, and very interesting as well."

"As I told Wesley in the car, I'm going to take it slowly this time."

"Sure," Paul replied with a doubting smile. "I'll believe that when I see it, and I might get my chance very soon because here they come," he added as he heard Karen and Debbie just before they appeared around the corner of the hallway.

"We're ready," Karen announced as she and Debbie walked into the living room carrying their winter coats.

"Okay," Paul said. "We'd better head back to the Athletic Club for the festival. You're in for a real treat, Debbie," he concluded as he moved to help Karen with her coat.

"I've heard a few things about, what did you call it? the Athletic Club?"

"That's right," Paul answered. "The River Road Athletic Club."

"Karen's told me about it," Debbie continued, standing in the middle of the living room as Paul cautiously gestured to Ron who stood frozen in his tracks, "and I'm looking forward to seeing it for myself," she said as Ron caught Paul's eye and stepped forward to help Debbie with her coat. "Thank you," she said in response to his offer and handed it to him.

"It's my pleasure," Ron answered, slipping the white, fur-collared coat over her arms and onto her shoulders, all the time trying to act calm and collected—even though his heart pounded harder than ever as he stood close to Debbie and caught the enchanting fragrance of her perfume.

"Are we ready then?" Paul asked as Debbie buttoned her coat. "We have to get back to the Club before our guests arrive."

"I think we're ready," Ron answered. "You can lead the way."

"Okay," Paul said, moving toward the front door and opening it wide. "After you," he said as Karen led Debbie through the open door and out into the December chill, followed by Ron and Paul who locked the doorknob on the inside and closed the door behind them.

"On to The River Road Athletic Club," he said, following the three of them up the steps leading to his Fury waiting for them at the curb as Wesley's watchful eyes followed Ron and Debbie around to the back seat on the driver's side.

Paul and Ron opened their doors almost simultaneously as Karen slid under the steering wheel and into the middle of the front seat while Debbie ducked into the back seat and moved over next to Polly as Ron slipped in next to her and closed the door.

"Well," Wesley exclaimed as he moved closer to his passenger side door to give Debbie and Ron more room, "now that we're all here, let's get on with it. The Budweiser'll be running more clear than ever tonight. Right, Paul?" he asked as Paul closed his door and started up the Fury.

"No doubt about it. It'll be running clear."

"Who's your date?" Wesley asked, turning to look around Polly and at Ron and Debbie as Paul pulled away from the curb.

"Sorry," Ron answered. "I guess I forgot."

"That's understandable," Wesley said. "You must be Debbie."

"Yes," she answered.

"We've heard about you for a week. It's nice to meet you."

"Excuse me," Ron broke in before Debbie could respond. "Debbie, this is Rob Wesley, the other charter member of The River Road Athletic Club. And this is Polly, his companion for the evening. And, you two, this is Debbie Wright."

"Your companion for the evening?" Wesley asked as Paul turned left onto Main Street leading back to Lebanon.

"That's right," Ron answered with an embarrassing look at Wesley. "I guess you could say that."

"Hi, Rob and Polly. It's nice to meet you."

"Hi, Debbie. It's Polly McKenzie. Ron isn't big on last names."

"I'm sorry. I'm used to you just as Polly."

"Hi, Debbie," Wesley added. "And you can call me Wesley. Nobody ever calls me Rob. Maybe we'll get used to you just as Debbie. Right, Legend?" he asked with a twinkle in his eye.

"Maybe," Ron answered, embarrassed, as Karen moved a little closer to Paul, who stole a quick glance into the back seat through the rear view mirror, smiled knowingly, and headed out of Corvallis and over the bridge toward Lebanon and The River Road Athletic Club in anticipation of the Friday night festival.

## XVII

The 20 minute ride back to Lebanon passed uneventfully, except for the fact that Ron's heart continued to jump back and forth between his chest and his throat with irregular beats that he sometimes felt had to be audible in the back seat. Nonetheless, he was able to talk to Debbie along the way and learn that she was a Lebanon girl and a graduate of the high school as well. She and Karen were classmates who just this year decided to live together on their own in a Corvallis apartment. She was a year-and-a-half away from graduating with a degree in general studies, and she had no idea of what she was going to do after graduation. Ron knew the feeling, although his major was more specific, but he was fortunate enough to have discovered student teaching during which experience he began to discover himself. Judith Griswold proved to be right about Debbie working part-time in the library for the holidays, and he was determined to proceed with caution, as he told Paul and Wesley. Still, he couldn't help telling her he was glad she decided to work at the library. She smiled and said she was glad as well as he settled comfortably in the back seat, placing his hands harmlessly on his knees in front of him.

Polly sat next to Debbie and continued to rest her head on Wesley's left shoulder as he kept his left arm around her. He sat straight with his eyes focused on the road ahead, only occasionally turning to acknowledge Polly's attempt at conversation or to steal a glance at Ron and Debbie. Karen sat next to Paul in the front seat, but he kept both hands on the steering wheel, confidently guiding the Fury through the sharp turns of the Corvallis highway west of Interstate 5. Safely out of the curves, Paul relaxed and headed for the freeway overpass and the flat, straight-line road to Lebanon. Ron could hear the pleasant hum of tires in contact with the blacktop as his heart, at least for the time being, returned to his chest to beat regularly, and his nose picked up the bewitching scent of Debbie's perfume.

At almost eight o'clock Paul pulled the Fury into the driveway of The River Road Athletic Club, where none of the scheduled guests had arrived as yet. Wesley had told Steve Carlson about Ron and his "vision of delight," and Ron was both excited and apprehensive about Debbie meeting Steve and Sue. Steve was a far cry from the college boy Debbie was used to, and the Athletic Club's Friday festivals didn't present mirror reflections of college keggers. The regular guests had put those years behind them to begin the working phase of their lives. Ron had put his college days behind him as well and he could be a man with the best of them. But no matter how hard he tried in his 23-year-old manhood, he couldn't control the location and beating of his heart when his eyes discriminately settled on a vision of delight with the power to disturb the heart. He wanted Sue to meet Debbie, but he didn't know how Sue would react to her. He trusted her vision, but he knew only Debbie herself could dispel the foolish rapture that had engulfed him.

"Well," Wesley said as Paul turned off the ignition, "this is it. It's festival time," he continued as he opened his passenger side door to let Polly out. "Every man for himself from here on out," he added, leaving Polly to close the door as he quickly walked toward the front door of the Athletic Club. "Well, Polly, are you coming?" he asked as he opened the door and turned around to see if anyone had followed him.

"I'm coming, but you have to give me a chance to get out of the car."

"You have to be quick around here. C'mon," he signaled as Polly stepped out of the back seat and closed the door behind her.

"Is he always so enthusiastic?" Debbie asked as Ron and Paul opened their doors.

"When it's running clear," Paul answered, helping Karen out of the front seat, "he's always that enthusiastic. No moss grows on Wesley. You can count on that," he concluded, closing his front door as Karen slid out from under the steering wheel.

"But that's Wesley," Ron said, helping Debbie out of the back seat and closing the door behind her. "What you see is what you get, and you'd better see clearly."

"Does Polly see clearly?" Debbie asked, standing next to Ron.

"I don't think so. She's a little too vulnerable and desperate. I think she's playing by different rules. But she'll have to find out for herself, I guess."

"It is cold out here, you know," Karen said, looking at Paul. "Don't you think it would be nice if we went inside?"

"You're right," Paul answered. "Shall we go inside then?" he asked, stepping aside to let Ron and Debbie go ahead of them.

"It looks like a nice house," Debbie said. "I'd like to see it," she added, tightening her fur collar around her neck.

"I'll show you around," Ron said, gently placing his right arm on the small of her back to walk her toward the door as his heart jumped to his throat once again. "They can follow us," he added, looking back at Karen and Paul as he and Debbie walked, together, up the sidewalk and through the open door into the warmth of The River Road Athletic Club, neatly picked up in honor of Ron's "vision of delight" and the remainder of the Friday festival guests.

"It's running clear," Wesley announced as Ron and Debbie led the way into the recreation room. "The best beer we've ever had," he exclaimed, hoisting his wide-mouthed paper cup in tribute. "Is everyone ready?"

"Debbie?" Ron asked, mentioning her name directly to her for the first time.

"Okay," she answered, "but I probably should take my coat off first."

"I'm sorry," Ron said. "Here, let me help you," he added, slipping her coat off her shoulders and down her arms as Paul did the same for Karen. "I'll put them in my bedroom," he said, taking Paul's coat as well as Karen's and walking into his bedroom just to the right of the fireplace hearth.

"Are you going to leave yours on, Leg?" Paul asked as Ron walked out of the bedroom.

"I forgot," he answered, embarrassed and preoccupied with Debbie and the beating of his heart as he unzipped his coat and threw it on the bed with the rest. "There, I'm ready," he proclaimed as he joined the others gathered in the middle of the recreation room.

"Here, Polly, this is for you," Wesley said as he handed her a full cup of beer.

"Thank you," Polly said, accepting the cup.

"And, Karen, this is for you."

"Not too much, Wesley," she said.

"This isn't too much," he replied, handing her a full cup as well.

"And finally, Debbie, this is for you," he concluded, handing her a full cup, too. "Legend, you and Sorenson are on your own. The keg's sitting on the patio running clear. Help yourself."

"Thanks, Wesley," they answered in unison, moving toward the keg. "I think we can handle it," Ron added as both he and Paul found cups and filled them to the top before walking back into the recreation room, closing the sliding glass doors behind them.

"To Greater Northwest Living," Wesley said in his favorite salute, elevating his wide-mouthed cup in his right hand.

"Greater Northwest Living," Ron and Paul answered, elevating their cups as well.

"Well," Wesley said, "I see three cups still lowered. Are you ready."

Karen looked at Debbie, who blushed and looked back at Karen. Then Polly smiled and proclaimed, "We're ready," as she elevated her cup.

"Greater Northwest Living," the three of them said somewhat tentatively, raising their cups as high as they could.

"That's it," Wesley said as they all drank. "And now a few sounds to make it official," he added, moving to his stereo and selecting the appropriate record.

Ron and Paul both knew what was coming and they were ready. As the stereo needle caught the grooves of the record, the three charter members of The River Road Athletic Club, with Ron forgetting his irregular heartbeat for the moment, locked arms and joined Manfred Mann in his impassioned tribute to the indomitable spirit of 'The Mighty Quinn.'

"Is Wesley the 'Mighty Quinn?'" Debbie asked as a relative calm settled in over the Athletic Club while they awaited the arrival of the Friday night regulars, highlighted by the appearance of Steve and Sue Carlson and Ken and Judith Griswold.

"I don't know," Ron answered as they sat together on the couch resting along the outside of his bedroom wall. "But of the three of us, I suppose he has to be. He's in a class by himself, believe me."

"I believe you," Debbie said, laughing. "I've never seen anyone like him."

"'The Mighty Quinn' just seemed to belong with us this year, and I have to say that so far it's been one of the highlights of my life."

"Are all three of you going to be here next year?" Debbie asked, taking a drink of her beer.

"I don't know, but I doubt it. Wesley's seriously thinking about quitting teaching, and if he does, he'll certainly leave Lebanon. And Paul, well, you can see for yourself. He and Karen aren't exactly a casual couple. And he's not Wesley nor is she Polly."

"I know," Debbie said. "I think they're pretty serious."

"Well," Ron said, drinking his Budweiser, "Paul's a good man. I don't think Karen could do any better."

"I know she doesn't think so. As far as she's concerned, he's the one. And what about you? Are you going to stay in teaching?"

"If I didn't teach, I don't know what I'd do. I belong in teaching, but it's not easy. Things are changing and so am I. Nothing is as definite as it used to be, it seems, and I'm still figuring out who I am with regard to teaching. I'm not sure where I stand, but I have to stand somewhere. Sometimes I can really be torn, but I know I'm a teacher. Wesley says anyone can teach English, and in a way he's right. But he's wrong at the same time. I don't think just anyone can teach English the way it should be taught."

"Do you know how it should be taught?"

"Not exactly, but I do know that teaching English has to be more of an inspiration than anything else. If a person's inspired, the rest will follow."

"You mean the way English should be taught?"

"I think so," Ron answered.

"Do you think it's safe?"

"What?" Ron asked in return.

"Your approach to teaching," Debbie answered.

"I don't know, but life is never an adventure for anyone too interested in safety. I think you have to plunge into it and take your chances. You have to follow the path of your heart regardless of the dangers. It's the way to experience life."

"Maybe you're the 'Mighty Quinn,'" Debbie said as she took a sip of her beer and lifted her eyes toward Ron.

"I just want to be Ron Petrich, that's all. That song, together with The River Road Athletic Club, makes me smile, but I'm not interested in being 'The Mighty Quinn.' I'm just interested in being Ron Petrich, which means I'd like another beer, and I'd like to show you around for a few minutes. Are you ready? Would you like another beer?"

"I would like to see the house more closely, but I'll wait on the beer. You go ahead, though."

"Okay," Ron said, standing up from the couch and offering Debbie his right hand. "A quick trip to the patio, and I'll show you around."

"Okay," Debbie replied, accepting his hand as Ron's heart pounded at their touch. "I'm ready," she added, getting up from the couch as Ron gently clasped her left hand in his right hand and walked toward the sliding glass doors and the concrete patio on which rested the Budweiser keg, Wesley's "nectar of the gods."

Ron had a chance to show Debbie the house before the scheduled guests arrived, and he was able to explain the color television set to her and why he had the responsibility to buy it after Paul proved to be primarily responsible for the house and Wesley had provided the stereo. He told her how he had come to Lebanon just last January, when he only owned the clock radio he had won in a high school composition contest, but now he had stepped up in the world with his color television. She was impressed with the television and with the house in general after he gave her the grand tour, starting with the living room and kitchen and ending with the three bedrooms. Ron felt more comfortable in her company during and after the tour, although his heart still pounded uncontrollably whenever his eyes focused on her radiant beauty. He tried to remind himself that he was a 23-year-old man who shouldn't be acting so foolishly, but under the spell of Love he had no choice.

After Ron showed Debbie around The River Road Athletic Club, the festival guests began to arrive, and he settled into the evening, introducing Debbie to a variety of people—some of whom he liked and some of whom he disliked. Some guests appreciated and respected the Athletic Club while others saw it as a place they could use with little room for such appreciation. The unappreciative and disrespectful always performed the loudest, and Ron had no respect for those revelers. Still, no one ever could accuse any charter member of the Athletic Club of shying away from the keg. When he was alone, Ron could make the rounds with the best of them, but he was more selective when in the company of a date. And in the company of Debbie Wright he was even more so. He wouldn't leave her alone to be at the mercy of the indiscriminate revelers feeling their Budweiser.

The Carlsons and the Griswolds arrived shortly after the first guests made their appearance and Ron didn't waste any time introducing Debbie to them. He could tell his friends intimidated her because she wasn't used to parties where the people in attendance were beyond their college years. Besides, Ron had told her that the Carlsons and the Griswolds belonged to an elite class, as far as he was concerned. Still, the initial meeting proved to be pleasant and Debbie appeared relaxed, if not overly confident, in their presence. Steve said they had heard about her before they had ever seen her because Wesley had told him at work that Ron had come across her at school and that he could talk about nothing else for a week. She blushed when Steve mentioned the high school library but said she had noticed Ron as well. Steve told her he was happy to meet her and easily could see why Ron might feel compelled to talk about her. Debbie felt the blood rush to her cheeks as Sue told Steve that maybe he'd better have another beer. And all the time Ken Griswold stood by quietly and mysteriously as Judith sipped her brandy and waited for the appropriate moment to play her guitar.

The evening unfolded in typical River Road Athletic Club fashion, with guests filling the living room and the recreation room as well as the kitchen. Wesley left Polly to her own devices as he made the rounds, making sure that each reveler had a full cup of beer and announcing to everyone that they should feel free to drink heartily because there was more where that came from. To Wesley, making a second run to the Town Tavern meant a triumph for Greater Northwest Living. Ron usually accompanied him, but this time, once Wesley had collected the necessary money, he hardly noticed his absence. As usual, Ron was feeling his Budweiser, but he was well-schooled in the morality of temperance. And he didn't fall in love with Debbie because of the Budweiser. Such love lasted only as long as the effect of the beer. In this case, however, that same beer—Wesley's "nectar of the gods"—only helped to release what already had been brewing in his heart.

He was determined to take it slowly this time, as he continually reminded Wesley and Paul when they inquired about his condition throughout the evening. For the most part Ron was oblivious to the rest of the guests, choosing to spend time, exclusively, with Debbie who proved to feel just as comfortable with him as the evening wore on. They enjoyed each other's company, and more than once their eyes met for extended periods of time. During such meetings Ron's heart always, and uncontrollably, found its way to his throat and he hoped Debbie's did the same. Several times they danced to the slower music of The Wee Five and The Mommas and the Poppas that Wesley played on the stereo, although they didn't hold each other in the same clinch that Wesley and Polly affected nor did they dance with the familiar closeness manifested in Paul and Karen's togetherness. Neither of them took any formless liberties on their first date. But they danced close enough for Ron to feel the softness of Debbie's cheek against his own face and for his nose to pick up the still bewitching scent of her perfume. Ken Griswold stood in the corner between the kitchen and the sliding glass doors, observing Ron in action as Judith played her guitar in the living room, sometimes joined by Paul, and Steve and Sue stood on the other side of Ken, closer to the doors and the keg, where Sue paid particularly close attention to Ron and his vision of delight.

The bathroom Paul and Ron normally shared was reserved for the female guests; and well into the evening, following The Mommas and the Poppas' rendition of 'This is Dedicated to the One I Love'—that Ron always felt paled in comparison to The Shirelles' original version—Debbie excused herself, shortly to be joined by Karen who had temporarily left Paul in the living room playing his guitar duet with Judith. Left alone for one of the few times that evening and aware of the watchful eyes of Steve, Sue, and Ken, Ron took the opportunity to find out what they had concluded so far.

"Well," he said as he approached the three of them standing in the corner with Ken leaning against the wall and Steve leaning against the sliding glass doors, "what do you think?"

"I think I need a refill," Steve answered, grinning as he slid the doors open, letting in the crisp, December air. "It's the best beer I've ever had," he added, imitating Wesley.

"Have you ever had a bad one?" Ken asked as Steve filled his cup and stepped back into the corner, closing the door behind him.

"Probably not. But I do have to say that it runs more clear at the Athletic Club than it does anywhere else except, maybe, for our back deck. Now I can think more clearly about Ron's, or should I say the Legend's, inquiry."

"I'll tell you what I think," Sue said. "But first of all I'm interested in what you think."

"I think I'm done for again," Ron said as Judith and Paul played in the background and tried to sing Simon and Garfunkel's 'Bridge Over Troubled Water.' "What can I say? When I look into her eyes, it's all over. I shouldn't look at her, but I can't help it. I wish I were different, but I'm not. Sometimes I wish I could be more like Wesley. Nothing bothers him. Or I wish I could be more like Paul, who's always calm and more in control. But I look at Debbie, and something comes over me that reminds me of the stories I teach about knights and their ladies and how their hearts beat uncontrollably at the sight of their beloved. Love, and never the beloved herself, always makes those knights foolish. That's exactly how I feel. Do you see what I mean?"

"Nope," Steve answered. "I don't trust anything about stories of knights and their ladies. I only trust the river and what I can build with my own hands. I might believe in love, but I don't believe in the love you describe. Budweiser has made a fool out of me more than once," he added, looking down at his cup and smiling, "but never love."

"Ken, how about you?" Ron asked. "Do you see what I mean?"

"A little, but I'm not sure. I have to say you're fun to watch. Is this how you earned your title of the Legend?"

"I suppose so. I enjoy the title as much as anyone would, but I'm just an ordinary individual who's somehow moved by the power of Love. It's an overwhelming passion and rapture, and as corny as it may sound, it truly does come from the heart. It's like one heart in possession of another. Tonight, with Debbie, I can feel it as powerfully as ever, and I can't hold back. It's like magic and I have to follow its course. Sue, what do you think?"

"I think you may be too much for Debbie. I'm not sure she's a match for you, although she's awfully attractive. Beware of the blonde sphinx syndrome. She may be fragile and shallow, and as she gets to know you, she may become afraid. You're not the safest man in the world, you know, to anyone interested in security. I think anyone can be governed by the love you mention, but I don't think all of us allow ourselves to be. It's scary and I don't know about Debbie. But you have to find out. And to find out, you have to follow your heart. You have to follow that natural path and see what happens."

"I don't think I can do anything else. But I would like to be more careful this time. Maybe you're right, Sue. Maybe the others were afraid."

"The others?" Ken asked, still leaning against the wall.

"I can tell that Debbie likes me and that she enjoys being with me, but in my past experiences, I always end up being left in the cold. Maybe fear does play a part."

"Fear of what?" Ken asked, moving away from the wall.

"Fear of the adventurous path of Love," Sue answered. "It's not the well-traveled path, and sticking with Ron means walking that path. That's his charm, which then scares the timid that, I'm afraid, includes most of us. If we truly believe in anything beyond the level of expediency, we believe in marriage. That becomes our religion. But Ron believes in Love, and if Debbie does, too, they'll be compatible for life.

However, if Debbie believes in marriage or if she's another woman of expedience, for whatever reason, they won't be compatible for long."

"So, what do you think so far?" Steve asked.

"I haven't observed her long enough, but I think I can safely say that she's interested in more than expedience. Whether or not she's ready for the adventure Ron promises remains to be seen. She could be too shallow and fragile or she could be just the woman such an adventure requires."

"How do you know so much about this subject?" Steve asked, looking her in the eye.

"I don't think those stories Ron mentions are lies, for one thing," Sue answered. "And for another," she added, flashing her inviting smile, "life with you has been more of an adventure than you might think."

"I think I need another beer," Steve replied. "You ready, Ken?"

"Why not?" he answered, moving toward the sliding glass doors. "I can't dance."

"What about you, Legend?" Steve asked.

"I have to take it easy on the beer. I think I've had enough for right now. Besides, with this second keg, I'm sure some will be left when I get back from taking Debbie home."

"You must be enraptured by love or something," Steve said from the patio as he opened the spigot, filling his cup and Ken's as well. "I'm not used to you holding back."

"Usually I don't, but tonight's different and Debbie's different. Some night when I'm alone, we'll 'let it all hang out,' as Wesley says."

"I don't think that'll be anytime soon," Ken said, smiling, as he took his full cup from Steve.

"Maybe not," Ron said. "We'll have to wait and see."

"Well, don't wait too much longer," Sue said, nodding her head in the direction of the fireplace. "Debbie looks fairly alone over there with Karen."

"You're right," Ron acknowledged. "I'd better get over there. See you all later," he concluded as he turned and walked toward the fireplace.

"Greater Northwest Living," he heard Steve proclaim as Debbie smiled at his return.

"Steve's having a good time," she said as Ron turned and stood by her right side,

"He always does. I've never met anyone like him. He's an honest man and someone to trust. And he likes his Budweiser. I've always felt honored to drink with him."

"I'm okay here with Karen if you'd like to talk with him a little more."

"No, that's all right," Ron said, feeling the blush in his cheeks. "I think I'll stay here."

"I guess that means I can rejoin Paul in the living room," Karen said. "I like to listen to him play his guitar with Judith. Isn't that her name?"

"Yes," Ron answered.

"I like her," Karen said. "She has a nice sense of humor."

"I know. And she's a dedicated teacher. I don't know what I'd do without her in the faculty room."

"What about her husband? Is it Ken?" Debbie asked. "He seems awfully quiet."

"He is, but he doesn't miss anything. He's a great observer. He and Steve make a good pair, and I like being around him. I like his humility."

"And Sue?" Debbie asked.

"Steve's awfully lucky. Sue's an authentic woman. She and Steve deserve each other, and both of them, in different ways, are good friends of mine. And I trust her insight."

"Well," Karen said, "I'm going to leave the two of you alone now. I hear Paul warming up to play his rendition of 'Teen Angel.'"

"I think a lot of people hear the same," Ron said as he watched the remainder of the revelers leave the music of the recreation room and head for the living room and the crowd gathered around Judith and Paul. "Do you want to join them, Debbie?"

"I like it here by the fireplace," she answered as Karen turned and walked toward the gathering crowd. "But I'll join the others in the living room if you want to."

"That's okay. I like it here, too," Ron said, catching Steve's eye as he and Ken and Sue left their corner to join everyone else in the living room.

"You have a nice house and I like this fireplace," Debbie said, sitting down on the elevated stone hearth.

"Yes," Ron said. "It's a great place, and it's been a good year," he added, sitting down next to her at her right side and holding his cup of Budweiser in his right hand. The room emptied quickly, the stereo music stopped, and Ron made no attempt to replace the stack of records on the turntable.

For a few minutes Ron and Debbie sat side by side on the stone hearth, each alone with his or her own thoughts as the sound of Paul's voice accompanied his famous guitar rendering of 'Teen Angel.' Although most listeners saw 'Teen Angel' as more of a novelty song, the devotion of Love, that the songs of Ron's high school era celebrated, curiously reinforced his own feelings with regard to Debbie and the actual Religion of Love that, he discovered, helped to define him. He thought of Ricky Nelson's 'Hello, Mary Lou' and had to recognize it as the anthem of the 20th century expression of Medieval courtly love. Ron was a Medieval courtly lover living in the 20th century, and nobody really understood, although Paul—and most likely Sue—came close. He wasn't sure Debbie understood or would understand, but if such love were natural to him, it had to be natural to everyone. He wasn't a special person.

The courtly love of Amor had to identify a way of life that flowered amidst the marriage-ordered society of the Middle Ages, but it must have always been around waiting its chance. And the Church supported the social structure built on marriage with the sanctioned marriages having little to do with one individual's discriminate love for another individual. But the Love that struggled to blossom amidst a contrary social order only drew laughter or disbelief by 1967. The post-Vatican II Catholic Church did nothing to recognize a social order built on the Amor of the courageous courtly lovers who responded to the call of Love, even if it meant an eternity in the Church's fires of Hell. Belief in the reality of those fires may have subsided in the latter half of the 20th century, but Ron still walked alone in a land and in a time where that very Love of majesty and creative power elicited laughter at best.

Still, he remained locked in its power and committed to its path. He sat on the stone hearth next to Debbie Wright, in the presence of his beloved, knowing that, at least for him, the eyes and the heart agreed which meant that true love was born. But only true lovers know of the connection between the eyes and the heart, and only true lovers do not fear the promise of adventure. He felt sure that Debbie wasn't another child of expedience and thought she could be a child of Love. But he knew she was a product of a social order known to produce children of marriage. The more he knew himself, the more he hoped Debbie matched his devotion. For now, anyway, the rapture was sweet. He turned his head toward her and their eyes intertwined.

"I know it's cold outside," he said as Paul continued with his rendition of 'Teen Angel,' "but I'd like to show you the back yard and the canal. Is that crazy?"

"Not at all," Debbie answered, smiling and looking directly at him. "I'd like to see it while the moon is so bright. Besides, I have my winter coat with the fur collar. I don't think I'll freeze."

"Wait here then," Ron said, getting up from his seat on the hearth. "I'll get our coats."

"I won't go anywhere," Debbie answered as Ron stepped into his bedroom. "I like it here."

"Well, here we are," Ron said as he quickly returned to the stone hearth, carrying the coats.

"Thank you," Debbie said, standing up and turning her back toward Ron so that he could slip her coat over her arms and onto her shoulders.

"It's the chivalrous thing to do," he said as he fixed her coat on her shoulders.

"What was that?" she asked, buttoning her top button.

"Nothing," Ron answered. "I just said it was my pleasure," he added, slipping into his own blue winter coat. "Shall we go?" he asked, gesturing toward the sliding glass doors with his left hand. It was late into the festival and only the true believers remained, gathered around Judith and Paul in the living room. Wesley and Polly were nowhere to be seen as Ron opened the sliding glass doors, and he and Debbie stepped out onto the concrete patio.

"I'm glad it's not raining," she said, looking up at the bright light of the full moon. "I like these clear and crisp evenings."

"So do I," Ron said. "Mrs Williams, from the Gables Motel, used to say the same thing about Montana winters."

"Do you know Mrs Williams?"

"Yes. She was my main ally when I first came to Lebanon last January and didn't know a soul. I stayed at the Gables when I interviewed for the job with Dr Harrison and Mr Polk. I don't know what I would have done without her. She made me feel at home, just as if I never left in the first place. Do you know her?"

"Not really, but I know of her. I think everyone in Lebanon knew her, and I never heard anyone say an unkind word about her. Didn't she move to Montana?"

"Yes. She grew up in Billings, but she moved to Butte and now runs a motel there. She used to tell me that she missed the clear, crisp nights of Montana winters. I don't think she ever fully adapted to our rain."

"I don't notice it too much, but I can understand what Mrs Williams meant about clear, crisp nights of Montana winters. Shall we step off the patio so you can show me the canal?"

"Sure," he answered as he felt his heart move toward his throat. Be calm, he told himself, and go slow. Be careful, he thought. "C'mon," he added, reaching for her left hand with his right. "We'll stand under the filbert tree," he said, nodding in the direction of the canal bank.

"Okay," Debbie said, stepping off the patio and giving Ron her hand. "Lead the way," she added as Ron walked slightly in front of her toward the canal, gently clasping her left hand in his right hand as his heart beat faster and lodged itself securely in his throat.

"There it is," he said, pointing with his left hand at the running water glistening in the moonlight. "Nobody's jumped into it yet during one of our Friday festivals, but I wouldn't put it past some of our guests. But it's nice to have the canal in the back yard," he continued, moving closer to Debbie. "Are you cold?"

"Just a little," she answered a Ron dropped her hand and put his right arm around her shoulders. "That feels better," she said, snuggling closer to him so that he could feel the side of her body next to his. "Can I ask you a question?" she inquired, welcoming Ron's arm around her.

"Sure," he answered, turning to meet her eyes. "Go ahead."

"I've been wondering. Why do your friends refer to you as Leg or the Legend?"

"I knew you were going to ask me that," he said, shaking his head.

"You have to admit it's unique. I've never heard anyone referred to as the Legend. How did you acquire that title?"

"It's not quite as arrogant as it can sound."

"I don't think it's arrogant. I think it's curious and interesting."

"Well," Ron continued, keeping his right arm around Debbie's shoulders, "you know how guys can get together and exchange stories of their past as a way of getting to know one another?"

"Yes," Debbie answered, listening carefully and smiling with her eyes as Ron's heart pounded.

"Paul and Wesley and I exchanged stories after I met them, and in the course of relating my past to them, I made the comment, humorously of course, that I was a legend in my own time. They laughed and the name stuck. But it really doesn't mean any more than that."

"The stories you told must have been interesting, though, for the name to stick," Debbie said as her eyes continued to smile.

"I don't know, but that's how I became the Legend. It's fun, but I'm just who I am. That's all. I don't want to be anyone else."

"I don't know much about the Legend, but I like being here with you," she said, gently laying her head against his right shoulder.

"I like the moonlight," Ron said, turning to his right in response and moving his arm to the small of her back where he could feel the contour of her waist through her coat.

"So do I," she said, meeting his eyes as both of them stood parallel to the canal under the moonlight gently filtering through the barren branches of the native filbert tree. It wasn't the crystalline bed of Tristan and Isolt, but it was a canopy of Love nonetheless. And they moved closer together under its protection.

Don't say anything, Ron told himself as he stood with Debbie under the canopy. Just go slow and enjoy the moment. Don't push it and don't rush into anything, he cautioned himself as he drew his arms up Debbie's side until his hands found the warmth of her fur collar. His heart beat a thousand times a minute as he looked into her moonlit eyes and told himself not to make any future commitments just now. You have to make it harder, he told himself. You can't make it seem like you can't live without her, he added. You told Wesley and Paul this experience would be different. Now live up to what you said, he continued as Debbie moved closer to him. "I like your collar," he said, gently pressing the fur against her cheeks.

"So do I," she said in response as Ron moved his hands from the fur collar and down the length of her arms until they found the small of her back. He put his arms around her back as she slipped her arms around his neck, and they embraced in the shadowed moonlight.

Don't say anything else, Ron told himself. Just kiss her and leave it at that and maybe call next week, he continued, talking to himself as he felt the closeness of her body pressed tightly against his—winter coats and all. But he looked into her eyes as she looked into his, and the power of the rapture was too much to resist. He forgot what he said to Wesley and Paul and he forgot his promise to himself. His thoughts only were of Debbie and the magical power of Love. "Would you like to go to a movie tomorrow night?" he asked before he even realized it.

"I'd love to," Debbie answered as she tightened her arms around him, still looking into his eyes as the full moon illuminated their natural canopy.

"I'll pick you up at seven," he said, and as his heart pounded in his chest and throat, they kissed tenderly and honestly, sealing the enchanted moment forever.

# THE DECISION

## XVIII

While the Religion of Love certainly renders one foolish, in the tradition of Shakespeare's "wise man," it just as certainly does not render one frivolous, as Ron's life as a high school English teacher proved. It's true that Wesley was fond of saying anyone could be an English teacher, but no one could conclude that such a comment inspired Ron. The Religion of Love provided him with all the inspiration he needed, and in keeping with it, his ties, sport coats, and slacks served as his priestly vestments. His classroom was his altar, and his religion reminded him of his responsibility to lead his students along the path of the unbounded adventure of learning. But Lebanon was a Protestant town steeped in the boundaried confines of the Bible, and Ron was a Catholic just as steeped in the more expansive imagery and symbolism of the Holy Sacrifice of the Mass. With the subsequent reform of the sacrificial altar, as a result of Vatican II, Ron struggled to discover and preserve the unbounded expansiveness of that imagery and symbolism. He kept his struggle private, but being such a catholic teacher in Lebanon's boundaried environment created a teaching situation built on a foundation of honest conflict.

He was familiar with the stories of the Bible, but he wasn't schooled in them in the manner of his Protestant counterparts. Supported by the ritual of the Mass, he was schooled in the Roman Catholic catechism which clearly outlined a way of life—a philosophy—that promised to lead the believer to eternal life in Heaven in the presence of the Beatific Vision of God. Ron pledged to obey that philosophy, solidly built on St. Augustine's concept of original sin in the Garden of Eden. But he never experienced any way of life built on obedience to the biblical authority devoid of the magic of consecrations, transubstantiations, and beatific visions of his Catholic past. As a result, he tended to view biblical stories, even the formative story of Adam and Eve and original sin, in a manner similar to how he viewed stories made up by the English and American writers he was supposed to teach. His church's post-Vatican II emphasis on pulpit sermons, celebrating a life of social and community service in the name of religion, forced him to question the understanding of life and responsibility the previous church authority had taught him. Such curiosity set him apart from his teaching peers and initiated the conflict of duties that would determine the course of the continuing adventure of his life.

He was aware of his social duty to respect and to adhere to the standard curriculum of his high school English department, but such a plan didn't always accommodate his childlike curiosity, consistently awakened by the magical, silent sermon identified with his pre-Vatican II Catholic Church. He was curious about the origin of language, for example, and the senior English curriculum called for a two-week study of the development of the English language as an introduction to the standard survey of English literature from 'Beowulf,' the epic poem from the Anglo-Saxon past, to the present day—at least to the 20th century. The accompanying teacher's manual came complete with lesson plans and guidelines showing the teacher how to present the material to the students. If followed to the letter, the introductory section on the development of the English language easily could be completed in the allotted two weeks, allowing the teacher to proceed on time with the rest of the curriculum plan.

Ron respected the curriculum and its time allotments, but never having studied the development of English himself, he couldn't stifle his curiosity about the development of language in general. He brought that curiosity to his classroom and asked his students about the origins of language, as much for the benefit of his own quest as for theirs. He didn't know what answers to expect from high school seniors who very seldom, if ever, entertained such a question. But that's the purpose of a classroom, he thought, and he asked the question—only to be greeted with the immediate answer that identified the biblical story of the Tower of Babel as providing the definitive answer.

Ron didn't know the exact answer, or answers, to his question, but he was certain the Tower of Babel didn't provide anything so conclusive. He respected his student's sincere belief and didn't know how to respond. He didn't want to tamper with a student's faith because he didn't think he had that right. Besides, he had nothing substantial, as yet, with which to replace it should he be instrumental in its destruction. Had the student given the answer in a flippant manner, he could have reacted against the flippancy, if not in favor of the answer itself. As it was, he didn't know what to say, beyond commenting that such an immediate and definitive answer represented only one way of dealing with the question.

From then on, however, he was careful and began to sense his separation from, and even opposition to, any way of life built on such an answer. He couldn't simply let it go as just another passing comment because he found such unquestionable, biblical certainty destructive to the unbounded adventure of learning. It was in September, almost three months before he met his "vision of delight," and already the conflict, which would plague him throughout the year of The River Road Athletic Club, had begun in earnest. And it didn't take long for Wesley and Paul to become involved.

Wesley would have preferred to keep up his break-neck pace every night of the week, and Ron wasn't above trying his best to keep up with him. But at times the three of them found themselves home together at the Athletic Club with no poker night and no Friday festival to anticipate. On such a night their conversations centered around school and teaching—most often around Ron's school and his teaching. And on this particular Monday night in mid-September, almost three months before Debbie Wright, their conversation quickly turned to Ron's teaching life at Lebanon Union High School.

"Well, Legend," Wesley said after the three of them had cleared the dining table and placed the dishes in the dishwasher and before Ron retired to his bedroom to correct papers and prepare himself for the next day, "how's LHS treating you in your first full year?"

"Not bad. I don't feel as much like a rookie this year. I'm not an accomplished veteran by any means, like the two of you, but I'm getting there. At least I'm getting to know the school and the town better. It's interesting but not so easy."

"What do you mean?" Paul asked.

"You guys know that I was raised a Catholic," Ron answered, warming to the occasion, "and that I took it as seriously as I could, for whatever reason."

"That's the understatement of the year," Wesley said. "I'll never forget last spring when you missed Mass to go to the coast. I'd never seen anything like it."

"That's because you Protestants aren't quite as well-schooled in the virtue of obedience as we Catholics," Ron said, smiling.

"What do you mean by that?" Paul asked. "I used to take religion pretty seriously myself. But since then I've learned that science makes more sense."

"I know about you and religion and science," Ron said. "You've forced me to think about many things since I've known you, and you're a formidable challenge. But blatant disobedience is as grave a sin as a Catholic can commit. Sins of the flesh, as I call the most common variety, very rarely are sins of disobedience because we can cite so many excuses for falling victim to them. We don't always participate in those acts with the full consent of the will in defiance of God."

"But what if there's no God?" Paul asked.

"Then I guess there's no sense of sin. But I can't believe there is no God or that there isn't something to God. We might have to redefine

God in relation to the truth of your science—and I'm working on that—but life without God, whatever it means, would be missing something I don't want to live without."

"Yes," Paul said, looking Ron in the eye, "but can you prove, scientifically, that God exists? How do we know that Christ ever existed?"

"I wish you wouldn't ask such easy questions," Ron answered, shaking his head. "But I don't think God is scientific. I think scientific discovery can help lead us to a more mature understanding of God, although I can't say what that is just now."

"But you will someday, I'm sure," Wesley broke in, throwing back his head to get his hair out of his eyes. "If you don't, you'll kill yourself trying."

"Maybe," Ron said, smiling, "but I can't think of any idea more important or more interesting."

"Still," Paul persisted, "what if Christ never existed?"

"What difference does is make?" Ron asked in response.

"What difference does it make?" Paul asked, exasperated. "If Christ never existed, then it's all fake. It's just made up."

"So what?"

"So what?" Paul replied, lifting his eyes to the ceiling. "If something's made up, it's not real. It's not true."

"I'm not so sure about that."

"What do you mean?" Wesley asked.

"For the sake of argument," Ron answered, "just assume that Christ lived historically. Okay?"

"Okay," they both answered simultaneously.

"I think that historical Christ would be irrelevant today," Ron continued.

"Why?" Paul asked.

"Because we live in a different historical time, and any historical figure is trapped in his historical time."

"Would there be another Christ then, by any chance?" Paul asked, still fixing his eyes on Ron.

"I don't know. But I think it has to have something to do with the imagination. For now I guess I'd call this other Christ the Christ of the imagination. I don't understand them thoroughly enough yet, but this Christ reminds me of the stories I teach. And I'm learning more everyday."

"That's nice," Wesley said, "but what does it all have to do with knowing the school and town better, and what does it have to do with the virtue of obedience?"

"Wesley's right, Legend," Paul said. "What's the connection?"

"You see, I had a hard time going to the coast last spring because I knew I'd have no excuses, such as youthful curiosity, for example, for missing Mass, for committing a sin of the heart. Do you understand? It's an act accompanied by the full consent of the will which makes it as close to a defiance of God as you can get. It wasn't easy for me to go to the coast that day."

"Yes, but you went," Wesley said with a broad smile.

"I know, but, believe me, it wasn't easy."

"So, why did you go?" Paul asked.

"Because the Church, the modern Church, had nothing of power to draw me to it."

"What kind of power?" Paul asked. "I can understand scientific power."

"I don't know what to call it, but we used to call the Mass the magic show in the days before the Second Vatican Council. The magic wasn't scientific, but it was there. I could feel it. But I haven't felt it since the conclusion of the Council. And that's why I wasn't disobedient when I accompanied Wesley to the coast that Sunday."

"What do you mean?" Wesley asked.

"If the magic had been there, I know I would have gone to Mass first. I can be many things, but I can't be disobedient. Without obedience, however we ultimately define it, there can be no love. And without love we are left with only sound and fury, as far as I can tell. Anyway, I wasn't disobedient when I went to the coast, and thus I avoided the sin of the heart. I was bothered for quite a while but not any more. In fact, I think today's Church is disobedient and therefore guilty of that sin of the heart. How can I obey such a Church?"

"I suppose you can't," Paul answered. "It makes sense when I listen to you explain obedience. Maybe you Catholics weren't so bad after all."

"I don't know about that, but I think there's a difference between church and religion, even if I can't explain it. Before the Vatican Council I think I always associated the Church with religion. And I sought to obey religion, which now appears to be more tolerant and more understanding than church."

"So then, what's religion?" Wesley asked.

"I think religion is Love. But don't ask me to explain it just yet. Give me a few years. It's going to take some time."

"So, we should obey Love?" Paul asked. "Isn't that right?"

"I think so, but it's still unfolding for me. I'm just beginning to understand what I've always tried to obey. I don't know why, but I always have. And I feel a certain kinship with Adam and Eve in the Garden of Eden."

"You don't believe that story, do you?" Paul asked incredulously.

"Not scientifically or historically anymore," Ron answered, "but I'm not willing to dismiss it, either. Lately I've entertained the thought that maybe Adam and Eve did the right thing in the Garden."

"But nobody did anything in any garden. Don't you see?" Paul asked.

'Yes, I see. But the fact that nobody did anything in any garden doesn't make the Garden of Eden story a lie. That story's the foundation of our religion, and if it's a lie, so is our religion. And I can't dismiss religion as being a lie to be replaced by science. In fact, I don't know too much about other bible stories, but I doubt if any of them are meant to be scientifically and historically true, and certainly not the story of the Tower of Babel."

"Who cares?" Wesley asked. "It seems pretty irrelevant to me anyway."

"I know what you mean," Ron said, "but I came face to face with the Tower of Babel today."

"Is that what you meant about getting to know the school and the town better?" Paul asked.

"Yes, and I'm still shocked. I've never heard anyone refer to a bible story as being a record of such solid historical facts—other than the story of Christ's birth, death, and resurrection, that is. Because of our need for redemption for original sin, that story, taken as historical fact, always made sense. But I can't easily accept the doctrine of original sin anymore. As historical fact, even the story of Christ doesn't ring true. But the Tower of Babel is something else again."

"How did the Tower of Babel come up in English class in the first place?" Wesley asked.

"Have you ever been curious about the origins of language?" Ron asked, countering with a question of his own.

"Now that I think about it," Wesley answered, "not particularly. What about you, Paul?"

"I've thought about it a little, I guess. And there has to be a satisfying, scientific answer."

"Not according to one of my students or to her teaching authority, either," Ron said. "And furthermore, I'm sure not according to Lebanon."

"What do you mean?" Paul asked.

"I asked one of my classes about the origins of language. The curriculum calls for me to teach a section on the development of the English language, and, besides, I've been thinking about it myself."

"I see," Wesley said as his eyes lit up, "and one of your students responded with a reference to the Tower of Babel. Even I've heard of that story, and no one ever expected me to take religion seriously—anyway not as seriously as The Wall Street Journal and life's sensual pleasures."

"So," Paul said, sitting on the edge of his chair, "what happened. I'm curious."

"As I said," Ron answered, shrugging his shoulders and lifting his palms to the ceiling, "I asked about the origins of language, expecting either nothing or some answer having to do with cavemen and grunts and groans or something like that. But this girl, in all seriousness and with total commitment to belief, identified the Tower of Babel as the answer."

"What did you say?" Wesley asked.

"At first I didn't know what to say. I was completely surprised. But I had to accept her commitment, even though I couldn't accept the answer. An occurrence as complex as the development of language demands an answer just as complex. My student's answer left no room for adventure or exploration."

"Neither would such an answer regarding the Garden of Eden story," Paul said.

"That's exactly the problem I'm referring to. The school and Lebanon, I think, would be more inclined to accept an interpretation of religion more closely related to such an historically definitive answer. On the other hand, I'd be more inclined to accept an interpretation more closely related to a scientific answer to the same question. A scientific answer allows for some investigation and adventure. It would be more expansive. Thus any interpretation of religion that followed would be equally as expansive."

"Lebanon isn't the most expansive of towns," Paul said. "It's solidly built on the Grange Hall and the Protestant Church. And both are well entrenched."

"May I ask what all this has to do with teaching English?" Wesley asked. "What's the big deal. Can't anyone teach English anywhere?"

"English, referring to literature, is an expression of the imagination," Ron said. "To study it, then, is to study the depth of the imagination and to learn its secrets. The issue here is bigger than the Tower of Babel. If that story isn't true, in accord with my student's belief, then religion isn't true either. And religion has to be true in some way. You can't just throw it out. You can throw out the bath water, but you'd better keep the baby. I wish Lebanon were more expansive. I think I'm more expansive personally, and I'd like to teach English in a school and in a town where I could be compatible with both."

"And you don't think you can be compatible with Lebanon?" Wesley asked.

"I don't know for how long."

"Then it's easy," Wesley said, shrugging his shoulders.

"How?" Ron asked.

"Quit teaching," Wesley answered, smiling and turning the palms of his hands toward the ceiling.

"But I'm a teacher. Don't you understand?"

"I'm a teacher, too. But I'm not going to teach math and music all my life. This year certainly could be my last."

"What about you, Paul?" Ron asked. "You must understand."

"I think I do, but I don't think teaching's worth the effort. The rewards just aren't there."

"But if I don't teach, I don't know what I'll do. If I hadn't discovered student teaching and the fact that I actually could teach effectively, I don't know what I would have done after college. I'm a teacher, pure and simple, and I think I have to make a stand as to what direction my career will take. Everything's confused. Some people are growing their hair long and some are keeping it short. And somehow the length of a person's hair has become associated with moral behavior, or the lack of it. I don't want to look like a hippie freak. On the other hand, I don't want to look like a crew cut jock, either. And even I wore a crew cut from the fourth grade until my senior year at Seattle U. But hair style wasn't an issue then. Life was stable, and we didn't have to worry about Christs of the imagination and the Garden of Eden and the Tower of Babel. But now we do. It's exciting and scary at the same time."

"And it's all because of science," Paul said.

"Not exactly. I think it's all because we want to understand, or at least some of us do, and that desire has led to science. I have nothing against it because I prefer the flush toilet to the outhouse. But life can't be all science. You can't have science at the expense of religion any more than you can have religion at the expense of science."

"Well," Wesley said, standing up from his chair and running his right hand through his thick, blonde hair, "I don't think you can have much of anything at the expense of beer. Can I interest either of you enlightened thinkers in a cool one?"

"I can be interested," Ron answered.

"So can I," Paul followed.

"All right then, before we continue, three Budweisers coming up," Wesley replied as he turned on his heel, stepped into the kitchen, opened the refrigerator door, and reached in for three refreshing cans of Budweiser. "Here you are, Legend. And here you are, Paul," he added as he set up the cans. "Now we can continue," he announced, sitting back down in his chair at the dining table.

"I don't know," Ron continued, opening his Budweiser and taking a long drink. "I wish I could stop thinking about ideas like science and religion. It's too confusing. Sometimes I wish I'd never seen the inside of a Catholic Church with all its magic that preaches one, continuous silent sermon that I'm just beginning to understand. Sometimes I think we'd all be better off if we believed in the Tower of Babel as firmly as my student does. But that understanding is too narrow, and I know the literature I'm supposed to teach is more expansive. And if I teach it with the curiosity it deserves, I may be instrumental in destroying the faith reflected in my student's answer to my question about the development of language. I didn't realize teaching would be so complicated. But then

I'd never come face to face with the kind of belief I encountered today. It's attractive in its simplicity."

"Maybe," Wesley said, "but it doesn't allow you to drink beer. Thus I'll have none of it," he added, taking a long swig of Budweiser. "I don't think I can be converted, but at least you Catholics can drink beer."

"You're right there," Paul said. "I guess it can't be all bad, even if it isn't scientific and true."

"But it is true," Ron said. "It just isn't scientifically true. But that doesn't make it a lie. If religion's a lie, we only have science and economics left—neither of which inspires me to any great heights. How did we survive before science and economics?"

"Hummm," Paul said. "I'll have to think about that."

"I'll drink to that," Wesley broke in, lifting his can to the ceiling. "Any takers?"

"I'll go along with it," Ron answered, smiling as he elevated his can.

"Me, too," Paul added, following suit.

"To religion and science and life's sensual pleasures," Wesley said.

"To religion and science and life's sensual pleasures," Ron and Paul echoed as the three of them drank together.

"Now that we've settled that issue," Wesley said, setting his Budweiser can on the table, "what else is new at LHS? We all know nothing ever happens at the junior high."

"That's because you guys still labor in the minor leagues. I work in the majors. Things happen in the big leagues."

"What's happening besides the Tower of Babel controversy?" Paul asked.

"Another issue does make me think," Ron answered, hesitating slightly.

"Don't be so hesitant," Wesley said. "It's not like you. What's going on?"

"The two of you know Judson Heath, the football coach, don't you?"

"Who doesn't?" Paul asked in response.

"How can you miss any football coach?" Wesley asked.

"Anyway, he's taken me under his wing, you could say. Maybe he thinks he's my father. I don't know. But he's always been more open to me than has anyone else on the faculty, with the exception of Judith Griswold and Mr Polk, the principal."

"But I thought you were a baseball man," Wesley said. "You keep that baseball glove on your dresser as if it were some kind of sacred object. What are you doing running around with the football coach?"

"That glove is a sacred object. It was my dad's last and my first. If the Athletic Club caught fire, I'd save that glove first. And I am a baseball man and I don't exactly run around with the football coach."

"What's the problem then?" Paul asked as the three of them finished their beers.

"It's not exactly a problem. It's just that sometimes I'm torn."

"I can see this is going to call for more Budweiser," Wesley said. "You guys ready?"

"Sure," Ron answered as Wesley stood up from the table and returned to the refrigerator, "but I have to teach tomorrow."

"All of us have to," Paul said as Wesley walked back to the table carrying three more Budweisers. "But I think we can handle one more as you tell us about Judson Heath and being torn."

"No problem," Wesley said. "One more won't kill us. What are you torn between?" he asked, sitting down once again.

"Judson Heath and the coaches' room and Judith Griswold and the faculty room," Ron answered, opening his beer.

"I have to say that I don't understand that one," Wesley said, savoring his Budweiser. "Do you, Paul?"

"Not exactly," he answered, taking a drink of his beer. "But I'm sure the Legend will explain. Right, Leg?"

"I'll try," Ron answered, taking a drink himself. "But it won't be easy."

"It has to be easier than trying to explain the connection between science and religion," Wesley said. "At least I know Judson Heath and Judith Griswold."

"That's true, but I'm not exactly torn between the two of them."

"But you just said you were," Wesley replied. "Didn't you hear him, Paul?"

"I heard him. But remember, the Legend's an English teacher."

"What's that supposed to mean?" Wesley asked.

"It means that he doesn't always say what he means."

"Now I'm totally confused," Wesley said, shaking his head and reaching for his beer. "At least Budweiser is easy to understand. I can grab it and drink it. I can believe that."

"It's not that complicated," Ron said. "I'm torn between what Judson and Judith and their respective rooms represent. I'm not exactly torn between them as individuals. That's all."

"Oh, now I get it," Wesley said with a sigh as he turned his attention to his beer.

"Before we get too confused," Paul said, "you'd better get on with it. What's the problem?"

"Well," Ron answered, inching up in his chair and warming to the occasion once again, "sport always has been important to me. I think it's an institution like church, and I think I've always looked to both for inspiration. I think I believed in sport as strongly as I believed in church."

"What does this have to do with Judson Heath and football?" Wesley asked.

"Baseball always has been my favorite and most trusted sport, but the institution of sport—whether high school or college—has been built on the foundation of football rather than on baseball. Therefore, in our schools we've granted our football coaches special status. It's no accident that Judson Heath is the most imposing presence at the high school, even more so than Mr Polk—although he's never intimidated or surpassed by Judson's presence. But if someone didn't know the school, he'd assume Judson Heath, and not Mr Polk, to be principal."

"Go on," Paul said as the three of them lifted their Budweisers.

"Mr Polk reminds me of an authority who has yet to be discovered," Ron continued, "and Judson Heath reminds of an authority who's always been recognized. Only now I think that authority's becoming obsolete. The structure of life that granted the likes of a football coach heroic status is cracking and we're questioning everything. We no longer take anything for granted."

"Just how does Judith Griswold fit into this picture?" Wesley asked. "It's not as clear as a can of Budweiser, and even you have to admit that."

"That's right, and it's not exactly running clear to me, either. But I think Judith Griswold represents a contemporary reaction to the institutional authority we associate with Judson Heath and his social standing."

"And you think the idea of hair length is directly related to the crumbling of this structure?" Paul asked.

"I think so. I know Judith's more sympathetic with the long hair crowd than Judson is. Everyone on the football team has to have a crew cut. I realize I wore that style myself at one time, but I chose to. I don't know what I'd do if someone ordered me to get a crew cut for any reason. There's more at stake here than hair length. It's not just a matter of taste and popular style."

"What is it then?" Wesley asked.

"As I mentioned earlier, I think it's more a matter of morality and its subsequent behavior. Somehow short hair has become associated with moral bearing, and athletes are supposed to be expressions of the preferred morality. So we have coaches like Judson Heath demanding that their players wear short hair in contrast to the lack of moral bearing they associate with long hair. The whole issue is divisive, and the high school's split into two camps. We have the faculty room at the north end of the school and the coaches' room at the south end. And the two ends, the two rooms, don't interact."

"Where do you belong?" Paul asked as the three of them drank from their Budweiswer cans.

"That's the question I have to resolve. I don't know where I belong. Sometimes I think I belong in the coaches' room because I'm a product of the structure it represents, and I feel as though I should defend it. And sometimes I think I belong in the faculty room because I can't turn my back on someone just because he doesn't wear a crew cut."

"What are you going to do?" Wesley asked.

"I don't know yet, but I do know that I have to stand somewhere. And as an added complication, Judson wants me to join his coaching staff."

"You coaching football!" Wesley exclaimed. "You coaching football!" he repeated. "Doesn't Judson Heath know you?"

"I told you about the institution of sport, and how I respected and believed in it just as I did with the Church. So under normal circumstances I don't think coaching football would be out of the question. Besides, Judson made me feel more welcome at the high school than anyone else did."

"What about Mr Polk?" Paul asked.

"He basically left me alone, but he certainly didn't abandon me. He was around as always, but he was quiet. It's hard to believe he once was a football coach, although I don't think he'd walk the sidelines today. I interviewed with him last winter and discovered that he's essentially a baseball man. He's a Cardinal just as I'm a Yankee, and a picture of Stan 'The Man' Musial hangs in his office. Mr Polk's an interesting man, but I don't know exactly where he stands. I know where Judson and Judith stand."

"Maybe you have to find out," Paul said. "Maybe Mr Polk stands where you're going, only you aren't there yet to understand."

"Do you two ever make any sense?" Wesley asked. "I thought you were a scientist, Paul, and scientists are supposed to make sense."

"I am a scientist, but I'm not all science."

"Well," Wesley said, "I'm all out of beer. Can you two handle one more?"

"One more," Ron answered, "but that's it. I don't want to get started tonight. I hate to go to school with a hangover. It's tough enough to teach when I feel good. But I should be able to handle one more Budweiser. How about you, Paul?"

"I'll take one," Paul answered. "It tastes good tonight, but I think I'll stop with this one, too," he added as Wesley returned from the refrigerator carrying three more cans.

"How can anyone stand where the Legend's going, only he isn't there yet to understand?" he asked, sitting back down at the dining table. "Why does he have to go anywhere? Why can't he just teach and let it go at that?"

"But I teach English," Ron said.

"So? Why don't you teach English with Judith and coach football with Judson?"

"Because I only can serve something I believe in."

"Do you believe in football?" Wesley asked.

"I don't know. I used to," Ron answered, turning to take a sip of his beer.

"You used to believe in church, too," Wesley said, smiling and drinking from his can of Budweiser.

"I know."

"Do you believe in English, in literature?" Paul asked.

"I think I'm going to literature only I'm not there yet to understand," Ron answered with a smile, knowing that Wesley would groan and throw back his head in exasperation.

"I've heard everything now," Wesley said, acting in the expected manner. "Look, it's simple. Are you going to join Judson's staff or not? That's the question."

"I honestly don't know. I've always been impressed with the majesty of football, and I'd like take part in the charge onto the field, onto the gridiron. I think Judson feels the same, but I think he might be too wrapped up in morality these days. If all the music and the colors and the charge onto the gridiron supports a morality I can't believe in, then I can't coach football, regardless of how impressed I might be. But I just don't know. Maybe I should coach baseball."

"I can see you dressed in baseball knickers more easily than I can see you decked out in football pads," Paul said.

"Maybe, but I just don't know."

"When do you have to make your decision?" Wesley asked.

"Not until next year. Judson wants me to attend a couple of coaching clinics next spring and then go from there. I think I'll go."

"Would you have to get a crew cut?" Wesley asked, running is hand through his thick hair.

"I don't think I could live with that requirement."

"Does the faculty room have such requirements?" Paul asked.

"That's just it. I like clarity. Unlike the clear-cut requirements of the coaches' room, whether or not I approve of them, the faculty room lacks discipline. Something has to fill the cracks and create a new structure just as solid as the old one used to be. Right now, as I think about it, I'm tempted to choose the faculty room, but I can't dismiss the lure of the coaches' room."

"Maybe Mr Polk could help," Paul said.

"No, I have to decide for myself, but I think Mr Polk's watching my every move. He knows the situation, and he knows I have to make the decision on my own. And as I do, he knows it'll be forever. It's a tug-of-war and I only have until next spring."

"I know what you need," Wesley said.

"What?" Ron asked.

"You need a beautiful girl to take your mind off this business."

"That really would complicate matters. You haven't seen anything until you've seen me rendered foolish by the power of Love."

"Maybe we'll get our chance," Paul said, finishing his Budweiser. "Stranger things have happened and the year's young."

"That's true," Ron said as he finished his beer. "But nothing's turned up yet."

"Don't despair," Wesley said, savoring his last drop of beer. "Anyone care to join me at the Elks Club to top off this evening of conflict and philosophy?"

"Not tonight, Wes," Paul answered. "I think I'll just stay home."

"I can't," Ron answered. "I have to read some papers. You know an English teacher's work is never done."

"Ha!" Wesley exclaimed as he stood up from the dining table and headed for the front door. "Anyone can teach English," he added with a smile as he opened the door, closed it behind him, and walked directly toward his blue Volkswagen waiting in the driveway, leaving Paul and Ron alone with their seemingly obscure, philosophical thoughts about science, religion, and conflict. Wesley's path lay clearly before him. He saw no conflict in the reality that blue Volkswagens and cold cans of Budweiser offered him.

# XIX

Ron's reality by no means excluded the likes of Wesley's blue Volkswagen and cold cans of Budweiser, and there was a time when his religion, supported by its catechism, clearly directed an individual life toward union with God in Heaven. But that time had passed. In its place he found a spineless path of social service that, devoid of the majesty of individual sacrifice, led nowhere. Ron liked clarity and spine, which explained his attraction to Judson Heath and the coaches' room—even if he found their version repulsive to his own emerging manhood. The faculty room offered a more palatable alternative to the coaches' room, but its spineless path, lacking the strength of discriminate, individual vision, mirrored that reflected in the post-Vatican II Catholic Church. And then there was the path of the ever present, but quiet, Mr Polk. Literature revealed that path, and in the process of discovering it, Ron also was coming to know himself for the first time.

Because he learned that the world of literature, of fiction, mirrored his experiential world, his journey of self-discovery involved discovering his fictional counterparts. If he, or anyone else for that matter, looked closely and carefully enough at the reflected images in the fictional world, he could see himself revealed in depth. And in his search to know himself Ron discovered—privately, of course—his first fictional counterpart in the person of Beowulf from the Anglo-Saxon epic of the same name.

He had read 'Beowulf' during his own high school days at Bellarmine in Tacoma, and upon his first glance at the story as a teacher, he didn't see beyond the killing of the monster, Grendel, and the exciting warrior adventure built around that battle. But he expected more of himself now, and after a patient second glance he discovered that Beowulf's story reflected his own, even though he wasn't a warrior and even though he lived in an historical time hundreds of years removed from that identified with 'Beowulf.' Still, as he looked patiently, in the manner of an authentic teacher, he couldn't help recognizing a story that illuminated the connection between the individual and the virtue of obedience. And he couldn't help realizing that such a story reflected his own. He kept his discovery to himself, not telling either Paul or Wesley, because he found it hard to believe that he actually could be Beowulf—which meant that he actually could live as Hero.

Ron had been raised on the virtue of obedience that he was supposed to direct toward the Church which, as Christ's Church, was supposed to represent the earthly expression of God's Law. Beowulf, too, was raised on that virtue, but he was a pre-Christian, pagan warrior who, unlike Ron, knew no institutional church. His obedience, then, was directed toward his king, who played the role of Ron's church in that he functioned as the authority to which Beowulf owed obedience by virtue of his warrior status. Like Ron's personal story, Beowulf's revolved around the relationship between the individual and authority and the subsequent social expectation to obey. Without obedience there could be no order and structure. Obedience was a pre-requisite for love. It was a matter of duty—and the Hero was devoted to duty. Upon patient, second glance Ron found 'Beowulf' to be an interesting, fundamental story that reminded him of another, even more familiar, formative tale.

Beowulf's story that examined the individual in relation to the virtue of obedience reminded Ron of Adam and Eve's experience in the Garden of Eden. According to his church, he inherited Adam and Eve's original sin. Therefore, duty called him not to repeat that sin of disobedience. But he was troubled when he compared the two stories. He recognized a disturbing contrast between the authority Adam and Eve disobeyed and the authority Beowulf obeyed. He looked patiently at both authorities, God in the Eden story and the Danish king, Hrothgar, in Beowulf's story, and discovered that he liked Beowulf's obeyed authority better than he liked Adam and Eve's disobeyed counterpart. Such a discovery scared him to death. God in the Eden story, Adam and Eve's disobeyed authority, was God—The One True God and Creator of the Universe. And he liked Hrothgar better than he liked God.

Both Beowulf's Hrothgar and Adam and Eve's God possessed the spine to either command or demand obedience. Adam and Eve's God demanded obedience with the imposed penalty for disobedience being expulsion from a world without pain and death into a world marked by both. In contrast, Beowulf's Hrothgar commanded obedience with no threat of expulsion from anything, as if pain and death constituted a monstrous, but necessary and natural, part of life just as it's experienced. After Beowulf had killed Grendel, the monster who had ravaged Hrothgar's land, the noble king, grizzled by many winters into living proof of what he had to say, reminded Beowulf that he, too, had to die. When faced with that monstrous necessity—for which no one was to bame—Beowulf should affirm it and seek "eternal gains" as the way to achieve immortality and to defeat death. Where God spoke to Adam and Eve supported by the majesty of the threat of punishment, Hrothgar spoke to Beowulf supported by the majesty of compassion, leaving Beowulf free to obey or disobey. Hrothgar knew that only obedience inspired by love, free from the coercive power of fear, could be authentic.

He told Beowulf a story about another warrior, Heremod, whose heart was more disobedient than obedient. As a result, his life was marked by misery and chaos that eventually led to his "slaying of his table companions." No one imposed punishment on Heremod for disobeying, but he did have to endure punishment he created for himself. The path of disobedience he freely chose, contrary to that reflected in Hrothgar's experienced wisdom, initially led to success but ultimately to despair for Heremod and his kingdom. He chose the path of rewards rather than that of responsibility, the path of "eternal gains." Heremod sought "temporary" gains and paid the price for disobeying the creative path of obedience to Hrothgar's wisdom of experience.

Like Hrothgar, Adam and Eve's God stood firmly as an authority with spine and majesty. But Eden's God relied on fear with any subsequent obedience being of more benefit to him than to the individual. On the other hand, Beowulf's Hrothgar relied on benevolence with any subsequent obedience being of more benefit to the individual than to him. In obeying his benevolent authority, Beowulf obeyed a natural law. Furthermore, he didn't obey out of fear of imposed expulsion from anything. As Ron looked patiently, more for himself than for his students as a result of the barrier the Tower of Babel erected, he concluded that Beowulf obeyed out of love—with its sacrificial demands raising it to the level of religion.

Then he couldn't help thinking about Adam and Eve's plight. Hrothgar should have been God, he thought, because he had everything to do with majestic compassion and love that sought to free the individual and had nothing to do with fear that sought to enslave the individual to authority. Adam and Eve only could obey God out of fear, he reasoned. If I can't like God as much as I can like Hrothgar, Adam and Eve couldn't have obeyed God freely out of love. I can see how Hrothgar can be an incarnation of love, but I don't see how God can be. And He's supposed to be the True God and Creator of the Universe. If Beowulf, in his obedience, is my fictional counterpart, Adam and Eve, in their disobedience, are my fictional counterparts as well. They had to disobey God to obey Hrothgar, and in their story Hrothgar has to appear in the form of the serpent. Beowulf's no threat to Hrothgar, who sought to pass on his wisdom to give him the chance to live as Hero. Isn't that just like the serpent?, Ron thought to himself and for himself. How can it be wrong to encourage individuals to know both good and evil? To want them to become as gods? To want them to seek "eternal gains" without forcing them to choose under threat of punishment and banishment from paradise?

What about Christ?, he questioned, privately once again and still worried about the Tower of Babel barrier. Like Beowulf and me, Christ is obedient, he continued, but he's obedient to the New Law and not to the Old Law. Eden's God represents the Old Law and its serpent represents the New Law. Christ must be the serpent fulfilled, Ron reasoned. His New Law, ironically, is Hrothgar's pagan law. I have to include the stories of Adam and Eve and Christ in the fictional world that already includes the story of Beowulf. I have at least three fictional counterparts, he decided. And with chills still crawling up his spine, he concluded that maybe the serpent has been the authentic God of Eden all along.

He didn't talk to anyone about his fictional counterparts, but he realized that if they belonged to him, they could belong to anyone. He also knew that his students could be the primary beneficiaries of his thoughts and, at least, tentative conclusions. But he held back in the face of the Tower of Babel. He wasn't afraid, but he didn't think he had the right to teach literature in a manner that could destroy any student's traditional faith. Ron wasn't convinced of anything at the young age of 23 but he was learning to know himself, in depth, for the first time. At the same time he was learning to know the universal individual just as deeply.

If my fictional counterparts suggest that I have the capacity to live the majesty of obedience as an Adam, as an Eve, as a Christ, as a Beowulf, anyone does, he thought. The Old Order, built on the exclusion of Adam and Eve and Christ from the fictional world and built on the doctrine of original sin, hasn't disintegrated yet, although it's severely cracked. Maybe when that order has sufficiently disintegrated, I can freely teach what I'm, privately, just beginning to understand. In the face of the undeniable disintegration of the Old Order, of which I am a proud product, maybe I can teach the fictional world, the world of literature, as being inclusive of the stories of Adam and Eve and Christ, he concluded, still feeling the chills. Then maybe I can give them a chance to work their magic—if anyone remains open to it.

But for now, in the fall and early winter of 1967, Ron's discoveries were best kept secret. He didn't feel comfortable discussing them, not even with Paul or Sue who may have been open to them, because he was well-schooled in the evil of pride, which identified Adam and Eve's sin in the Garden. But when Ron included their story in the fictional world and saw the authority of God in relation to that of Hrothgar in 'Beowulf,' he saw pride revealed in God and not in Adam and Eve. If humility is the majestic opposite of pride, he thought, Hrothgar is an incarnation of it and his call to Beowulf, which corresponds to the serpent's call to Adam and Eve, is a creative call to a life of humility that Beowulf is free to disobey at his own peril. But no one simply walks away from obedience to a church and a belief designated, for almost 2,000 years, as the path leading to the beatific union with God in Heaven. And given Ron's thoughts, it didn't take an impossible leap of the imagination to see Judson Heath as an immediate, earthly expression of Adam and Eve's God.

Maybe it's easy to disobey a mere football coach, but it's not easy to disobey anyone surrounded by an earthly imitation of the Heavenly majesty afforded God and His authority. Earthly institutions, with their hierarchical structures, reflect the celestial institution, and Judson carried that authority with him, making him the most imposing figure in the high school. He stood tall as an authority of the Old Order and as a defender of its moral bearing built on the premise of original sin and its companion belief that excluded the stories of Adam and Eve and Christ from the fictional world. Reflected in its crew cut requirement, a sense of discipline identified the Old Order, with the only alternative appearing to be the undisciplined chaos reflected in the flowing locks of the emerging Hippie Order. The Old Order was built on responsibility and disciplined obedience in relation to the premise of original sin, while the hippie opposition, lacking any foundational premise, was built on rampant irresponsibility and undisciplined expedience that created the deceptive pretense of freedom. In the face of that emerging Hippie Order, Ron was flattered by, and attracted to, Judson Heath's invitation to join his football coaching staff.

What Ron could see in Beowulf and in Adam and Eve and Christ, when he included their stories in the fictional world, a person schooled in the irrefutable historicity of the Tower of Babel could not. Furthermore, such a person could not include the stories of Adam and Eve and Christ in the fictional world without branding them false as a result. Confronted with such facts, as well as with indifference and failed historicity, Ron remained alone with his thoughts and adventurous discoveries. And he made no public avowal of any kind to his individually recognized belief in the obedient path of Love until that moonlit December night when he rode with Wesley and Paul to Corvallis to meet Debbie Wright, his "vision of delight."

Debbie never had encountered anyone like Ron, and given their different historical pasts, they weren't exactly made for each other. But throughout the remainder of the year of The River Road Athletic Club the two of them were inseparable, and, for Ron anyway, every day meant adventure. The consecration of such love in marriage represented the fulfillment of his motivating dream, but he couldn't ignore the divisive split between the coaches' room and the faculty room, overseen by the quiet presence of Mr Polk. If it weren't for that nagging conflict, which he had to resolve, he knew that he would simply settle in Lebanon, hopefully with Debbie, forever. But because of its lingering presence, the flowering of the love that blossomed, that moonlit December night, under the natural canopy of the filbert tree definitely remained in question.

## X X

Ron knew he didn't have to face any final resolution of his conflict until after the spring coaches' clinics Judson Heath wanted him to attend with the established members of his staff. In the meantime, he enjoyed the complex foolishness of love with Debbie, much to the delight of Paul and Wesley, and for the most part his weekends were devoid of any references to anything resembling the Tower of Babel. Debbie knew of his conflict and listened intently to anything he had to say, but she had little light to shed on his path of resolution. Her own life was without such conflict, and the Ron she wanted to see represented the fulfillment of her dream. Both of them basked in the glow of the filtered moonlight of their filbert tree, but for Debbie and her limited pulpit vision, its promise ended in marriage and in a life mostly bathed in bliss. She didn't know it, and neither did Ron as yet, but her fictional counterparts could be found more in the likes of Jay Gatsby's Daisy Buchanan than in the likes of Christ's Mary Magdalene.

All the time Ron's mostly private journey of self-discovery continued, and early in the spring of 1968 he added Huckleberry Finn to his list of fictional counterparts. Never in his formal education, not in high school and not in college, has he been asked to read 'The Adventures of Huckleberry Finn,' and as an American, he couldn't see how his formal education in literature could be complete without a thorough study of Mark Twain's masterpiece. Gaining confidence in his ability to recognize the experiential truth of literature, he was eager to examine the fictional work that Ernest Hemingway, with whom his formal education had familiarized him, had identified as the book from which "all modern American literature comes." Fortunately, Lebanon's senior English curriculum, which called for the study of a novel in the spring, afforded him the opportunity. Technically, he was supposed to choose an English novel, with the American novel belonging to the junior survey of American literature, but his department chairman approved his selection of 'Huckleberry Finn' on the basis of the fact that Ron's current students hadn't read the entire story as juniors.

Like the lives of his previously discovered fictional counterparts, Adam and Eve, Christ, and Beowulf, Huckleberry Finn's outward life—or outward adventure—bore no resemblance to Ron's corresponding experience. But on the universal level of the inward adventure, all their stories, experiences, and adventures were one and the same. And being well-schooled in the virtue of obedience, they encountered authority to whom they recognizably owed the loyalty that necessarily accompanied that virtue. But in the on-going adventure of life, only Beowulf, the pagan expression of the responsible individual, confronted an authority more benevolent and commanding than tyrannical and demanding. Only Beowulf didn't have to disobey to obey. And, privately, Ron had identified Beowulf's Hrothgar with Adam and Eve's serpent as well as with Christ with whom he associated the fulfillment of the serpent authority.

Huckleberry Finn's story of obedience centered around himself, the Christian pulpit authority of the Widow Douglas and Miss Watson—with both seeking to "sivilize" Huck—and Jim, Miss Watson's runaway slave who, ultimately, became Huck's companion in adventure. According to the popular understanding Ron brought to his study of 'Huckleberry Finn,' Tom Sawyer played the role of Huck's friend and confidant. But given his newly discovered understanding of himself and his fictional counterparts, he quickly saw Tom more in contrast, rather than in comparison, to Huck. For all his playfulness and charm, Tom wasn't well-schooled in the virtue of obedience and thus did not belong in the company of Adam and Eve and Christ and Beowulf and Ron

Petrich. Given several opportunities to prove himself worthy of Huck's company, he proved himself otherwise every time, finally leaving Huck alienated and alone, ready to "light out for the territory ahead of the rest because Aunt Sally, she's going to adopt me and sivilize me, and I can't stand it. I been there before."

Huck's statement at the end of his adventures served as a revelation for Ron. He could see that if Huck allowed himself to be "sivilized," he would have to live in obedience to the very authority Adam and Eve had to disobey to be free. Huck's Christian pulpit authority certainly wasn't an expression of Beowulf's Hrothgar, a fact which only contributed to the irony. Authentic civilization, which Huck would not resist or desert, had to be built around obedience to Hrothgar's compassionate wisdom. That wisdom illuminated the path of "eternal gains," the path of Love, which, in the context of Ron's discovered fictional counterparts, proved to be more pagan than Christian. So, Hrothgar's call, compassionately issued to Beowulf, was the call to be civilized, not "sivilized." And it was a call Huckleberry Finn didn't hear from any authority outside that of his own noble heart. The time line extending from Adam and Eve to Huck Finn clearly taught Ron that established authority, with the exception of Beowulf's Hrothgar, still existed more for its own benefit than for that of the individual. Ron's own time was no different. Past the mid-point of the 20th century the path of obedience to Love still wasn't the well-traveled path.

With regard to Huck's story, Ron's discovery centered around the culminating incident, toward the latter part of the book, where Huck's definitive moral dilemma surfaced. He had to decide whether or not he should reveal the whereabouts of Jim, the escaped slave who, as far as Huck knew, still was being sought by Miss Watson, Jim's owner. Ron could see that this dilemma represented the essence of Huck's adventure because it illuminated his conflict of obedience where he had to "decide forever betwixt two things." He had to decide to do what was right in reference to Jim who, to Huck's knowledge, was an illegal runaway. He had to decide whether he should turn Jim in or "steal" him away from Mr Phelp's farm. The established authority, the Christian pulpit authority—Huck's "God" in Adam and Eve's Eden and Christ's Pharasaic authority—told him to do the right thing and turn Jim in. But another authority, that of Love—around which was built the Religion of Love founded on the serpent's and Hrothgar's compassionate call—told him to do the right thing and "steal" him away. But if Huck decided to obey the authority of the Religion of Love, the fires of Hell awaited him.

Ron's pulse quickened as he contemplated Huck's dilemma. If obedience is a prerequisite for love, he asked himself, what authority does Huck obey? How deep will his love be if he avoids Hell and obeys his social authority? How deep will it be if he, in spite of the consequences of experiencing an eternity in Hell, obeys the authority of his own noble heart? According to what Ron had learned from studying his previously discovered fictional counterparts, Huck's love would reach greater depth, and would require more majestic and compassionate sacrifice, if he decided to "steal" Jim away. In Huckleberry Finn's clear dilemma Ron could see the path of right, the path of Hrothgar's "eternal gains," the path of authentic civilization — as well as the path of Love, the path of the Grail in the Medieval romance—reflected in the path of obedience to Huck's awakened noble heart. And his own heart leapt in exhilaration when Huck looked at the note he had written to Miss Watson, obediently revealing Jim's whereabouts, studied it closely, and said finally and forever: "All right then, I'll go to Hell"—and tore it up.

If we weren't faced with the Tower of Babel barrier, Ron thought, his heart still pounding in exhilaration at the recognition of Huckleberry Finn's courage, we all could see the greatness of the individual revealed in Huck and in my other fictional counterparts who have to be our fictional counterparts, who are supposed to be our fictional counterparts. But is it my responsibility to tear down that barrier? I think it's my responsibility to teach what literature reveals, regardless of existing barriers, he thought to himself, but it's not my responsibility to break them down. I think they're breaking down on their own. The structure they supported is cracking. Besides, I'm not ready, yet, to publicly teach what I've privately discovered. I can't clearly explain it right now, he continued to think to himself. I'm still learning. But I know for a fact that I'm no Tom Sawyer. He knew Jim already had been freed and he didn't tell Huck. Instead, he concocted this elaborate, charming scheme that put the lives of both Huck and Jim in jeopardy. Huck had everything at stake, but Tom only thought of his own entertainment. Even after being shot, he still doesn't learn anything. He's not worthy of Huck's company, and I never again will listen to any complimentary comments concerning Tom Sawyer. Adam and Eve and Christ and Beowulf and Huckleberry Finn—that's who we're supposed to be. To achieve that level of obedience is to live our destiny and to earn our freedom.

Ron knew the time would come when his private revelations would burst forth publicly, but he also knew now wasn't the time. Still, he felt confident that when the Old Order had sufficiently disintegrated, he could help illuminate, as a result of having discovered himself in his "true" fictional counterparts, the path that would lead to the building of the New Order. And it wasn't the path outlined by the spineless and accommodating post-Vatican II Catholic Church. Instead, it was the sacrificial, majestic path of obedience to the Serpent of Eden repeated in Christ's story and in Bewoulf's story—but most clearly and most emphatically in Huckleberry Finn's story. For now, however, Ron still had to deal with Judson Heath whom he couldn't easily dismiss—any more than Huckleberry Finn could easily dismiss his Christian pulpit authority.

Debbie, Paul, and Wesley were aware of Ron's upcoming commitment to attend some football coaching clinics, and of the three of them Debbie was foremost in not being able to picture him in such company. She could see him in the faculty room, she told him when he tried to explain his dilemma to her, but she couldn't see him in the coaches' room amidst what she labeled "macho behavior." He tried to explain to her that such behavior didn't attract him to the coaches' room in the first place. Its sense of order and discipline accounted for his attraction. He tried to explain its clarity to her and said that he might be able to stand up for it but that he wasn't sure.

Part of him, he said, felt like he belonged in the faculty room where he saw none of Debbie's "disgusting macho posturing" but that he wasn't totally attracted because he saw little clarity and discipline. He found nothing to stand for, he didn't think, besides taking up arms against the evils of "macho posturing," with the reaction against that evil resulting in what he called the "guilt-imposed feminization of the male." Debbie said maybe the male needed that "feminization" and Ron agreed in principle but not in practice. He told her didn't consider himself macho by any means but that he didn't consider himself a "trendy, feminized male," either. And Debbie said that as far as she could see, he belonged in the world of the faculty room and didn't understand why he had to attend any coaches' clinic in the first place, and he told her that he had to see for himself before he made up his mind forever. And she told him she didn't really see the problem. He belonged in the faculty room and that was that.

According to Wesley, Ron didn't have to be committed to either the coaches' room or the faculty room. He just had to remain on the path of "Greater Northwest Living," which Ron found exciting and entertaining but, ultimately, unsatisfying. No one could walk that path any better than Wesley, nor more comically, but even he couldn't walk it forever. Sooner or later, he would have to settle into the mercenary path to which it led. Ron felt he deserved better, but he wasn't sure Wesley thought the same way himself. He seemed to know where he was going, and to him the mercenary path was clear and perennially noncommittal.

Paul, on the other hand, saw Ron's dilemma, although he didn't see any exact solution. His own path was that of marriage and involvement in mercenary concerns, but more so religiously than conveniently. Basically, Paul was religious and disciplined, but science had destroyed his faith in his pulpit Christianity—which he didn't seem to mind losing. He listened carefully during his discussions with Ron concerning the significance of the made-up world of story, but he couldn't overcome the hurdle of disbelief in anything made up. His new religion, replacing that of his Protestant pulpit, was that of science—complete with its calculated and rational wonder. Still, he appreciated Ron's position with regard to the worlds of the coaches' room and the faculty room and, if nothing else, anxiously awaited the outcome of his experience with a football coaches' clinic. He told Ron he couldn't see him as a football coach but that he could understand his attraction and could further understand his need to find out for himself

The Carlsons and the Griswolds were curious observers of Ron's dilemma, with Sue and Judith both failing to see the merits of football to begin with. Judith, of course, was firmly entrenched in the world of the faculty room in dedicated opposition to that of the coaches' room, come what may. Sue, removed from both worlds, leaned toward a social-political ideology built on an idealistic premise of rational cooperation for which Ron could find no solid foundation in his newly expansive, made-up world of fictional counterparts. Steve remained a man of the natural world, skeptical of any intellectual speculation, choosing to believe in something as solid and as trustworthy as fishing. And Ken remained the quiet, mysterious observer, waiting to see if everything would fall into place, at which time he'd still remain the same quiet, mysterious observer. At any rate, all six of them had gathered at the Carlson's country dream house on a sunny spring Saturday to await Ron's report of his findings concerning the coaching clinic he attended earlier in the day with Judson Heath and the rest of his coaching staff.

Ron had left his Camaro at the high school and had driven up to Portland with Judson, who managed to prime him for his first experience with the fraternity of football coaches. Because of the University of Notre Dame's solid Catholic identity, football and the Catholic Church were not so strange bedfellows, and next to baseball's Hall of Fame, Notre Dame's was dear to Ron's heart. He was well-schooled in Notre Dame lore. And it was this football lore, rather than any football fact, that drew him to the game and to the coaches' room and now to a coaches' clinic with Judson Heath—the personification of the world of football fact. Still, surrounded by the aura of Ron's football lore, Judson seemed larger than life itself in the manner of the pope or a cardinal in the Catholic hierarchy. Judson was aware of his status with Ron, and he had taken him under his wing—as much for his own benefit as for Ron's.

On the drive up to Portland he and Judson talked with ease about football and the majesty of the colors, the bands, and the fight songs, with Ron giving special attention to the Notre Dame fight song which, he told Judson, still sent chills up his spine whenever he heard it. He was convinced that he would run through a brick wall for the Notre Dame blue and gold if he had the chance, all the time spurred on by the song and the pantheon of heroes it supported. Judson knew of Notre Dame's legendary Four Horsemen and of Knute Rockne and Frank Leahy, the school's just as legendary coaches, but the blocking and tackling in support of the traditional morality of the game of life, more than any legendary appeal, attracted him. And the clinic itself had been devoted to that blocking and tackling in support of that very morality. Ron had neither seen nor heard any mention, however oblique, of the majesty of his world of football lore. The world of football fact, supporting an obsolete and disintegrating social and moral order, was the topic of the day, and during the silent ride back to Lebanon Ron and Judson had little to say to each other. When Judson pulled into the faculty parking lot, Ron was glad to see his red Camaro but still somewhat saddened to realize that a once cherished world had been stripped of its grandeur, revealing its individuals to be seemingly light years removed from Hrothgar's path of "eternal gains."

After saying goodbye to Judson, thanking him for the trip to Portland and the clinic, and telling him that he'd see him on Monday, Ron stepped into his Camaro, started it up, and headed for the Carlson's country dream house just a few pastures removed from The River Road Athletic Club. He had learned to like Lebanon, but it hadn't come to mean as much to him as did his Old Town neighborhood in Tacoma. And he hadn't developed any depth of feeling for the surrounding Willamette Valley, either. Every now and then he still ate dinner at Bing's Kitchen, but, although it remained Lebanon's restaurant, it never became his. He recognized landmarks such as the Lebanon Lumber Company that told him where to turn on his way to the Carlson's, but no Lebanon or Willamette Valley landmark ever came close to matching the affect power of Tacoma's Union Station or Stadium High School or even Rankos Drug Store. He lived and worked in Lebanon and he respected the community. But its Grange Hall foundation, supported by the Protestant pulpit, never penetrated to his heart to allow him to embrace it in the manner he had embraced Old Town and its Slovenian Hall foundation, supported by the Catholic altar. For Ron Lebanon was The River Road Athletic Club and the Carlson's dream house. He felt as though he belonged when he pulled into their driveway late that Saturday afternoon following his clinic experience with Judson Heath and his football coaching fraternity.

# XXI

Ron recognized Wesley's blue Volkswagen, the Carlson's green Volkswagen bus, the Griswold's brown Toyota station wagon, and knew that The River Road Athletic Club faithful were waiting for him. He also knew that wherever the faithful gathered, with Wesley having engineered the gathering, Budweiser would be available. The spring sunshine filtered through the boughs of the tall firs, encouraging the emergence of the Willamette Valley greenery, as Ron stepped out of his Camaro, smiling in eager anticipation of Wesley's proclamation of "running clear." He closed his driver's side door, walked toward the fence, and through the gate that connected the house with the neighboring pasture. He continued walking along the side of the house until he turned the corner and saw the faithful sitting comfortably on the Carlson's sunlit back deck gathered around the tapped aluminum keg resting just as comfortably in its expansive bucket of ice.

"Well," Wesley exclaimed as he spotted Ron rounding the corner of the house, "it's running clear and look who's here, Knute Rockne. C'mon up here, Legend," he continued, reaching for a wide-mouthed paper cup, "your chair's waiting for you, and I'll be happy to draw you a cool one," he concluded as he filled Ron's cup. "The best keg we've ever had," he proclaimed as he handed the full cup to Ron just as he stepped onto the deck. "Greater Northwest Living," he saluted as Ron accepted the cup.

"Greater Northwest Living," Ron repeated, raising his cup to meet Wesley's as the rest of the faithful looked on with amusement. "No doubt about it," he said, savoring his long drink of Budweiser, "the best beer I've ever had," he added as he sat in his chair next to Sue and Steve at the end of the deck nearest the back door.

"Well, Leg," Paul said, "we've been waiting. How was it?"

"Yes," Sue added. "Have you been converted?"

"Are you Judson's right-hand man now?" Judith asked.

"Give him a chance," Steve said, looking at Ken, who smiled and nodded his head in agreement. "Let him swallow his beer first."

"C'mon, Knute, fill us in," Wesley said as Ron settled into his chair. "How was it?"

"I can tell you one thing for sure. I didn't see any Knute Rocknes, not in the coaching world of football fact."

"What do you mean?" Sue asked as the rest of the faithful waited for Ron's answer.

"I mean," Ron answered, taking another drink of his beer, which just may have been the best beer he'd ever had, considering his experience with the football coaching fraternity, "that Knute Rockne belongs to the world of football lore, and I didn't see any evidence today of any coach in the world of football fact ever growing into the lore's significance."

"I don't know much about the worlds of lore and fact," Steve said, "but I would like to know just what happened."

"First of all," Ron said, answering Steve's inquiry, "football lore is part of the made-up world of story and football fact simply is the world of football experience that we see before us. I think the gap between the two worlds is unbridgeable. The world of football lore doesn't provide the inspiration for the world of football fact."

"I knew you'd say something like that," Ken said as he took a deliberate drink of his beer and smiled in recognition. "Does that mean that you and Judson don't see eye to eye?"

"I think so. The world of Knute Rockne, the Four Horsemen, and Red Grange, as the 'Galloping Ghost,' inspired me. I hoped I would find some of that world alive today, but I didn't. Judson's as inspired by the world of football fact as I am by the world of its lore. So, you're right, Ken. He and I don't see eye to eye."

"I still want to know what happened," Steve said, "regardless of any relationship between football lore and football fact. So, what happened?" he asked, emptying his cup of Budweiser and heading toward the keg for a refill.

"I knew I was destined for a long day when they introduced the keynote speaker who entered the auditorium to the most thunderous standing ovation I've ever heard."

"And it wasn't for Knute Rockne of your football lore?" Ken asked knowingly.

"No way," Ron answered, shaking his head and raising his wide-mouthed cup. "Light years separate this guy and the Knute Rockne of that lore. I couldn't join the chorus of cheers."

"Tell us," Judith said. "Who was he?"

"Wesley and Paul should know."

"It had to be the Beaver mentor, Dolph Karstens," Paul said, smiling. "Power football at its best. That's the Beaver way."

"Maybe, but now I know why you Beavers are so obnoxious and almost on a par with the Husky fans in Seattle with their University of Washington. Husky fans are the most obnoxious people on the face of the earth, and you Beavers run a close second."

"You don't see our Beavers having much trouble with your Oregon Fighting Ducks these days," Wesley said between drinks of his beer.

"I only adopted the Ducks because the two of you were so disgusting in your adoration of the Beavers and their so-called 'mentor,'" Ron replied, emptying his cup and moving toward the keg to draw a refill.

"Coach Karstens must not be one of your favorite people," Steve said.

"He never was, and I suppose he's sunk even further after what I saw today."

"Just what did you see?" Judith asked. "I think that's still the main question we're trying to get answered."

"I bet the ovation you mentioned was in response to Karstens' stand on the hair issue at Oregon State," Sue said.

"That's right," Ron said. "That's exactly right," he added emphatically. "I could have handled the ovation more easily if it had been in recognition of his success with the power football that Paul mentioned. But he wasn't even introduced as the champion of power football. His introduction as the courageous champion of upright moral bearing resulted in the thunderous ovation."

"But he did take a stand by requiring crew cuts of his players and by refusing to allow mustaches," Steve said. "You have to give him that."

"Maybe so, but he didn't take a stand for anything representing true progress. If anything, he took a stand in defense of a moral bearing and discipline that's becoming obsolete. That bearing and discipline had its day, but today I learned that we can't retreat into obsolescence and call it progress. Such a retreat is more destructive than creative. But you know what really troubles me, more than anything else?" Ron asked, warming to the occasion.

"I bet it has to do with religion," Sue said, taking a more cautious sip of her Budweiser.

"What does football have to do with religion?" Wesley asked, not exercising any caution as he raised his cup to his lips.

"I think we can find religion in the world of football lore just as we can find it in the world of literature I'm supposed to teach. And I think if we move toward the discovery of that religion, we move in the direction of authentic progress. But if we embrace the world of football fact, just as it is, and elevate it to the status of religion, we condemn ourselves to decadence, as far as I'm concerned. There's no way I can take part in such a condemnation."

"And that makes you angry," Ken said, smiling as he continued to drink his beer deliberately.

"I guess it does," Ron replied with a smile to match Ken's.

"But why?" Judith asked. "Why should it matter to you?"

"Because," Ron answered, trying to look everyone in the eye, "I would like to be able to belong. But I can't. Do you see?"

"Hummm," Steve answered. "No wonder I like to fish. You just cast the line into the water and wait for the action. It's clean and neat, without any controversy. Besides, I find it comforting. I don't know why, but I do. At least it's not made up. There's no lore about it and mustaches and hair length are of no consequence."

"Today I saw, firsthand, that the world of the football coaching fraternity isn't so neat and clean," Ron said. "And I saw, firsthand, that in the eyes of the members of that fraternity short hair and clean-shaven faces can reflect an individual's moral bearing."

Following Ron's last comment a pensive calm temporarily settled over the faithful as they all faced the fact that they would have to deal with an emerging world far more chaotic than that which had spawned them. It seemed as though their world had changed more drastically in the past three or five years than it had in the previous three or five hundred. Without any unifying force to hold them together, beyond that of The River Road Athletic Club, they all could go their separate ways, leaving their unity behind only as a memory of what was. Ron spoke for all of them when he said he'd like to be able to belong.

Of the different paths that identified the faithful as they sat on the Carlson's back deck, Steve's fly fishing probably was the most solid, even if he didn't understand it himself. Judith's faculty room only would lead to confusion because it lacked clarity and spine. Sue's social ideology would prove to lack the satisfaction of authentic religion. Ken's deliberate mysteriousness would carry him through most anything. Wesley's mercenary path would lead him to prosperity if nothing else. And Paul's more religious commitment to marriage and its accompanying mercenary path would lead him to a series of financial adventures within the boundaries of his committed marital state. That left Ron, united with the faithful now around their Budweiser keg, but ultimately alone, discovering the sacrificial demands of humility and love—the Religion of Love—and waiting for the appropriate time to commit himself to their illumination for anyone who might still be interested. As any keen observer could have predicted, Wesley finally broke up the pensive calm that had enveloped The River Road Athletic Club faithful.

"What else happened at this clinic, Legend?" he asked. "Did you learn anything about football?"

"Come to think of it, I really didn't. I don't know any more about teaching football now than I did before I went to the clinic. But I do know more about teaching moral bearing through the medium of football. As long as we celebrate the likes of Dolph Karstens as the heroes of the coaching fraternity, I don't want to have anything to do with it."

"Judson won't like that," Paul said.

"I know, and as late as yesterday, his reaction would have bothered me. But no more. I'm not part of that world and I don't belong in it. I have to tell Judson the same and go from there. I can't accept the talk about football being the game of life. No one can tell me that life is as simple as a football game. I think football, and sport in general, resembles church. It's an institution that once was surrounded by majesty similar to that which identified the Catholic Church. But it's different now. The majesty has eroded, revealing the mediocrity of the individuals it once ennobled. Stripped of that majesty, the Dolph Karstens of the world, I discovered, aren't very impressive. They don't represent any movement toward anything as clear and as disciplined as the disintegrating, orthodox moral order used to be."

"Dolph Karstens alone couldn't have put you in this mood," Judith said as Ron and the male faithful drank from their wide-mouthed paper cups. "He's not that important. Something else must have happened."

"You're right," Ron said. "In the first session of the afternoon I had to listen to Jack Parks, the head coach at Portland State. That was the last straw."

"What did he have to say?" Paul asked. "Portland State's not exactly a powerhouse, and Parks isn't exactly a household name like Dolph Karstens has become with the Beavers. What harm could he have done?"

"You all know that I like to cuss. In fact, I don't trust anyone who frowns upon such creative use of language. But I do believe there's a time and place for cussing—a simple fact that Jack Parks has yet to learn."

"Go on," Paul said. " You're right. You can cuss with the best of us."

"Parks addressed the coaching fraternity, in this professional, supposedly adult, setting, as if he and his fraternity brothers—me included—were holding forth in some locker room. And," Ron continued, "the fraternity lapped it up as if Jack Parks stood tall and proud as an expression of a real man. But such manhood has no regard for proper form and decorum. And as I read it, the world of football lore doesn't celebrate the authenticity of that manhood. The Old Order, once unquestionably reflected in the solid institutions of sport and church, is rapidly disintegrating. If we are to preserve football, as the popular foundation of the institution of sport, with any dignity, we have to grow into the world of its lore. But I don't see any hope for such growth. If there were visible hope, the likes of Dolph Karstens and Jack Parks would not have been accorded the admiration they received today. Football will remain with us, but the world of football fact certainly doesn't deserve to be elevated to the status of religion."

"You're in rare form today," Steve said, shaking his head and taking a drink of his beer. "But you always return to the issue of religion. I think we're better off without it, if you want to know the truth."

"We're better off without obsolete religion and we're better off without the world of football fact being celebrated as religion," Ron countered, drinking his Budweiser. "But we're not better off without religion."

"So, where do we find religion these days?" Sue asked. "We're supposed to find it in church."

"I know, but I don't think we can trust that institution any more than we can trust the institution of sport. Neither could have been built on a solid foundation."

"What should be the popularly recognized foundation of the institution of sport, Leg?" Paul asked.

"I think," Ron answered, taking a deep breath and a healthy swig of his Budweiser, "it would have to be baseball."

"Why baseball?" Judith asked.

"I'm not sure I know why, at least not yet. But I sense it. I know baseball isn't such a fashionable sport these days, but it's always exerted a powerful hold on me. And my experience today only strengthens that hold. I've never spoken of life in terms of it being a game, but if there is a game of life, it has to be baseball. In terms of substance and what I'd have to call psychological depth, whatever that may mean, football pales in comparison to baseball."

"That may be," Steve said. "But who cares?"

"That's just it. I don't think many of us do. And I think all of us should, even though I can understand why we might consider sport to be a somewhat frivolous activity. But religion's a different story."

"Nothing frivolous about religion. Right, Legend?" Wesley asked with a twinkle in his eye as he raised his wide-mouthed paper cup in celebration.

"You're right there, Wes," Ron answered, shaking his head. "Religion is the foundation of human life. And any life is only as solid as the foundation on which it's built."

"But doesn't the science that you and Paul discuss make religion frivolous in comparison? Wesley continued.

"Science only makes religion frivolous when it's offered as science," Ron answered. "I'll never accept the premise that says science makes religion frivolous," he added, taking another drink of his Budweiser.

"So, what's the popularly recognized foundation of church with regard to religion?" Judith asked.

"According to the Garden of Eden story the character called God fills that role," Ron answered. "But we live in 1968 now, and it's impossible not to question the truth of that foundation. Paul's science has succeeded in expanding our understanding of our world and the universe beyond the boundaries authorized by any institutional church."

"And that expansion weakens the foundation?" Judith asked.

"It must. Otherwise, we wouldn't be living in the midst of such chaos and disintegration that results in making heroes out of the likes of Dolph Karstens."

"And now for the next, logical question," Paul said. "In view of scientific progress and discovery what should be the popularly recognized foundation of church?"

"That's a tough, and scary, question," Ron answered. "But if we look at the Garden of Eden story, in light of the impact of contemporary scientific discovery and space exploration, I think we discover the serpent. I honestly believe the primary question facing the Western world today is: What if the serpent is God?"

"And you've asked that question?" Steve asked.

"Yes, but only recently and only privately. I think we have to ask that question if we hope to preserve the affect power, the magic, of our Christianity. But I don't think Lebanon is ready for it yet. And neither are towns built in its image. I'm not sure any of our cities, regardless of size and personality, are ready for it."

"But Lebanon and other towns and cities will be ready someday?" Sue asked.

"I think so, but only when the disintegration of the old moral order is complete, or at least more advanced."

"That gives you some time to figure out religion, the Christian religion, from the serpent foundation. Right, Leg?" Paul asked with a knowing smile.

"That's right. I can't help it. We need both science and religion. We can't have either one at the exclusion of the other."

"I don't know what all this has to do with Greater Northwest Living," Wesley said.

"Or with fishing," Steve added.

"But," Wesley continued, standing up and stretching his arms toward the sky and holding his now empty wide-mouthed paper cup in his right hand, "it's still running clear, and as far as I'm concerned, religion can wait until another day. Anybody ready?" he asked, moving toward the keg.

"I'm ready," Ken answered. "I need some help digesting all that I've listened to. I grew up in the same church as Ron, but for some reason the affect wasn't quite the same. I have to think about it."

"I'll draw one for you while you think," Wesley said, taking Ken's cup, filling it to the top, and handing it back to him. "Steve, what about you?"

"I'm more than ready," Steve answered, handing his cup to Wesley. "Why don't we ever talk about fly tying or something concrete?" he asked as Wesley handed him his full cup.

"Sue, how about you and Judith?" Wesley asked.

"None for me, thanks," Judith answered. "I'm not much of a beer drinker no matter how clear it's running. I'll sip a little brandy at the party tonight."

"No more," Sue said. "I'll wait until later when the rest of the guests arrive."

"Paul?" Wesley asked, extending his right hand.

"Not now. I have to pick up Karen pretty soon. I'd better wait until later."

"That leaves you, Legend," Wesley said, extending the same hand in his direction.

"I have to pick up Debbie pretty soon, too, but I'll have one more to Greater Northwest Living," he said, handing his cup to Wesley.

"Spoken like a true believer," Wesley said as he took Ron's cup and held it under the tap. "Here you go," he added, handing him the full cup. "Greater Northwest Living," he toasted, raising his cup to the sky.

"Greater Northwest Living," Ron and Steve and Ken answered in unison.

Maybe the year of The River Road Athletic Club would fade into memory of what once was, but not yet. After the final tribute to running clear and Greater Northwest Living—with or without the support of Wesley's nectar of the gods—the faithful dispersed in their various directions. But they would return to the Carlson's country dream house after sunset to continue the celebration and further partake in Wesley's celestial "nectar."

By the time Ron returned with Debbie, who was staying at her family home in Lebanon for the weekend, the regular Friday night crew from the Athletic Club was intact, only transferred to another location. The setting was different, but the rhythm of the evening remain unchanged, with the exception of the fact that the Athletic Club's faithful had grown accustomed to Debbie who no longer was a stranger. Ron returned with her to find all of the celebrants gathered around the keg sitting, still comfortably, on the Carlson's back deck. But as the evening wore on, Wesley and the always dependable Polly became conspicuous by their absence. Judith had joined the singing group with Paul and Karen, this time relocating to the Carlson's living room. Ken and Steve had settled into chairs at the kitchen table, discussing the merits of fly fishing. Sue had wandered into the living room to observe the singing group. The more obnoxious revelers either had retired for the evening, victims of their orgiastic appetites, or had gone home in advance of enforced slumber. And Ron and Debbie found themselves standing alone but bathed in the spring moonlight, this time filtering through the boughs of the Willamette Valley tall firs.

## XXII

"Now you can tell me all about your experience at the coaches' clinic today," Debbie said as they leaned against the front edge of the back deck with the fingers of Ron's right hand interlocked with those of her left hand.

It was spring and Debbie's fur-collared winter coat had given way to a white cardigan sweater that protected her from the moonlit chill in the air. Her face remained as radiant as ever, and the white cardigan rested comfortably on the contour of her breasts. She was wearing a blue cotton skirt that stopped slightly above her knees, accentuating her nyloned, not yet suntanned, legs; and her soft, yellow blouse complemented her cardigan and highlighted her beckoning, blue eyes. Ron tightened his grip on her hand as his eyes met hers.

"You know," he said, "you're still beautiful, winter or spring, filbert trees or tall firs. It doesn't make any difference. I still can't believe how we got together. If you could have seen me that day I came home and told Wesley and Paul about my vision of delight in the library," he added, shaking his head.

"I didn't exactly refer to you as a vision of delight," Debbie replied, "but I did tell Karen about you. And I hoped we would go out somehow."

"Well, we did," Ron said, smiling, "and I'll never forget that night last December. Finding your picture in Wesley's yearbook was like a dream come true. My heart still beats a thousand times a minute when I think about it. Such a meeting just doesn't happen."

"It did with us," Debbie said, squeezing Ron's hand, "and I've never met anyone like you. I don't know where it's going to lead, but I'm awfully glad I met you," she added, smiling at Ron as his heart responded in kind.

"So am I," he said, trying to control his heart as their eyes intertwined, "and maybe we should just let it go naturally and follow along."

"Maybe, but I do want to know whether or not you're going to coach football."

"There's no chance," Ron said, shaking his head. "Not after today."

"Why not?"

"I learned, conclusively, that I don't belong in the football coaching fraternity."

"What happened?" Debbie asked with concern.

"You remember the hair-length issue we've talked about?"

"Yes."

"And you remember talking about Dolph Karstens and the hair and mustache controversy at Oregon State?"

"Yes," Debbie answered once again.

"Dolph Karstens was the featured speaker at the clinic, and as I told the Athletic Club faithful earlier, he was greeted with a thunderous standing ovation. I could have handled a polite reception, but this was an ovation reserved only for an authentic hero. I knew he was going to be the speaker, but I didn't expect the coaches to welcome him as their champion in the battle to preserve the honor of traditional moral values. I expected them to welcome him as a successful football coach who has turned power football into a consistent winner at Oregon State. But then I didn't completely understand the connection between football and moral behavior before today. We should allow the game to speak for itself. We shouldn't cloak it in moral and patriotic dress as if it were America personified. And to top it off, in the afternoon I had to listen to Jack Parks, the head coach at Portland State, insult me and everyone else."

"How did he do that?"

"I like to cuss when the time is right, but I've never equated that colorful use of language with manly, or adult, behavior. However, Coach Parks addressed his assembled colleagues in language more appropriate for their locker rooms than for a professional gathering of adult men who happen to be football coaches. All in all, the entire day was more disgusting than anything else. I've attended my last coaching clinic, believe me."

"But maybe this one was an exception."

"I don't think so. All clinics might not be carbon copies of this one I attended, but I know they're similar in tone. We've made football synonymous with moral bearing as if it were God's sport or something. It's confusing enough to think about the nature of God these days, but elevating football to the level of the deity is too much. If we're going equate a sport with God, we should choose baseball. At least it reflects enough substance to do justice to the concept."

"You've lost me," Debbie said, shaking her head. "I told you that I've never met anyone like you, and you continually prove me right. You're amazing. You can be funny and seemingly light-hearted, and then in no time at all you can be talking about God and God's sport. It's all part of your charm, but sometimes you lose me along the way."

"I don't mean to," Ron said, turning to look at her. "But our structure of life is falling apart, and I'm trying to figure out where I belong. With the structure intact I accepted football just as football, and the majesty of its colors and marching bands and fight songs worked like magic. But today I saw football fervently celebrated as if it represented some kind of righteous crusade that crowned the likes of Dolph Karstens and Jack Parks as its heroes. That's not what football meant, or means, to me. Besides, I'm no crusader. The search to discover a moral standard compatible with our age of scientific exploration and discovery should be quieter, and it shouldn't center on football any more than it should center on the pulpit."

"You've really lost me now," Debbie said. "Where is that guy whose heart beats a thousand times a minute at the mere sight of me?"

"He's right here," Ron answered. "And only a guy whose heart beats so fast at the sight of his beloved can get so passionate about the chaotic state of civilization in the midst of the disintegration of the established moral order. It's part of our religion."

"What do you mean? I thought you were raised Catholic."

"I was. And the Catholic altar celebrated the religion I'm referring to—not the Catholic or Protestant pulpit and certainly not football. The Religion of Love is more compatible with baseball's inspiring depth than with football's disillusioning emptiness. Maybe I don't understand such thoughts well enough yet to adequately explain then, but when my eyes first caught sight of you, my heart didn't disagree. And according to the Religion of Love, as celebrated by the Medieval troubadours, true love is born when the eyes and the heart agree. I experienced that phenomenon with you. Do you see?"

"I think so," Debbie answered.

"And when you experience something, it's easier to believe in it. I might not know the full meaning of rapture, but to be in your presence, especially on that magical December night, has to come awfully close."

"But what about all this talk about football and morality and the Religion of Love?"

"Talking about them simply is a logical extension of a person for whom the heart is the center of passion. It's just who I am. I feel the same way about literature as I do about the altar and baseball. If we hope to discover authentic morality that's compatible with a scientific age, we have to search the world that includes baseball, the altar, and literature. I reacted so strongly to the clinic today because I learned that popular sentiment doesn't lean toward my interpretation. And I wish it did. Or I wish I leaned toward popular sentiment. Do you understand?"

"To some extent. But I have one main concern."

"What's that?" Ron asked, still holding onto Debbie's hand.

"Where is this passion going to lead you?"

"And you're interested in where it's going to lead you?" Ron asked in return.

"I guess that's part of it," Debbie answered. "Where is it going to lead?"

"I don't know. The path isn't clear yet. But I know I don't belong in the coaches' room. I've established that much."

"What about the faculty room?" Debbie asked hopefully.

"I think I'll feel more comfortable there for now."

"What do you mean for now? Can't you just teach English like everyone else and enjoy life?"

"I have to say for now because the faculty room doesn't present a permanent, creative alternative to the entrenched, obsolete morality of coaches' room. I can't embrace either path. And when it comes to just teaching English, as the teacher's manuals say, I can't help realizing that those secure days are rapidly passing. Do you understand?" he asked hopefully.

"I don't know. I love you, but I just don't know," Debbie answered, dropping her head and squeezing Ron's hand.

"I love you, too, but as corny as it may sound, I have to follow my religion and its path of adventure. I can't disobey my religion."

"But I don't know if it's my religion. I didn't grow up as you did. Your religion isn't as clear to me and it's scary besides."

"Are you afraid?"

"I wish I weren't, but I think I am, even though I don't want to be."

"Maybe you'll get over your fear," Ron said.

"Maybe," Debbie replied, "but I just don't know. I wish you could just teach English."

"That's just it. I don't want to do anything else. I just want to be an English teacher, but I think teaching English means teaching the

Religion of Love. If that's the case, I still have some ground to cover. Are you going to come with me?" he asked as he and Debbie turned to face each other directly.

"I don't know. I just don't know," she repeated as she felt Ron's arms tighten around her waist and responded by lifting her arms around his neck. "I want to go with you," she continued, looking him in the eye, "but I just don't know. I wish there were no third path that has to be so untraveled. I wish we could choose one of the two well-traveled paths. Then our lives would be easier. Do you see?"

"Yes," he answered, holding her close to him and feeling the warmth of her body close to his. "But it's the path of Love that counts. It doesn't discriminate but it is discriminate. And it's supposed to be the well-traveled path. Maybe if we follow it, it'll be well-traveled eventually and not quite as scary."

"Maybe," Debbie said, "but I can't be sure. And I have to be sure," she added, pressing herself close to Ron, not wanting to let go but afraid to hold on forever.

"I can't guarantee anything, I guess. "But I wish I could."

"However, I do know one thing for sure," Debbie said, still pressing herself close to Ron, "no matter what happens."

"What's that?" he asked, holding her tightly in the glow of the spring twilight that seemed to settle on the boughs of the tall firs.

"No matter what, I'll never forget that magical moment when we stood together under the filbert tree in the Athletic Club's back yard."

"No matter what, neither will I," Ron said as their lips met in honest celebration of that enchanted moment when the promising, December moonlight softly filtered through the filbert tree's barren branches and blessed their natural canopy of Love.

## XXIII

Ron wasn't afraid to make decisions, but he didn't mind delaying his confrontation with Judson Heath until the end of the school year. Like Huckleberry Finn, his most recently discovered ficitonal counterpart, he knew his decision had to be forever. There could be no turning back, regardless of any conclusion Debbie might reach. In his mind he could handle Judson the individual, but in actuality he still came dressed in his authoritative cloak as an intimidating representative of a way of life that the Lebanon community, for the most part, celebrated as the path of righteousness and nobility. And the remainder of the community embraced the way of life identified with the faculty room as the path of honor and commitment. Like any obedient heart—like any Adam or Eve or Christ or Beowulf or Huckleberry Finn—Ron wanted to follow the right path and not merely the convenient alternative. He couldn't respect Tom Sawyer.

Judson's authoritative presence reminded him of that which Huckleberry Finn had to face and finally disobey. Ron knew that obedience to such a well-intentioned path did create a sense of order and structure, but he also knew that such an authority ultimately proved to be more interested in its own welfare than in that of the obedient individuals who dutifully embraced it. In effect, the shepherd acted as if the flock existed for his benefit and not the other way around. He acted in his own best interests and not in those of his sheep. He needed his sheep so that he could be the shepherd. He had no other identity. When Ron thought of Judson and the coaches' room in this light, the faculty room seemed welcoming and attractive. But no shepherd directed the faculty room alternative, leaving the sheep to do whatever they desired with no accountability to anything or anyone. Any shepherd who did appear sought to accomodate the sheep, revealing his lack of spine. Judson's authoritative presence, that demanded obedience through the imposition of fear, certainly wasn't spineless in contrast. But Ron was searching for an authoritative presence with commanding spine that sought obedience through the awakening of love that had to be the essence of the human heart. He was searching for serpent spine.

His thoughts turned to Mrs Williams, his motel woman from the Gables who left Lebanon for what she thought to be the more morally expansive city of Butte, Montana. He was sure she had experienced a similar dilemma in reference to authority and the virtue of obedience. But she didn't demand anything from him nor did she take any steps to accommodate him. Mr Polk had told Ron that she had faced death. As a result, she built her way of life, even if it ultimately clashed with that offered by the Lebanon community, more on the dictates of her own experience than on those imposed by any church or social authority. She was born from the collective belief of the Church into her own, individual belief, even if she couldn't explain the transformation.

And his thoughts turned to Mr Polk as well, whom Mrs Williams had recognized as a man of compassion as well as a man more interested in embracing responsibility than in merely wearing the crown. She knew that Mr Polk, and not Judson Heath—for all his authoritative presence—represented an expression of the "authentic learned man" that Ron, as a teacher, felt himself called to be. Mr Polk, who identified with neither the coaches' room nor the faculty room, once coached football, but a portrait of Stan 'The Man' Musial, a baseball player, adorned his office wall. Baseball matched the depth of his character and became his sport. Unlike Mr Polk, Judson Heath needed football. That was the difference. And Mr Polk, a man with spine of his own, quietly commanded, rather than demanded, respect.

If Ron Petrich owed allegiance to anyone associated with his Lebanon community, he owed it to Mr Polk and to Mrs Williams, who sought allies amidst the copper mines and slag heaps of Butte, Montana. As his historical counterparts, they gave him strength and courage, and they had to be living expressions of the creative serpent that lived in the garden of his individual soul. Maybe he didn't have to challenge Hell in the manner of Huckleberry Finn, but he did have to face the prospect of alienation from the social order structured around the collective belief.

Then there was the matter of Debbie Wright. Ron couldn't help thinking of the movie 'High Noon' where Gary Cooper faced the possibility of losing "his fair-haired beauty." Ron faced the same possibility, and he knew that if keeping Debbie meant disobeying his religion, he'd have to lose her. He didn't want her simply to folllow him, and he couldn't impose his religion on her. For the two of them to live together in love, Debbie had to be able to make her choice free from any coercion. He honestly didn't know what she would do, but he knew what action he had to take to return the sacrifice, whether conscious or unconscious, of his fictional and historical counterparts.

The end of the year of The River Road Athletic Club marked the end of Wesley's teaching career. He had decided to pursue a career in the business world and was resolved to search for greener pastures and greater opportunities in Chicago, which was a far cry from Lebanon, Oregon. Ron would miss him, and he never would forget the rallying cry of "running clear" and the triumphant toasts to "Greater Northwest Living." Polly would have to find someone else on whom to pin her hopes, but Ron couldn't help thinking she should have known better.

The end of the year of The River Road Athletic Club also marked the end of Paul Sorenson's single life. He and Karen were to be married in the summer just as Ron had expected earlier in the year. Paul was Karen's marital dream come true, and as far as Ron was concerned, she couldn't have made a better choice. He would miss Paul and his scientific insight and penetrating inquiries into the mysteries he saw as being primarily scientific in the first place. He would teach one more year, until Karen finished school, and then he, too, would answer the call to search for greener pastures.

And the end of the year of The River Road Athletic Club marked the beginning of the second life of Ron Petrich. He knew what he had chosen, and with the end of the year he knew he had to make his choice public. His decision, that he already had made in the sacred privacy of his own heart, didn't mean he had to leave Lebanon—at least not yet—but it did mean he would have to lose his "fair-haired beauty" if she didn't embrace the same path of obedience. Without Debbie, which remained to be seen, he would be left with the Carlsons and the Griswolds and, for one year anyway, with the Sorensons. He wouldn't be alone necessarily, but the life of his second birth was destined to be more alienating than that of his first.

The last teaching day of the 1967-68 school year, and for all practical purposes the last day of The River Road Athletic Club, arrived. As could be expected, Wesley spoke up to break the morning solemnity of the occasion.

"Today's the day you have to face Judson Heath, Legend," he said as the three of them sat at the dining table, finishing their coffee.

"I know," Ron answered. "I've run out of days."

"Are you scared?" Paul asked.

"No, I'm not scared. I just wish I didn't have to face anybody. I wish I naturally and comfortably belonged to something."

"Then you wouldn't be the Legend," Wesley said, brushing back his hair with his right hand. "And who would you be otherwise?"

"He's right, you know," Paul said. "Who would you be?" he asked as Ron adjusted his necktie knot.

"I don't know, but I wouldn't find myself in danger of losing my 'fair-haired beauty.'"

"That's enough of the Gary Cooper stuff," Wesley said. "If you weren't the Legend and if you weren't a believer in your Religion of Love, whatever that is, you wouldn't have to lose her in the first place. I don't know, maybe we all ought to be Legends. But I have no regrets. This has been a great year. I'll never forget it. I don't know if the Budweiser ever will run as clear anywhere else."

"It did run clear, didn't it?" Ron asked, smiling.

"And often," Paul said. "Maybe all three of us could use a break."

"Maybe," Ron answered, "but I'll miss the Friday afternoon sounds of 'The Mighty Quinn' and 'Lady Madonna' and 'I Just Dropped In (to see what condition your condition was in.)' I don't know how we ever survived," he added, shaking his head."

"You survived because you found your vision of delight," Wesley said. "I'll never forget that night when you first met Debbie. And you were going to go easy this time. Who were you trying to kid? You had no chance."

"I know, but Debbie didn't make a fool out of me, remember."

"I'll remember," Wesley said, laughing. "Love made a fool out of you. Isn't that right?"

"That's right. And 'the wise man knows himself to be a fool.'"

"It's the fool who 'doth think he is wise,'" Paul added. "See, I've learned something from you."

"You learned it from experience. I just happened to quote Shakespeare's expression of it."

"Maybe," Wesley said, "but you also did a fine job of living the quotation. You should come to Chicago with me. You can look just as foolish there."

"Hummm," Ron said. "Maybe I'll come for the summer if things don't work out with Debbie."

"If you lose your 'fair-haired beauty,' you mean?" Wesley asked.

"That's right."

"Are you going to lose her?" Paul asked.

"I don't know. What do you hear from Karen?"

"Not much, but I know it's not easy on Debbie. She's never met anyone like you, and she doesn't know where it will lead. I don't think she's as well-schooled in the Religion of Love, as you call it, as you are. I think she'd like to follow you. But she's afraid."

"That's just it. It's not as simple as following me. She can't follow me and be an individual in her own right. She has to discover and follow the Religion of Love. Then both of us can live in Love. Does that make sense?"

"Yes," Paul answered, "but I don't think too many of us live in Love as you present it."

"Maybe not, but if we don't, it's not because we can't. That's why the Religion of Love, clearly expressed in the world of literature, is worthy of belief. It's a matter of faith. It's something I hope for, for example, and something I can see, something I can argue for. If the Word is Made Flesh in Christ, that Word has to be Love. And that Incarnation can occur more than once."

"Why does everything come back to the same point with you?" Wesley asked. "It never fails. You can go from running clear and Greater Northwest Living to something like the Incarnation—is that what you said?—faster than anyone in existence. No wonder Debbie's perplexed. She's probably wondering: 'Who is this guy?'"

"She probably is," Ron said. "But you know something?" he asked, adjusting his tie once again.

"What?" Wesley and Paul asked together.

"I don't think it's that hard to go from running clear and Greater Northwest Living to the Incarnation, the essence of Christianity. It's more a matter of how much time an individual is willing to spend thinking about it."

"And these thoughts aren't new to you?" Wesley asked.

"No. They're lifelong thoughts somehow awakened, first of all, by what I call the silent sermon of the Catholic Church and later awakened in earnest by that church's Second Vatican Council. That church and its path to union with God never was very far removed from the world of my everyday experience. As a result, I thought about that sermon and its truth all the time."

"And now you're getting closer to conclusions, to convictions. Is that right?" Paul asked.

"Yes," Ron answered. "I think I've reached the end of my first life, and I'm about to begin my second life. I experienced my first birth and now I'm experiencing my second birth."

"Well, "Wesley said, looking at his watch, "I wish you luck because it's about time."

"You're right," Paul agreed, checking his watch as well. "Time flies when you're having fun, and talking to the Legend is always fun."

"Yes, but perplexing," Wesley said, standing up from the table. "This is my last day," he added, straightening his tie and heading for the front door and his waiting Volkswagen. "See you guys around three for one last tribute to 'The Mighty Quinn?'" he asked before he walked out the front door.

"We'll be there, "Paul answered.

"I wouldn't miss it for anything," Ron said.

"Not even for the Incarnation?" Wesley asked as he flashed his trademark smile and closed the front door behind him.

"He does manage to get in the last word, doesn't he?" Ron asked as he stood up from the table and put on his sport coat that he had draped on the back of his chair.

"That he does," Paul answered, laughing. "If he didn't, he wouldn't be Wesley. The River Road Athletic Club couldn't have been the same without him."

"That's for sure. Nobody has been anything like that 'Mighty Quinn.'"

"Well, Leg," Paul said, putting on his sport coat and moving toward the front door, "time to go. You coming?"

"Right behind you," Ron answered, grabbing his grade book off the top of the dining table. "We've come a long way since September. What a year," he added, shaking his head.

"You're right there," Paul said, opening the front door. "But we have one more tribute to running clear and Greater Northwest Living."

"That's right. One more," Ron said as he followed Paul out the front door and closed it behind him.

## XXIV

Ron's drive along the pasture road to River Road, through town, and eventually to the high school was no different from any of his previous trips to work. And except for the fact that today marked the last teaching day of the 1967-68 school year, his morning routine at school was no different, either. But he knew that on this day he would have to confront Judson Heath individual to individual for the first time. He knew the confrontation would occur after lunch, and he knew its results would "forever" determine the course of his life as a teacher. Even though Judson no longer presented the imposing figure he did before his institution had been stripped of its grandeur, Ron didn't look forward to lunch at the end of his fourth period class. For the first time he wished he had made a lunch that he could take to the faculty room and eat with Judith Griswold, with whom he had no impending confrontation. But he hadn't made a lunch because he never did, and he couldn't be cowardly and skip lunch altogether. Given the circumstances, Lebanon Union High School became a very "close place," indeed—Ron's immediate answer to Huckleberry Finn's fictional predicament—when the bell rang at the end of fourth period, finally signaling the inevitable.

The teachers' lunch room was located at the back of the student cafeteria and off to the left of the student serving line. As usual, Ron waited for the crowded hallways to clear before he went to lunch. He had learned to avoid putting his life at risk by walking through a hallway jammed with hungry high school students, Usually, he simply smiled and waited for his chance, but today he just waited. Finally, the hallway outside his door emptied, the banging of locker doors ceased, silence returned, and Ron made his move toward his classroom door. He opened it, stepped out into the empty hallway, closed the door, locked it, and began his walk down the wide, tiled hallway toward the cafeteria located across form the main office and behind the south wall of the expansive foyer that held the trophy cases celebrating the triumphant heritage of Lebanon Union High School.

He never liked this walk to lunch because he had to cover the length of the student cafeteria to get to the faculty lunch room. He always wished for a more private entrance that would eliminate the public parade through the throngs of high school students released from the confinement of their various classrooms. Ron wasn't aloof, but he didn't like to mix with students in their world, which he found to be loud and obnoxious. He remembered his high school world, marked by the black-robed and cloistered Jesuit presence, to be quieter by its very nature.

He never walked the halls of a public high school during his student days, but he was sure that students then, and in the decades preceding, weren't as loud as their contemporary counterparts. But then, he thought, we and they didn't live amidst chaos and disintegration, either. We and they lived amidst order and structure. If Ron didn't miss its imposition, he learned that he did miss the order and structure itself. Faced with the emerging chaos, he couldn't retreat into the clarity of the obsolete moral order championed by the likes of Dolph Karstens and those created in his image and likeness. Nor could he embrace the spineless and confusing path of accommodating order championed by the faculty room liberals who were fortunate enough to count authentic believers, of the stature of Judith Griswold and Sue Carlson, in their numbers. Not knowing exactly where he belonged, he reached the cafeteria and walked quietly, and anonymously as possible, down the long and narrow north aisle toward the secluded confines of the faculty lunch room.

When he opened the door, he found the regulars already seated in their places as if no day were different from any other. With the exception of Judson Heath, who was seated against the east wall at the end of one of the long tables, the regulars basically were faceless men, never any women, who taught as best they could with whatever conviction they could muster and waited until they could retire to their farms or to their projected life of leisurely travel. They simply were school teachers, comfortable in the days of the established Old Order that granted them the same respectful status their institution enjoyed but uncomfortable in the days of the disintegration of that order which made them appear to be nothing more than "raisins," wrinkled and stale, in the eyes of the liberated numbers of high school students. Naturally, the faceless men looked to Judson for leadership and helped elevate the likes of Dolph Karstens to his undeserved status of hero. Ron could feel the still private, but discomforting, tension as he accepted his hot lunch entree from the cafeteria server and found a small, empty table somewhat removed from Judson and his faceless followers. He never did like roast beef and mashed potatoes for lunch, but today's plate seemed less palatable than any previous servings.

He didn't feel like talking and was thankful that he had arrived late enough to find a place where he could sit by himself, unobtrusively, without any semblance of arrogant isolation. If anything, humility, and not arrogance, isolated Ron, or was beginning to isolate him—although the ignorant easily could choose the latter from their Tower of Babel perspective. He nodded hello to his now faceless colleagues as he took his place at his table, taking special notice of Judson's smile and nod of the head in recognition of his expected presence. Usually, Ron arrived in the lunch room in time to sit with the faceless group, and when he had finished his lunch, he'd accept Judson's invitation to follow him to the coaches' room. He'd finish out the period and remain there into his preparation time when, eventually, he'd find his way to the faculty room at the opposite end of the school. But the coaches' room no longer beckoned to him, and the faculty room no longer held out the promise of backboned clarity he expected as he faced his gravied mashed potatoes and cardboard-textured roast beef in agonizing silence.

After a few minutes the now faceless crowd had diminished, leaving Ron alone with his lunch and Judson Heath, who was the last of the faceless to finish his meal. He wasn't faceless yet, but Ron no longer saw him as an imposing authority worthy of the obedience that always would be a prerequisite for love. When he saw the individual Judson in comparison to his fictional and historical counterparts—and, finally and inevitably, in comparison to himself—he wasn't impressed. Thus when Judson approached his solitary table, Ron no longer felt either honored or intimidated.

"Are you finished?" he asked, towering above Ron, still seated at his table, working on his mashed potatoes and gravy and roast beef.

"Almost," Ron answered. "I can't quite handle this stuff today," he added, putting down his knife and fork.

"I know what you mean," Judson said, smiling in all his Bud Wilkinson, crew-cut glory and still looking down at Ron. "It certainly isn't food fit for any training table," he added in his Oklahoma drawl as his steely, glaring eyes lit up at the mention of the training table where males learned to be authentic men whose beardless faces and close-cropped hair identified them as the champions of the Tower of Babel morality.

"You can say that again," Ron said, wiping his mouth with his napkin. "I think I'll bring my lunch next year."

"Speaking of next year, we have to talk today about our plans. Next season will be here before we know it, and we have to be prepared."

"I know," Ron said, picking up his fork once again. "But maybe I'll take a couple more bites first. Things are lean at The River Road Athletic Club these days, and I need all the calories I can get."

"All right. I'll wait for you out in the hall by the benches in front of Polk's office."

"Okay. I'll be there in a few minutes," Ron said, not feeling comfortable with Judson's irreverent reference to Mr Polk.

"I'll be waiting for you," Judson said, depositing his empty tray on the serving counter. "Don't take seconds under any circumstances," he added as he shuffled his six foot four frame toward the door.

"Don't worry. One serving's plenty. I'll be out there in a couple of minutes."

"Okay," Judson said as he opened the door, stepped out into the main cafeteria, closed the door behind him, and walked as regally as he could down the narrow aisle toward the exit that led to the north-south hallway and to the benches sitting in the trophied foyer in front of Mr Polk's office.

Ron didn't follow him immediately. The path of destiny ran clear, and he knew he had to follow it, even if it meant losing his "fair-haired beauty." He took a deep breath as he thought of himself and Debbie Wright in company with Gary Cooper and Grace Kelly, before he stood up from his table and smiled in recognition of the reality of such movies. It doesn't matter if I lose my "fair-haired beauty," he said to himself as he grimaced at the sight of his now stone-cold mashed potatoes, gravy, and roast beef. I can't be afraid to live the path of wisdom and individual destiny, he concluded as he picked up his tray, and deposited it on the serving counter. Freshly resolved now, he opened the door to the faculty lunchroom, stepped boldly out into the now empty cafeteria, closed the lunchroom door behind him, and walked purposefully down the narrow aisle that led to the main north-south hallway and finally to his climactic confrontation with Judson Heath and the obsolete morality championed in the world of football fact.

The bell signaling the end of lunch had rung while Ron still sat in the lunchroom thinking about the universal, individual path of destiny, and the main north-south hallway was empty of any activity as he emerged from the cafeteria. He stopped and looked to the south in the direction of the gym and the coaches' room, and then he looked to the north in the direction of the exit and the faculty room. As he turned slightly to his right, he caught sight of Judson standing tall and crew cut with his arms folded across his chest, waiting for him next to the flat, backless bench sitting in the front of the trophied foyer. In the background he saw Mr Polk, knowingly leaning against the counter that ran in front of the main office as if he anticipated witnessing a moment of profound significance. Ron then took his first step to his right toward the tall, but less imposing, figure of Judson Heath.

"I see you made it," Judson said without smiling as he looked down at Ron, now standing at his left side.

"I didn't mean to keep you waiting. I just lost track of time, I guess," Ron replied.

"That's all right," Judson said. "It can happen to the best of us. C'mon," he continued, gesturing with his head in the direction of the coaches' room, "we still have plenty of time to talk about next year."

"I don't think so."

"What do you mean you don't think so?" Judson asked, turning to face Ron directly.

"I mean I'm not going to coach football, now or ever," Ron answered, looking Judson directly in the eye.

"When did you decide this?" he asked, standing with his hands on his hips.

"After the coaching clinic."

"What happened there? What did you expect?" Judson asked, shifting his weight to his right leg but keeping his hands on his hips.

"I learned that I don't belong in football and that if I were to belong in any sport, I'm sure baseball would be the one. And I don't know for sure what I expected. But I do know that I couldn't, and can't, embrace what I saw. I don't belong in anything I can't embrace."

"At least you can come to the coaches' room with me," Judson said. "You don't have to coach football to join me where you belong. You certainly don't belong in the faculty room. You're not one of them."

"Maybe not, but as much as I'd like to, I know I don't belong in the coaches' room. I think I would have once, just as I once belonged in the Catholic Church. I don't know if I belong in the faculty room, either, but at least I feel more comfortable there."

"You sound like a philosopher or something. What happened to the great Notre Dame fan who told me all about his devotion to the Four Horsemen and Knute Rockne?"

"He's still here. But, unfortunately, he doesn't belong in football or in the coaches' room. I have to be where I feel comfortable. I just never thought I'd have to make such a choice."

"But it's just a coaches' room," Judson said, shrugging his tight-end shoulders. "What's the big deal? Where's the harm in going to the coaches' room?"

"I know it seems crazy, and I don't mean any disrespect. But it's more than just a room, just as the faculty room is more than just another room. Both represent something bigger than the rooms themselves."

"You're talking about symbols, and I believe in fact. That's why I like football. It's hard and solid and factual."

"That world of football fact didn't attract me in the first place. I know that now. I don't belong in that world. If I belong anywhere, it has to be in the world of football lore. The world of football fact is light years removed from that which houses the likes of the Four Horsemen and Knute Rockne. If the distance between the two were less severe, I wouldn't have any problem."

"You talking like one of those intellectual literature teachers now," Judson said disgustingly as he thrust his hands into his pockets and shuffled his feet. "I still think you belong with me in the coaches' room," he continued, removing his hands from his pockets. "You coming?" he asked, taking his first step to Ron's left in the direction of the gym.

"No," Ron answered. "I can't."

"Well," Judson shrugged, "so be it. I hope you enjoy them," he added, nodding his head in the direction of the faculty room.

"I'll try," Ron said as Judson turned away completely and walked with measured strides down the long, expansive hallway that led to the gym and the coaches' room.

From his office-counter vantage point Mr Polk observed and studied the confrontation between Ron and Judson. Once they turned in separate diections, he stood up straight and motioned to one of the secretaries, pointing with his right arm in the direction of the gym. The secretary nodded in recognition and smiled as Mr Polk turned to his left and walked toward the backless bench sitting in the front of the trophied foyer. He stopped briefly to look down the main east-west hallway in the direction of Ron's classroom, turned again to his left, and continued with his authoritative walk. Ron, who had waited for Judson to disappear into the dimly lit gymnasium before deciding to join "them," had noticed Mr Polk's initial gesture out of the corner of his eye. Now, with his curiosity awakened, he stopped, turned to look back toward the main foyer, and saw Mr Polk nearing the cafeteria. But as Ron watched attentively, he turned sharply to his left into an auxiliary hallway, located midway between the coaches' room and the faculty room. Then, displaying the confidence of a man who knew where he was going and who was sure of the clarity of his commitment, he headed directly toward the sanctity and sanity of the boiler room.

Ron smiled in recognition, squared his shoulders, positioned his sport coat, adjusted his tie, and hitched up his slacks. Ready now, he reversed his direction and—without fear of losing his "fair-haired beauty"—walked resolutely toward that same sanctuary, trying his best to follow in the authoritative footsteps of his heroic historical counterpart.

The End

0-595-21641-2

Printed in the United States
203999BV00001B/357/A